P. Abbott

DUFFY:
Adventures of a Collie

A novel by Irving Townsend

JTN

J. N. Townsend Publishing
Exeter, New Hampshire
2000

Cover design by Design Point.

Printed in Canada.

Published by
J. N. Townsend Publishing
12 Greenleaf Drive
Exeter, New Hampshire 03833
800-333-9883
www.jntownsendpublishing.com

1-880158-29-9

Library of Congress Cataloging-in-Publication Data

Townsend, Irving, 1920-1981.
Duffy: adventures of a collie / Irving Townsend.
p. cm.
1. Dogs—Fiction. 2. Collie—Fiction. 3. Dog owners—Fiction. 4. Human-animal relationships—Fiction. I. Title.

PS3570.0938 D84 2000
813'.54—dc21 00-036378

10 9 8 7 6 5 4 3 2 1

Foreword

My father, Irving Townsend, spent the last year of his life working on *Duffy*. It was an ambitious project for him, telling the story of a dog's wanderings without anthropomorphizing his character. He wanted Duffy, who was based on our collie Elodio, to remain true to his collie nature—nothing more, nothing less. He believed the book was his best yet, and was hopeful his publishers would agree.

In December of 1981, he at last completed the manuscript and sent it off to New York. But *Duffy* was rejected by his publishers, and my father's heart broke. On December 17, he died suddenly of a massive heart attack in his home in the Santa Ynez Valley, California. He was sixty-one. Duffy's story remained unpublished until now.

My editing of this novel has been careful, yet respectful of my father's intentions. Some changes have been made, but always with the knowledge of the place and the dog my father envisioned. Although it has taken nearly twenty years to bring *Duffy* to print, I believe the timing is perfect. I trust my father would agree.

I also am quite certain he would have dedicated the book to Elodio, so I shall do so on his behalf.

Jeremy Townsend
October 2000

For Elodio

Chapter One

Duffy awoke at the outermost edge of morning. As usual, he had slept on a pad of sheep's wool spread across the window bench, his chin resting on the sill, his dark body cushioned by the pad, his curling brush tail dropping toward the floor of the master bedroom. As he opened his eyes, the scene before him was developing like a photograph, as pine tops, roof edges, and the bowed branches of the giant sycamore sharpened into deeper black against the lightening sky. Then he saw the cat, ghost white with a dark bull's-eye centered along its flank. Duffy gathered his rear quarters under him to watch.

The cat was making his way slowly along the sycamore branch all the cats used as a gangplank from house roof to the peeling trunk of the tree. As the cat paused to sharpen front claws at the center of the branch, Duffy shifted front paws to the sill to get a better look. Now the floating form of the cat with his brindled bull's-eye reached the trunk and headed in a graceful streak to the ground. There the cat walked slowly across the grass, tail taut, toward Duffy's window and along the walkway directly under his nose. As he sat up to follow the cat's progress, Duffy's tail moved slowly back and forth and a high soft whine of frustration escaped through the window screen. The cat paused, met Duffy's steady gaze, and then sat down to wash his face.

Duffy stood up on the window bench, tail gathering momentum as he fought his conflict. The urge to bark was unbearable. Just beyond his nose was one of three cats he could chase. Of the seven spring kittens born between hay bales the May before last, four refused to scatter when Duffy appeared in the yard. Instead, the four cats ran toward him, tails curling under his chin, sleek flanks rubbing against his legs so that he could hardly walk through them. Three, however, a fluffy black female, a white male with a calico cap, and the bull's-eye male now taunting him under the window, always dashed to the nearest tree the moment Duffy stepped outside. Cats who ran, challenging him to races he never won, delighted him. Why there should be two kinds of cats, Duffy had no idea, but the one below him was a chaseable cat, a cat who would never dare to wash his face inches away, if only Duffy could utter one sharp, clean collie bark.

But he couldn't bark. Barks were backed-up inside his chest like balloons straining to rise, and yet all he could do was to stare down at the confident cat and swallow back the bark he deserved. Behind him on the wide bed in the dark bedroom, the man still slept surrounded by the three small lumps, the three Lhasas who made up Duffy's indoor family. None of the sleeping shapes had moved, and until the largest one did, Duffy must not bark. He understood this as deeply as he felt the barks pushing at his throat. The man's anger, if Duffy should give in to his overwhelming urge to send the cat racing to the nearest tree, kept him silent.

As he watched, the cat continued past the window and out of sight around the corner of the house. Duffy settled back on the bench with a long low sigh, all that was left of the jubilant bark he had held too long.

He dozed. As soon as the bright crown of the rising sun appeared above the stable roof, sending shafts of morning light between the sycamore branches to the bed where the man and the small dogs slept, Duffy's day would begin. He felt secure about the day ahead. All his days were now divided into segments he could anticipate: a morning treat for each dog while the man ate breakfast, then an opened door to the yard, and the morning rounds to investigate every interesting corner of the property for traces of night visitors. Certainly, there would be at least one chaseable cat as the seven gathered near the kitchen door for breakfast. Then, before going back to the house there would be the walk along the dirt road, Duffy in the lead, the man and one or two small dogs following to the corner of the pasture where the cattle gathered in late summer for wafers of hay. All of this Duffy loved. All was familiar yet always new, as overnight his world changed. Old tracks crossed by strangers, yesterday's scents washed with morning dew; even the early September morning would carry its hints and promises to a lifted nose. Both the sameness of his days and their tantalizing differences gave to Duffy a sense of excitement he had not always felt. Best of all, he lived with a man who liked him, who never failed to show his approval when Duffy trotted toward him.

Still, Duffy was aware of something missing and disturbing about this Sunday morning. Not all of his days were the same, and this one should have been unlike most. Once each week the man's morning routine changed. The doors of the two small bedrooms were opened to air the rooms while the man made beds and vacuumed the carpets. Somehow this weekly attention to the small bedrooms coincided with the arrival of the girls to spend the night and the following day.

Duffy had learned to anticipate their arrival, to wait at the driveway entrance for the sight of the small car at the end of the dirt road, to be greeted by the high, sweet voices, the hugs and pats as the girls matched his joyous greeting with their own. Later, they would play with him, throwing a tennis ball as long as he returned it to be thrown again, or sit sunning themselves while Duffy stretched between them on the grass. That night he would share their beds, moving from one bedroom to the other until it was time to wake them for the Sunday walk. How he loved their visits! How he loved to feel their light hands, to hear them laugh and sing his name!

Yesterday the man had prepared the small bedrooms, and had taken Duffy and the Lhasas to the market in the pickup just as he always did on those special days when the girls came to visit. Duffy had stationed himself at the head of the driveway to watch for the small car, waiting until the man called him back to the house, but the girls had not arrived. Even now, as he waited for the day to begin, he knew that this should be one of those special mornings with his girls. Where were they? Duffy had received all the signals from the man, signals always before reliable. Duffy looked out at the empty yard, unable to understand.

It had taken many months of living with his latest family for Duffy to understand the ways of the man in his life, and how Duffy fit into this household of cats, little dogs, and occasionally young girls. He'd had to learn a new way of living involving freedoms and prohibitions unlike any he had learned before. Suddenly, he was welcome to accompany a human through every hour of his day, allowed to push nose first between the man's legs until the itching spot above his tail was scratched. Suddenly, he was free to run in great, widening circles whenever he felt the wild urge to cover ground. He found that he would be embraced and complimented upon returning at the sound of his new name, rear quarters waving from side to side with the violent motion of his heavy tail. His new security depended upon small acts he had never known: his dinner always served in the same place at the same time; the truck that never left without him; his place on the window bench.

Still, there were times even now when Duffy felt uncertainty and even fear. Just the other day, a late-August afternoon when the breeze failed to sweep away the flies, the man had moved through the house with a folded newspaper swatting and swearing at the flies. The sharp slap of the folded newspaper had awakened in Duffy a terror so real that he had run trembling from the room. And the sight of the man carrying his broom to sweep the floor on those special mornings before his girls arrived continued to worry Duffy. Never had the man hit him with a newspaper or broom handle, but somehow the sound of one, the sight of the other, sent him cowering from their reach. There were also times when the man went away without him for an evening. The Lhasas seemed unworried by these absences, curling into favorite chairs to sleep, confident that he would always return, but Duffy was never quite so sure. He had spent too many days and nights waiting alone behind a wire fence, sometimes until morning, for the human in his life to come back. Duffy hated to be left alone, even with the small dogs for company, but the humans he counted upon remained forever unaccountable.

Each of the humans Duffy had known had contributed in important ways to the dog he had become. Like his great coat, darkening and thickening with each annual shedding and new growth, adding color and texture but never quite replacing his old one, the humans in his three separate lives had added layers of experience and response, a part of which he carried always. His first life, no longer consciously remembered, had lasted less than three months. These were his puppy days at the breeding kennel. He was born in the early hours of a June morning, one of six siblings and the son of a champion. His sire, Mr. O'Shannon, had won the fifteen show points necessary for championship by competing with his peers in shows throughout the West. Among Duffy's forebears on his sire's side there had been twenty-three champions in five generations. His dam, Rachel's Golden Mist, was the daughter of great champions, so that Duffy's genes carried the breeder's carefully selected, painstakingly developed points of collie perfection.

Nevertheless, from the day he was born there were noticeable differences between Duffy and his brothers and sisters, differences which were to determine the rest of his life. He was the only puppy in the litter who refused to nurse at his mother's teat, a refusal which would, in a wild family, have resulted in his death. Instead, he was tube fed by a human until he was strong enough to make his way to the bowl with the rest. Also, although both his sire and dam wore the traditional sable and white collie colors, Duffy's puppy fur was sprinkled with long, dark hairs which, by the time he was half grown, marked his color as mahogony, a much rarer collie color. While his impeccable ancestry qualified him at birth for American Kennel Club registration, and his wide skull and short muzzle conformed to the latest official standards of acceptable fashion, one fault, apparent to the breeder's eye at birth, would disqualify him from the show ring. The small front teeth of his lower jaw protruded slightly beyond those of his upper jaw, a deformity known as malocclusion. This thrust of lower jaw beyond upper, hardly noticeable except when his chin was lifted, was enough to remove Duffy from puppies the breeder would keep or sell as potential champions.

The first weeks of his life were spent in the nursery room of one of the most unusual households any puppy has ever lived in. In a quiet, suburban section of a small city midway between San Francisco and Los Angeles, the last house on the block resembled from the street-side every other in the neighborhood: its wrought-iron fence protecting a barbered dichondra front lawn, its connecting garage closed, its recreational vehicle parked in an open breezeway. Only the collie's-head knocker on the rose-painted front door and the occasional muffled barking of large dogs marked it as the home of a collie breeder. Behind this conforming facade, the house, its human occupants, and the adjacent grounds had been converted to the raising and celebration of champion collies. Each room inside the house was separated from every other by a low gate behind which a collie, a tri-color or a sable or a blue, stood isolated until his coat dried or his temperature dropped or his long life ended in peace. The walls of every room were decorated with collie photographs, plaques, and silver trophies. Collie bric-a-brac, collie bronzes and collie plastics, collie highball glasses and collie coasters covered every table. Books and articles about collies filled the shelves of a small office where collie records and correspondence were filed.

The service rooms beyond the kitchen of the collie house had been converted into dispensary and grooming areas, complete with examining table, deep stainless-steel tub, glass-doored cupboards filled with metal combs and wire brushes, dental implements, syringes, and an array of medicines. The storage room beyond held hundred-pound sacks of dog food, feeding bowls, and bottles of dog shampoo. The yard behind the house was taken up with runs and kennels so intricately arranged that each of the two dozen dogs in residence would move through the labyrinthine system of gates and pens without necessarily encountering another dog. The motor home at the side of the house had been furnished as a traveling kennel, while the closed garage had been converted into a luxurious cattery. There, protected from the collies, a dozen cats rescued from the nearby freeway enjoyed upholstered climbing trees, cushioned nests, and every toy a cat has ever paused to pat.

This collie house, where not a loose hair fell to the floor, and a flea was as rare as a mouse in the cattery, became Duffy's first home. In it he was never alone, never beyond the sounds of other collies or the mysterious aroma of cats, but it was not his brothers and sisters or even the occasional visits of his mother, but the mistress of the kennel who became the center of his life. From birth, it was she who fed him every four hours night and day, who cleaned and combed the pablum from his fur, who later taught him all he knew. It was the human voice he listened for, the human legs he watched. Whether he would sleep in the pen with his brothers and sisters or stagger into the sunshine to meet the older dogs depended upon the human. That discovery and his allegiance to her became the very core of his being.

As Duffy watched, the man in the bed moved, shifting the Lhasas and waking them to yawn and stretch. Now sunlight filtered by the sycamore spread across the bed, an invitation Duffy recognized and accepted. He jumped from the window bench, shook himself and walked around the bed to stand before the man, watching him, waiting to be noticed. The man ran his fingers lightly along Duffy's nose, then held and rubbed an ear. Duffy's day had begun. Now the little dogs came to the side of the bed to greet him, and as the man rose, Duffy placed his front paws together, stretched back in a deep bow of satisfaction, and offered a soft cascade of barks.

Chapter Two

To Duffy, whose well-being depended upon the human in his life, his name meant everything. His name was the first word he learned. It became the sound above all sounds he listened for and welcomed because each repetition reestablished the vital connection every dog needs to feel secure. In a family of animals equally loved and acknowledged, only the precious syllables of each member's names spoken harshly or with love or even in passing satisfies a dog's need to reaffirm his place next to the human he reveres.

In the highborn society of blooded thoroughbreds into which Duffy was born, dogs are given names no dog could call his own, names intended to impress humans, not dogs. Duffy's great-grandfather's name, for instance, was Three Trees' Beau Blue; his great-grandmother's name was Shepard's Heiress O'Philamour. Imagine responding with typical collie pleasure to such cacaphonous showers of syllables!

But Duffy was denied, or perhaps spared, a patronymic. Instead, at the moment his second life was about to begin, he was named simply Sonny. This careless, rather unimaginative name did not, however, reflect a lack of concern for his welfare. Quite the opposite, in fact, for it was the kennel mistress's firm policy to select new owners for her collies as carefully as she selected their dams and sires.

Whether sold as future champions or given to people she believed deserved a collie, she chose her collie owners after thorough investigation. Then she continued to follow up on her choices. No puppy from her kennel was ever forgotten. She knew her dogs were worthy; she remained less certain of their owners.

Sonny, now a leggy adolescent, his first coat crowding out his puppy fur, his second teeth thrusting painfully through his gums, his pliant ears still refusing to follow directions, was to be no exception. In her collie files was a list of prospective buyers willing to pay high prices for young dogs to show and breed. Duffy's brothers and sisters would travel to Kansas and Texas and Alaska. Also, there were a few friends who, now and then, were rewarded with puppies because they would give them love and good homes. One of these was a young woman who worked as a physical therapist in the local hospital where the kennel mistress had received treatment. She lived alone in a small town twenty miles from the kennel, a point not in her favor because young collies like large families of playmates, but she owned her house on a quiet street. Dogs like permanent homes, and renters move too often and are always at the mercy of discriminating landlords. There was a fenced yard around the house, a condition insisted upon by the kennel mistress, where Sonny would be safe while the woman was at work. Finally, the young woman wanted a dog's company, and collie affection is notoriously lavish.

So it was that Duffy, still called Sonny, moved to his second home. At first, he was delighted. His new owner was young and willing to play his games. During their first day together she took him on a long walk through streets laden with the traces of other dogs. Best of all, for the first time in his life he had a human all to himself. His name and his dinner pan became unmistakably his.

His first day alone in the small fenced yard was to become one of those seminal days in a young dog's life when first encounters are indelibly imprinted upon his future patterns of behavior, but also when experience evokes elemental responses. A day, in other words, when Duffy became who he was to be. As he stood behind the crossed wires to watch the young woman drive away without him, he discovered for the first time what it felt like to be alone, which to Duffy could only have meant to be abandoned in a suddenly empty and meaningless world. His reaction to this sudden collapse of his new companionship began, as collie reactions often do, with his tail. Collie tails are among the most beautiful of all animal tails, proud banners woven of their colors and expressing always the state of their spirits. Collie optimism is worn at the turned-up tip where a graceful mountain of fur rides high. Duffy's tail tip, however, made a sharp left turn before rising, a quirk which gave his tail an extra fillip whenever it announced his interest. Now his tail fell between his legs. His soft eyes continued to watch the spot between houses where the car had disappeared, and his ears, taped and weighted at the tips to train them to break in the required collie fashion known as "tulip ears," stood half erect listening to the last sounds of the car a street away.

Then something new and wonderful happened. As Duffy sat watching through the fence, the empty street began to fill with children. From both directions they came, some on bicycles, others walking along the sidewalk in front of him. He had never seen small humans before, but as they passed, stopping to call and wave to him, he decided they were his favorite kind. He stood on his hind legs, his front paws against the fence, barking and wagging his tail. When a group of children stopped to watch, he ran in circles around the yard until the children walked on.

But his new admirers also left him, and once again Duffy sat down to wonder why. He watched them entering the building at the side of his yard, so each day of his first week he moved from the front fence to the side fence to wait. Several times each day the doors of the building opened and children of every size, some as small as he was, ran into the playground. If Duffy barked they would come to the fence to visit, poking small fingers through the wire to touch his nose, urging him to run his circles. Only when they passed him in the afternoon on their way home from school did he take up his place at the front of the house to wait, again alone.

As the autumn days grew shorter, Duffy's grew much longer. His morning and early-afternoon vigils were rewarded with the outpourings of children for recess and for lunch periods, but as their voices died away, the schoolyard, like the street, became another empty place.

Often it was dark when the young woman came home. Sometimes Duffy ate his dinner in the kitchen with her; sometimes she fed him in the yard, and then left him again to wait for her. Once or twice she came home so late that the moon was high and the night cold against his light coat. He was never allowed inside the house unless she was also there, so he chose a place on the back-door mat where his body warmed a sleeping circle.

Nor were his reunions with her always pleasant. Duffy, now half grown and able to rest front paws on her shoulders when he stood to reach his tongue toward her chin, was pushed away. When he repeated this exuberant greeting she reached for the broom and hit him sharply across his back with the handle. The pain was bad enough, but it was her anger, her shrill rejection, that destroyed for Duffy the relief he felt when at last she came home.

The misunderstandings between them increased. Paper-trained when he came to his new home, Duffy soon learned to use the yard to relieve himself. Except that now and then, in the middle of the night, he needed to go out. He slept on a folded blanket in a kitchen corner, so when the need for his first midnight trip to the yard became more than he could bear, he stood at the kitchen door and barked. The young woman, furious at being awakened just as she had fed him and gone to bed, ran into the kitchen to scold him. She would not open the door. Later that night Duffy chose a place on the living-room carpet much like the grass outside and left a dark pile. When the woman found it the next morning Duffy was dragged to the mess and slapped hard across his nose with a rolled-up newspaper.

After that the punishments happened more often. Duffy knew he must not bark when the woman was asleep. He also knew that he must not use the carpet. As his dilemma continued, so did the nightly pressure in his bowels. The morning rages, the stinging newspaper only made things worse. Duffy developed chronic diarrhea. He was banished permanently from the house, fed his dinner in the yard, and left to sleep on the back doorstep. Now only the arrival of the children at the fence reminded him that there were humans in the world who touched his head with love.

He had not been forgotten, however. The kennel mistress sometimes came to visit him. On several mornings when Duffy was alone in the yard she had stopped at the curb, come to the fence and run strong hands over him, adjusting the tape on his ears and speaking to him with the deep voice he remembered. Then, one rainy morning in early March, she arrived to find him soaked and shivering with nowhere to hide from the rain. That same evening she returned when Duffy's owner was at home. He heard the car and ran to the gate to meet her. Though it was still raining, he was not allowed to accompany her inside the house.

He ran to his place at the back door. From there he could hear the lifted voices as the women talked, the deeper voice angry, the lighter defensive. Then the back door opened. Both women stood under the kitchen light as rain slanted across its path to the yard.

"Sonny! Sonny!"

He heard the call and crept into the shaft of light, his coat stained dark, water dripping from his muzzle. As he appeared, the older woman stepped outside to fasten a leash to his collar. She reached down to him and Duffy rolled over, his instinctive surrender sign, a young dog's best defense.

He was pulled to his feet and led around the house to the front gate where he was guided into the back seat of the waiting car. Off they went, Duffy and his first human, turning down dark streets, tires squealing as the station wagon seemed to join the angry protests still ringing in his ears.

Rescued and returned to the collie house, Duffy received attention as unrelenting as the loneliness he had endured in the empty backyard. He was fed small portions of rice soaked in beef consommé twice each day with additional bowls of cottage cheese before he went to sleep at night in the same small room where he was born. He had to swallow spoonsful of Kaopectate for his diarrhea and Di-Gel tablets for his uneasy stomach. When his strength returned, he was lifted to the grooming table to be brushed and combed. His teeth were cleaned, his pads and nails clipped, and his whiskers trimmed. Once again his ears were taped and weighted in a last vain effort to remodel them. As he submitted to the daily doses of vile liquid, to the probing hands along his ribs, even to the thermometer inserted in his rectum, he also heard the forgotten sounds of praise and found the face he could lick.

Duffy was nine months olds, an age in a collie's life when his frame is set and finished, his markings defined, with only his chest and his coat remaining to thicken and deepen. He stood in the classic collie pose, white front legs meeting at his paws, white ruff rising from his chest to wreathe his head, long body tapering to the slope of his hips, rear legs set apart and back, brush tail the final flourish. He weighed sixty pounds, fifteen short of his adult weight, which he would not reach for another year. Otherwise, he was complete. It was now apparent that his coat would darken to black along his spine, but his flanks remained collie sable and his skirts a softer beige. His eyes, large for his breed and set in slanted casements, were amber rings within which deep pupils glowed with onyx light.

Restored to perfect health and groomed to show perfection, he joined his third family. Once again he rode in the rear of the station wagon with an older collie for company, but this time his destination was as unimaginable as his welcome. He was allowed to jump free into a circle of small dogs, strange little dogs with noseless faces and tails curling backward like teakettle handles. As he began his explorations they followed behind, as if at last someone had joined them with nose enough to discover the interesting places.

At a rail fence Duffy came face to face with the first horses he had ever met, a bay mare and her white colt, long, solemn faces that refused to return his bark. Off he trotted to trace the warm-milk smell of grazing cattle circling their flicking tails while they too ignored him. At the base of the sycamore trunk he caught the familiar smell of cat, although he still had never met one, and as he continued around the ranch house he came across traces of other dogs and stopped to cover theirs with his own proprietary scent. Fascinated by this wild bouquet of odors, he was also aware for the first time of limitless space, of paths and corridors leading to open fields and to a fenced corral where he stopped to drink at a deep trough. He found stables heavy with the smell of summer hay, spongey forest floors shaded by towering evergreens, and cat traces everywhere.

Duffy could resist the temptation no longer. He began to run. Around the house he went, leaping over broad hedges of juniper, racing at top speed through clusters of dogs and humans, their barks and shouts fading behind him as around he flew again. Then, tongue slipping to the side, his expression softening into a slanting smile, he stopped to be greeted by the man who would become the most important human in his life.

Now, two and a half years later, on this first Sunday in September, the middle morning of Labor Day weekend, Duffy led the way to the pasture corner where the cattle waited for hay to be tossed from opened bales by the roadside. Behind him at the driveway, the Lhasas and the cats sat in the cedar shade where the air still was cool. The sky was cloudless; the sun, well above the ragged spine of coastal mountains to the southeast, already warmed his back. The holiday silence was interrupted only by the intermittent squawking of an electronic bird call hidden in a vineyard, on the slope of a hill to the west, and timed to sound off at two-minute intervals, an amplified screech similar to a bluejay's scold, its scissoring alarm intended to frighten real birds from the ripening grapes.

As the man tossed hay wafers to the jockeying cattle a meadowlark rose from a grass clump near Duffy, slanting away in silent flight.

"Even a meadowlark is silenced by the electric bird, eh, Duffy?"

Duffy came to the man's side, wagging.

"Do you think birds would bother to sing if there was an electric bird in every tree?"

Duffy met the man's eyes, cocking his head.

"What if we put a barking record on the phonograph and turned it up loud. Would barking be any fun any more?"

Duffy barked. He always enjoyed these private consultations during their morning walks. The rising inflections as the man questioned him, the sound of his name in an important context, he knew required his response. Here at the end of the road, too far for small dogs and cats to walk, he was being asked something he certainly would agree with.

Back at the driveway entrance, Duffy was greeted by the Lhasas and the four unchaseable cats. As all reached the side door, the cats stopping to wait for the breakfast pan, the Lhasas hurrying inside ahead of him, Duffy heard the faint shouts of children. Neither the man nor the small dogs had noticed; Duffy was always the first to hear faraway sounds. He paused in the doorway to listen. Somewhere to the east, beyond the high fence separating Duffy's domain from the neighboring ranch, the high, clear voices of children rose into the morning air. Their cries reminded him of other small voices calling to him, urging him to come and play with them.

"Hurry up, Duffy," the man called.

Duffy stepped over a cat and slowly entered the house.

Chapter Three

It was shortly after noon, and quite by accident, when Duffy found the hole under the chain-link fence. At once he knew who had dug the deep trench and why. At the far end of the pasture lived the only neighborhood dog Duffy had ever met, a portly Labrador named Princess whom Duffy did his best to ignore, both because she was obsequious whenever they met and, worse, because she had been spayed. Princess had an obsession, however, which puzzled him. She was a tireless gopher hunter who spent her days nosing out gopher holes, then blasting headlong into the ground until her front quarters disappeared. In her endless search for the one gopher in all the world forgetful and disoriented enough to have neglected to provide alternate exits from its underground nest, Princess left large excavations everywhere. Often when Duffy walked to the end of the road in late afternoons he met Princess on her weary way home, her muzzle caked with dirt, and at each meeting the fat black dog approached him in a sidling wriggle until at his feet she rolled on her back in abject devotion. Duffy never knew how to act on these occasions, but he always wagged politely.

It was clear from the size of the hole and the pile of loose soil behind it that Princess' latest plunge into gopherland had carried her under the high fence which enclosed a world Duffy had never visited. He might never have come upon the trench, however, if this had been the kind of Sunday he had expected it to be.

But it wasn't. Resigned as he was to the absence of the girls, he had hoped when everyone went out at mid-morning that there would be the daily trip in the pickup, a ride Duffy always enjoyed because he passed so many interesting sights. With his head outside the open truck window, nose to the wind, he left a vanishing trail of barks at little girls on ponies, at work dogs riding in pickup beds, even at the woolly shapes of pastured sheep. But there had been no ride either. Instead, the man had walked to the small vegetable garden, a fenced-off corner of the corral, to work.

The rest of Duffy's family was equally uninteresting today. The Lhasas chose a sunny spot near the house to lie like small fur puddles. All the cats had moved to the roof where they would sleep at first on sun-warmed shingles, later moving under the canopy of the sycamore until late afternoon. Even the two horses stood head to tail under the limb of a Monterey pine to wait out the flies and the sun. Restless, still unable to understand why this day had turned out to be so disappointing, he decided to join the man. He slipped between the aluminum slats of the corral gate, saw him loosening the ground around the last stalks of summer corn, and decided to wander along the fenceline separating the east end of the pasture from the trampled paddocks on the other side of the chain-link fence.

He heard his name.

"Come on, Duffy. Let's go cool off."

He saw the man leave the corral to walk slowly toward the house.

He also heard again the laughter of children, louder and closer, just beyond the chain-link wall he faced. It was at that moment that he came upon the opening under a section of fence he had never inspected before.

Collies are among the most sociable of dogs, and Duffy was surely among the most sociable of collies. In his third home, however, opportunities for social calls to other humans were almost nonexistent. To be sure, there were infrequent visitors who came to repair a leaking pipe or a smoking appliance, or even on occasion to spend an evening, and these Duffy welcomed so vociferously that at first no one else could get a word in edgewise. And usually when he rode to the market or the post office in the pickup there was an admirer or two who stopped to speak to him. But for the most part his human contact was limited to the man, and to the weekend visits of his daughters.

From Duffy's many viewpoints along his daily rounds, he looked out upon a world of fences, the symbol of the new West, where a small house on a narrow lot becomes a ranch as soon as it is surrounded by a painted two-rail fence. Such was the house where Princess lived, at the end of the dirt road. Then there was the practical fence enclosing a large ranch across the road, a fence intended to protect the vineyards, where Duffy had never ventured. Finally, there was the high chain-link fence, an impenetrable wall around the pastures and paddocks of an Arabian horse ranch, a baffling network of wire-enclosed squares which for an equally baffling reason was called not a ranch but a farm. All these forbidding fences, as isolating as castle moats, warned Duffy to stay out. From his side of the chain-link fence he could see only cavorting horses and an occasional man pushing a wheelbarrow or riding a small tractor. He could see no house, no yard where children played. The world he lived in and the world he watched beyond it appeared to be a place where humans, if there were any, preferred to be left alone.

Nevertheless, as he stood before the passage under the fence, Duffy heard his welcome coming from somewhere beyond a long barn. He crawled easily through Princess's hole and found himself in a chain-link corridor running between a paddock where a stallion pranced and snorted and a bare pasture filled with mares and their spring foals. Duffy sent a shower of barks at the stallion, then continued toward the horse barn and the sounds of voices. He trotted jauntily around the barn, where he came upon a scene he could hardly believe. On the top of a gentle rise was a rambling, one-story house of white adobe with a sloping roof of Spanish tiles. The U-shaped house enclosed a multilevel patio with steps leading down to a swimming pool as blue as a square of sky, in which three children splashed a ball back and forth to each other.

And there was more to see. Where the ground fell away from the flowered banks of the pool lay a broad arena consisting of bridle paths around a fenced oval where a woman rode a white Arabian in a cantering circle. To the left of the oval, four horses tied by lead ropes to a turning center pole walked in a tight circle like a carousel on which the horses, rather than the platform beneath them, spun. As Duffy looked down upon this scene from the corner of the barn more humans appeared on the patio, wearing wide-brimmed hats and knee-high western boots. And then he caught the delicious odor of roasting meat rising in a plume of white smoke from a grill on wheels in the center of the lower patio.

If ever there was a scene into which a sociable collie fitted, the one Duffy looked down upon was it. Why there was not a dog in sight, of course, he never bothered to wonder. He made his way down from the barn wearing his best visiting manners, ears folded back, mouth slightly ajar, hips swaying to the tune of his tail so that he seemed to smile from one end to the other. There were so many people to greet that he had to choose where to go first. He decided to enter an open gate near the pool to stand on slippery tiles and wait to be noticed by the children.

They saw him immediately and two boys swam to poolside to greet him. He felt their hands on his back as water dripped from their noses to his. He heard their voices asking him excited questions. He stepped between them to the edge of the pool to look down into the shining face of a little girl. It was all just as he remembered. Children liked him and showed it in ways he understood. Now the girl joined the boys around him while Duffy continued to nose his way among them, so many legs and hands and voices at once that he offered his cascading bark of utter delight.

It was always Duffy's way when confronted by several humans to go from one to the next until all had received him. As the children jumped back into the pool, calling to him to watch them, he trotted up the steps to meet the tall man at the barbecue grill. The smell of sizzling steaks was overpowering, but it was the man Duffy had come to see. This, however, was not what the man thought.

"Where did you come from?" he asked, not unkindly.

Then, turning back to his grill, he added, "You better go home."

Duffy moved on. The two young women on the patio had been joined by a second man coming from the house. All three were now setting a long table for lunch, and as Duffy arrived to greet them each paused to speak to him, friendly acknowledgment he expected, but that was all. His high spirits would not be dampened by their failure to respond to him as the children had; he already understood the differences between adults and children. When the three returned to the house for more bowls and utensils for the table he was gently urged to go home, a suggestion unintelligible to him because it was made in passing as if they didn't really mean it.

The children were back in the pool. Duffy was on his way to rejoin them when once again he caught sight of the moving horses in the arena below the pool banks. There was the solitary rider astride her cantering Arabian, while the four riderless horses continued their slow spin around the pole. Duffy's life at the ranch had taught him that there were two kinds of horses, just as there were two kinds of cats. When a horse was without a rider, as the two horses in his pasture usually were, it paid no attention to him and was therefore not worth his attention. But when there was a human on its back a horse came to life. Duffy had discovered this when one of the girls rode the mare around the pasture while Duffy circled and barked. Always the horse responded, kicking up her heels and running away from him. It was a game he particularly enjoyed.

He trotted down the path outside the pool fence toward the rider. He squeezed easily under the rail of the oval fence, barking as he came, and just as he expected, the horse reacted. Duffy had no difficulty avoiding the nervous kicks. All he needed to do to keep things happening was to stand in the center of the training circle wagging and turning with the horse. Urged on by the barking ringmaster and reined hard by the flustered rider, the horse panicked. Head down, heels flying, he raced straight for the fence, cleared it easily and galloped off toward the barn, the woman clinging to his neck.

Duffy was pleased. There at last was a horse that was a real horse. He ran to the fence to follow up the hill when he noticed that the horse had stopped outside the barn, and that the woman was being helped from the saddle by one of the men, who had come running from the house. Duffy was as sensitive to sounds of outrage as he was to the odor of barbecuing steaks; both he could almost taste. Anger, whether directed at him or simply filling the air around him, stunned and frightened him. Now he heard it.

He turned then to investigate the strange behavior of the four horses walking nose to tail around the pole. Duffy had never seen a hot walker, which was used to cool off sweating horses after they had been ridden. Fastened by a lead rope from the center pole, each horse was led in a tight circle by his own momentum, circling as the horse behind him circled, turning the revolving top of the post. As Duffy approached the horses to find out why they moved so relentlessly without riders, the horses saw him and began to walk faster. But they couldn't hurry, they couldn't stop, they couldn't turn away. All they could do was send up shrill whinnies and kick out at him just outside their dusty path. They began to bump each other as, one after another, they pushed to get away.

The ordered procession fell apart. The horses turned rumps out to aim their hooves more accurately, while the ropes attached to their bridles pulled their heads inside the circle.

"Get away from there," came the shout as the woman ran down the path from the barn.

It was the rider. She looked very small now that she was off her horse, and as she came closer to Duffy, very terrifying. On her head she wore a black western hat decorated with pheasant feathers waving wildly around the crown. Her western shirt and tight jeans gave her the figure of a boy, but her voice, worn and harsh and very loud, was not a boy's voice. As she ran, silver jewelry on her wrists and around her neck and waist glittered in the sunlight like white, flashing eyes. Duffy watched her coming until she almost touched him with her riding crop. Then he scrambled out of her way, watching her angry black eyes. Dagger points of silver darted from her, and the tip of her boot rose toward him.

"OUT, OUT, OUT OF HERE," she bawled, chasing Duffy partway up the path to the barn.

Then she turned back to the horses, who were once again circling the pole as if nothing had happened. Satisfied that no harm had been done, the woman walked swiftly toward the house. As she passed the bank of the pool, the children met her.

"Did he hurt the horses, Grandma?" one of the boys asked.

"I'm calling Animal Control," she snapped as she hurried past them.

"He probably lives around here," the boy called after her.

"Grandma, they'll kill him before his owner finds where he is," the little girl cried as she ran after the woman.

"Serves him right. Dogs shouldn't be allowed to run loose."

Then the woman stopped and turned to call the boys. "Go up to the barn and find Luis. Tell him to tie the dog until he's picked up."

She hurried on, leaving the little girl to run after the boys.

Duffy watched all this from the hilltop near the barn. He saw the woman walk past her guests on the patio and enter the house. He saw the children making their way up the path toward him. As they approached he came wagging to meet them, certain as always that they had enjoyed the game as much as he had.

The taller of the two boys found the choke collar hidden deep in his ruff and pulled him along into the dark interior of the barn. Duffy followed without protest at first as the three children led him down a long corridor flanked by the half-doors of box stalls. As they walked along, the heads of curious horses appeared in each of the doorways, eyes and ears turned toward them. Duffy had never been inside a horse barn before. He walked beside the boy, his nose filling with strong scents of hay and horses. But as the children led him farther along, the sunlight from the entrance faded until they were in almost total darkness.

They stopped outside an empty stall while the smaller boy opened the plywood gate. Then the boy holding Duffy's collar pulled him toward the stall.

Duffy pulled back. He didn't want to enter the dark, square room. The boy grabbed his collar with both hands to pull harder, while the other boy pushed him from behind. As he was forced into the stall the collar chain slipped over his head, sending the boy who held it backwards into the thick straw covering the floor. The boy got to his feet, laughing and brushing straw from bare legs and arms. Then he joined the other boy and girl outside the stall and closed the gate, leaving Duffy inside.

"We'll come back for him after lunch," the taller boy told the others. "Don't tell Grandma where he is."

Duffy heard the children's voices as they walked out of the barn. Above his head at the top of one wall a square of sky cast faint light into the room. Otherwise, all he could see were four smooth walls enclosing him.

Somewhere buried in the loose straw near him was his collar with its metal license and rabies vaccination tags, his credentials and his only identification.

Chapter Four

"Duffeee!"

He heard the call. He recognized the voice. The repeated summons reached him through the small opening at the top of the west wall of the stall. The rising and falling syllables intensified, then faded as the caller moved around the perimeter of Duffy's ranch. Duffy faced the window, his head cocked, his eyes lifted as always to the sound of his name. He knew he was being called home and always before he had obeyed, sometimes reluctantly when just ahead a fresh scent beckoned, sometimes fearfully if he detected impatience in the voice. Had he strayed too far? Had he misbehaved in some unfathomable way? He stood now in the deep straw, willing to return home, waiting only to be allowed to.

Why was it that Duffy made no answering sound? His response to cats outside his window, to doorbells, to a girl with a ball in her hand was the signature of his breed. The collie bark comes easily and joyously. Yet it would have been easier for an abandoned kitten to make its whereabouts known than for Duffy to alert his caller. Collies respond; they don't reply. He was there and waiting. Wasn't that obvious?

Duffy had never cried for help. Once when a veterinarian had probed for a foxtail deep in his ear he had cried out. He was unusually sensitive to pain, even to anticipated pain, but his bark was saved for celebrations. He had never associated it with the inevitable appearance of a human to open a door or relieve the discomfort of a burr between his toes. If the stall gate must be opened to allow him to go home, in time it would be. He must trust the all-knowing human in his life.

He heard footsteps moving toward him along the center corridor of the barn. He turned confidently to face the stall gate just as a dark head passed followed by the high back of a horse. He heard heavy footsteps as the horse was led into an adjoining stable, then watched the man's head pass by again as he walked out of the barn. Duffy eased himself down into the straw to wait.

It was much later that he heard the children's voices. They were walking toward him and once again he stood wagging, knowing they were coming for him. The gate opened and the three children stepped inside, closing the gate after them and whispering soft greetings. Each had brought steak scraps folded inside a paper napkin and each took a turn holding the napkin under his nose while Duffy gulped down the juicy chunks as fast as he could. Each child patted his head before leaving.

"We'll be back," they promised, but Duffy didn't understand.

He lay on the straw bed, dozing but alert for sounds of the children returning for him. All he heard was the movement of horses in the stalls, stamping and pressing against the siding. Now and then above the turmoil of the heavy animals he thought he heard voices calling to each other, but they were far away and unfamiliar. At last, when even the horses seemed to have settled, he heard footsteps coming toward him. Then the low voices of men filtered across the open tops of the stalls. Horses were being led into the barn, and as gates slammed and animals subsided along the double row, the sporadic conversation drew near.

He stood facing the gate so certain of rescue that every now and then a soft impatient whine was driven from him, a noise he made while he waited behind a door at the very brink of welcoming his visitors. The gate opened. A man stood in the entrance, holding a horse by the lead-rope snap below the halter. He stared down at Duffy.

"*Caramba*!" The young voice was filled with surprise and fear. "Hey, Luis. There's a big dog in here."

A second man appeared in the doorway. Duffy was delighted. He leaped toward the men, forgetting his manners as he placed front paws on the chest of the young man holding the horse. And he barked. Just as he knew all along, his moment had come.

But the man Duffy chose to thank shrank back against the horse, while the older man stepped into the stall to push Duffy down into the straw so hard that the collie was knocked off his feet. As Duffy cowered, the man reached down to grab his collar. It wasn't there, so quickly he wound a rope around the collie's neck, using the fastener to make a loop. Then Duffy was pulled out of the stall.

As soon as the horse had been led in and the gate closed, the two men walked out of the barn leading Duffy along between them. They were speaking excitedly and glancing down at the dog as they came out into the sunlight at the barn entrance. Duffy went along willingly, listening and content to be accompanying the men wherever they led him. These were small men with soft voices and gentle dark eyes, and although he sensed fear in the younger man and uneasiness in the one who held his rope leash, there was no anger. They still had not touched his head with their hands or spoken his name, so when they paused outside the barn to talk, he nuzzled the hand that held the rope, a reminder that he was so glad to be with them in the sunlight.

The men started down the path toward the house. There were no children in the pool, no adults on the patio, and no voices to be heard, but as they neared the house Duffy saw the small woman with the angry worn-out voice coming toward them. This time she wore no hat. Instead, a cap of white hair, curled close to her head, bobbed in the late-afternoon sunlight. Walking faster than the men, as if to head them off, she met them before they reached the broad patio.

"Patron," the older of the men called, "we found this dog in the barn."

"The children must have put him there," she answered. "I've called Animal Control, but they can't pick him up till tomorrow."

She faced the men, her small feet spread as if to block Duffy's progress. "I want him off this place, Luis. He nearly caused a broken leg already."

Luis frowned, trying to reflect her horror at the thought of such a thing. Then, hoping to calm her anger, he smiled. "The horses are all in. Shall I let him loose?"

"No," she rasped. "He'll stay around and draw other dogs."

"I could keep him in my trailer overnight," he suggested.

"Luis!" She almost bit the tip of his nose as her small red mouth snapped at him. "I want the dog out of here tonight. I don't care what you do with him. Shoot him if you have to. But I'll have no dogs here. Even overnight. Even tied up. Do you understand me?"

And so it was decided. Except that nothing was decided. What were they to do with Duffy? Was he to be hidden in the foreman's trailer, parked beneath a pepper tree near the sheds and service buildings and close to the main house? What if the dog barked? If he were turned loose outside the chain-link gates would he not find his way in again, just as he had before? The foreman knew how intensely his employer hated dogs. When she bought the ranch she had insisted that the rail fences, common to every horse ranch in the valley, be replaced with the high, secure walls to keep out dogs. Perhaps, as sometimes happens, her hatred of dogs was aroused by her passionate fondness for the five pampered Persian cats who slept on her bed. He knew about those cats because, when his wife carried the breakfast tray to the woman's bedroom every morning, it must include extra bacon slices for the cats. They liked it crisp.

The foreman didn't know what to do. Was this a valuable dog? He didn't know that either. Neither of the men had ever owned a dog or wanted to own one. The younger man, hired as groom and handyman, knew even less what to do, and he was afraid of dogs, especially large dogs like Duffy with teeth he could see protruding from the lower jaw. But the younger man would do as he was told. He needed his job because he had no papers.

As the two men walked toward the graveled area where the ranch vehicles were kept, Duffy had to be pulled along. He kept stopping, resisting the rope around his neck, to turn his head back toward the empty pool and the vanished scene so exciting only a few hours ago. In the early evening silence he listened for voices, but the only sound he heard was the distant acceleration of a truck off to the west beyond the fences.

He couldn't know it was the pickup starting out again along the dirt road. His owner and the Lhasas were beginning another search, but to Duffy it was only a disappearing sound.

Chapter Five

Duffy left the Arabian horse ranch in the seatless back end of an ancient white Chevrolet sedan, one end of the rope collar tied securely to the door handle because the driver was afraid of being bitten by his passenger. They drove off along a rutted road, a back entrance used by employees and by trucks delivering hay and feed, a field away from the dirt road Duffy walked every morning and evening with his owner. It was nearly six o'clock, an hour in early September when the suspended sun gilds cropped fields, highlighting steeples and the snaggled sails of windless windmills, a golden time of rest and peace. Only the jouncing car and its wake of sunlit dust disturbed the stillness of the scene.

At the paved road the driver turned south, carrying Duffy toward the small town he and the man he lived with visited on daily trips to the post office. He knew the way over the valley floor toward the wall of coastal mountains, past farmhouses surrounded by fields of tomatoes and sugar beets ready for harvest, then along neat fencelines enclosing small ranches where irrigated pasture alternated with the summer's last alfalfa cutting. At the outskirts of the town, one-story houses on city lots lined both sides of the road, each fenced and offering to the passerby a glimpse of marigolds bordering a shaded patio. Finally, the crossroads corner, the town's center, halted the car before it sped on downhill toward a trough of lowland between the hill on which the town center sat and a mesa which formed the takeoff platform of the local airport.

The old car left the world Duffy recognized at the dusty entrance road leading to a settlement consisting of a public campground, a new and well-constructed community center, and a dozen more small houses scattered without apparent plan throughout the low-lying land. Here there were no white fences around the houses, no marigold borders. The houses wore coats of faded paint and were connected by a network of paths leading to the central building. The entire area was scored with deep trenches between ragged banks where runoff from the previous winter's rains had coursed through the settlement on its way to the river. The car followed the edge of one of these dry washes until it reached the last house tucked into the side of a bulldozed hill. There it stopped and Duffy heard the cries of children coming from the open doorway of the house. The driver left him tied and walked to the house, where a woman greeted him. Then two small children poked dark faces around the woman's skirt.

He watched the scene through the half-open window of the Chevrolet, standing on the floor waiting to be let out. But no one came to open the car door. The driver and the woman talked, turning now and then toward Duffy, but neither moved toward him as he strained against the rope. Then the man disappeared inside the house, leaving only the children in the doorway to stare at the collie as if he were some fierce, exotic beast they had never seen before. Duffy could bear his confinement no longer. He lifted his nose to the window and barked. The moment the children heard the sharp shower of barks they fled from the doorway. The great wild animal in the car was about to break loose and eat them.

The isolated community in which Duffy waited to be freed from his second cell that day was a tract of useless land set aside for the remnant population of descendants of the Chumash Indians, once a peaceful and highly artistic tribe inhabiting the central coast and inland valleys of California. So decimated by disease, Christian culture, and intermarriage with their Spanish conquerors that the last full-blooded Chumash member of this settlement had died a generation ago, the surviving families continued to receive the blessings of the Bureau of Indian Affairs. These included the strip of lowland, fees paid for the use of the campground, and the new building in which the tribal office was located.

The reservation offered the young Mexican alien a place to live. The house Duffy watched belonged to a Chumash man who had married the driver's sister. When the Mexican crossed the border the year before he had hitchhiked his way to his sister's house. Because he spoke English and had worked with horses, he found a job as groom and stable boy at the Arabian ranch. And in one year, living with his sister's family and saving his wages, he had been able to buy the white Chevrolet. Even though he usually worked seven days a week under the critical eye of a woman who seemed to like only horses and cats, his good fortune continued to amaze him. He was not about to risk losing this perfect job by refusing to take home a dog he didn't know what to do with.

Duffy waited in the back of the car for someone to untie him and let him out, but it became clear that no one was going to. And, although he never took his eyes from the open doorway of the house, not even the children reappeared to stare at him. He heard voices, and the odors of cooking food filled the air, but he never heard his name and even the food smell didn't interest him. And it was growing dark. The sun had sunk below the sill of western foothills, and as its direct light was withdrawn its absorbed light in living plants gave watered places a greener ghost light which would linger well after sundown. Darkness fell first in this crevice where the Indians lived, but as if to maintain its hidden profile, even the lighted windows of the houses were pale and flickering. Duffy couldn't see any movement, human or animal. Where were the dogs and cats belonging to these houses? He had never known a house without its sentinel dog or cat, but whenever he stretched his nose to the edge of the car window he caught no scent.

It was fully dark when he saw the men come through the lighted doorway into the small front yard. One he recognized as the driver; the other, taller and heavier, walked to the car window to look in at Duffy. The collie reached toward the man so that the tip of his nose poked beyond the glass of the window, and the man raised his hand as if to touch Duffy's head. But just as his fingers were close enough to lick, the man withdrew his hand in fear. He rejoined the driver to stand just out of reach, and the men continued to discuss the problem of the dog while Duffy wagged inside the car.

Other men appeared, walking along the paths from nearby houses to join in the discussion. Each stepped close enough to the car to look in at the dog, then stepped back to offer an exclamation. The woman and her children appeared in the doorway to listen to the men and to make sure no one let the dog out of the car. That Duffy was the center of attention was obvious, but why no one opened the car door or brought him a bowl of water was not. Nor would he have understood their debate any more than their fear of him.

"Is he a sheep dog?"

"No, no, man. Too big."

"He must belong to someone."

"He's got no license. Not even a collar."

"Does he bite?"

"Hey, man. Who's going to find out? You?"

And they all laughed.

The circle around the car continued to grow. Women and older children appeared. No one came forward, though, and Duffy's head finally disappeared below the car window while the discussion turned to dogs in general and the problems they created. Dogs the size of Duffy ate as much as a man, and children died from dog bites. One thing was decided: no one wanted Duffy.

The group around the car began to return to their houses, calling out as they left, wishing the young Mexican good luck with his dog. Just don't bring him back, they all agreed.

Duffy heard footsteps approaching the car. It was so dark that not until the young Mexican opened the front door did Duffy recognize him. The collie was silent now, and thirsty. So was the driver, although as they drove out of the reservation, neither understood the other's need. To the driver the big dog in the back of his car had become a much worse problem than he had anticipated. He had hoped to find a neighbor who would take him, but not only had all refused, their warnings worried him. His way of avoiding deportation was to attract no attention to himself. He had even been afraid to apply for a driver's license when he bought the Chevrolet from a friend of his brother-in-law because he would have had to sign his name and report his address. The dog in the back of his car would be noticed wherever he went. He must get rid of it tonight.

His sister, upon whom he relied for advice, was more terrified of dogs than he was, and had taught her children to fear all dogs. Not even overnight would she allow the dog to be tied in her yard. Soon the dog would need food. He had no money to waste on meat for dogs, whatever kind of meat dogs so big ate, but a sick dog, a starving dog would be a greater danger. North Americans, he knew, worried more about the welfare of their animals than they did about people like him. He needed to think, to drink a few beers and to talk to someone who knew about dogs.

Other than with the people he had met on the reservation—men and women who felt as alienated from the general population around them as he did, and who would no more have thought of betraying him to white authority than they would their tribal members—there was only one place he felt accepted and relatively safe. At the eastern edge of the small town was a bar called The Cutting Horse Café. Some years earlier a local developer had built a half-block replica of an Old West main street and the narrow, connected storefronts with ornate facades and a raised boardwalk ran the length of the frontage. The developer's intention had been to attract tourists from the city, and the shops had featured western jewelry, leather goods, a Chinese restaurant, and a western saloon. But the town was far from the highway, and the location of the Old West stores at the foot of the hill beyond the town's only commercial businesses, as well as their newly rundown appearance, attracted no tourists.

One by one the gift shops and restaurant went out of business until only The Cutting Horse Café remained open, not because of out-of-town customers, but because it soon became the nightly meeting place for hired hands of every breed, who gathered to drink and dance to the music of a husband- and-wife team who played, on drums and electric organ, every country song ever written and remembered. And because it was the only business open in this new ghost town, its blaring music, its shouted arguments, and many of its celebrants, spilled from its swinging bar gates into the country night without being overheard by the town's more sober citizens.

Introduced to the congenial atmosphere of The Cutting Horse Café by his foreman, the young Mexican had found a home away from home. In this company of horsemen and cattlemen whose combined savings amounted to less than the cost of a Thoroughbred yearling or a ribboned Arabian, the only credentials called for were a working man's knowledge of horses and a professional's contempt for city-bred ranchers. That he was an "illegal" made no difference to the drinkers at the bar. He had been accepted the first night when he bought a round and told about being ordered by the woman he worked for to brush the teeth of an Arabian stallion before it was to be shown at an important event. She had insisted that the horse's large yellow teeth would deny her the prize she deserved. She supplied a tube of Pepsodent, and stood by while each front tooth was polished.

Now he drove through the town's main street and down the hill toward the parking lot, enclosed by hitching rails outside the saloon. There, if anywhere, he would find someone to help him get rid of the dog. Meanwhile, he would enjoy a night of drinking with his friends, made even better because the next day, his foreman had explained, was a holiday when he could come to work later than usual.

He parked in front of the lighted doorway so that, if necessary, he could check up on the dog. Then, leaving Duffy tied to the door handle, he locked the car doors and entered the bar. Even though it was still early the two-piece band was pumping out another chorus of "Tie A Yellow Ribbon Round The Old Oak Tree," and the clatter of overlapping voices had reached a midnight crescendo. As he was recognized and greeted he felt happy and relieved. Here at last, the rope tying the dog to his car and therefore to him would be untied. He found a place between two occupied barstools and ordered his first Dos Equís.

When, if ever, does an animal resign itself to intolerable circumstance? In Duffy's case the answer seemed to have been the sight of the driver entering the bright, noisy interior of the bar. No longer did the collie stand to watch for the man's reappearance. Instead, with a soft sigh, he lay down on the floor of the car, as if he realized that this latest stop on his bewildering journey had no significance for him. And yet, like every animal immobilized by trap or twitch or tether, release remained as certain as life itself, and to Duffy the agent of his inevitable release was the human who had tied him. That was all he understood about his predicament. If he closed his eyes and drifted into brief periods of semi-consciousness it was not submission to his hopeless situation but an abiding trust in his alliance with an often puzzling species.

Not for long, however, could he resist rising from the car floor to watch the activity in the doorway of the bar. As the evening wore on the traffic through the swinging bar gates increased, always with loud shouts and a fresh wave of amplified music. The men inside carried their drinks outside to stand on the narrow boardwalk, to lean against the hitching rail or to wander aimlessly around the parking lot before reentering the bar. New arrivals in pickup trucks parked on both sides of the white Chevrolet, passing close to Duffy's window as they hurried inside. Perhaps it was because the inside of the car was thrown into deeper shadow by the splashing light from the bar gates, or perhaps it was simply because the last thing the customers of The Cutting Horse expected to see in the back of a battered sedan was a collie; whatever the reason, no one noticed Duffy or stopped to speak to him.

Then, suddenly, he was found. Through the doorway came the driver, holding a beer bottle, followed by a much larger man. They jumped from the boardwalk to the potholed surface of the parking lot and edged between the Chevrolet and the pickup next to it to stand outside Duffy's window while the large man peered in. Duffy raised his nose to the face under the frayed brim of a western straw, heard himself spoken to for the first time that night and felt the weight of a wide hard hand on his head.

"You all alone out here, boy?" came the drawling voice. "Nobody even buy you a drink?"

The man laughed and Duffy responded. He loved to be questioned. Here at last was someone not afraid of him. He strained against the rope to push his nose toward the long, shadowed face, his tail swinging, jaws opening and closing with the light smacking sound he used to answer friendly questions.

The man raised his beer glass to Duffy's nose.

"Here, boy. Take a sip."

Duffy managed to dip his tongue into the tipped glass.

"He likes it," the man shouted to the watchers at the rail. "Now that's a dog I could agree with."

Duffy withdrew his tongue, beer drops beading his chin. It was not the liquid he expected, but it was wet and cold and the man seemed pleased.

The two men continued to stand outside the car. Every now and then the large man would reach a hand through the window to rub Duffy's head and to offer him another sip of the prickly beer. Duffy licked the inside of the glass each time, still thirsty and very excited.

The men turned to walk back to the bar, but not before Duffy was given a reassuring pat. He watched them leave, unwilling to believe that his long wait was not about to end.

Finally, the lights inside the saloon blinked off and on and its human contents trickled through the bar gates into the summer night. The driver and his friend returned to the car, and the large man reached inside the window to unlock the door. He caught the rope and untied it, inviting Duffy to jump down. Then he led him to a pickup parked on the other side of the lot. While Duffy waited, the man opened the tailgate and boosted him into the bed of the truck. Then, slamming the tailgate shut, but leaving the dog untied, he climbed into the truck cab and with a shouted farewell to the Mexican he drove off up the hill toward the sleeping town.

Duffy had been sold to his new owner for ten dollars.

Chapter Six

Duffy's ride through the country night in the bed of the battered pickup lasted no more than half an hour and covered less than twenty miles. Yet it transported him into a world so different from any he had known that he might as well have traveled back in collie time to nineteenth-century Scotland. As he stood unsteadily in the truck bed, close to the sheltering wall of the cab and with only his nose tip tasting the wind, he was leaving a way of life in which he, like many of those around him, had become an actor playing a role. Like the Arabian horses he had watched cavorting beyond the chain-link fence, bred for purposes irrelevant to their size and stamina, and like the wealthy owners of stud farms and vineyards, men and women who played at raising foals and grapes, Duffy's breed, glorified and, some have said, ruined when Queen Victoria first gave it royal recognition, had become fashionable and had therefore been refashioned. It was no longer the work dog of the Scottish highlands, but a glamorous facsimile. Now Duffy was about to step offstage.

At the valley's eastern rim the conjunction of two steep ranges of scrub-trimmed mountains is bisected by a river bed whose westward course creates a basin where level acres have recently been subdivided into townsites and parcels fenced and nurtured for the breeding of expensive horses. This oak-studded delta widens as it stretches to the Pacific into rolling savanna, dry hills too far from county water lines, too overgrown with sage and nettle, too treacherous for the slender shanks of blooded horses. Once this wild country was the demesne of the *ranchero* who received it as a gift from a Spanish king, and who measured his boundaries by distant peaks and sold his sinewy cattle for tallow at two dollars a head. More recently and well within this century, this same land, where the ratio of feed to animal remains ten acres per grazer, could still be purchased by a man of moderate wealth willing to work from first to last light. Instead of ten acres fenced and fertilized, such a man could own ten thousand. And while the spread of small show ranches at inflated prices crept inevitably toward them, there were still a few outlying kingdoms where a thousand head of cattle calved in spring, fattened on wild oak grass, and lived or died according to the rainfall.

It was to such a ranch that Duffy rode along winding tarmac paths into foothills so far from the valley's population that not a house appeared along the way and only the twin wires of the telephone and power lines traced the starlit sky above his head. The pickup dove between dark pillows of barren hills, past the ghost faces of startled cattle until, at an apron of packed dust, it turned down into a glen surrounded by ranch buildings set under towering walls of eucalyptus, facing a centerpiece of the spreading limbs of an ancient bay. The pickup wound its way to a small one-story house with a screened front porch where it stopped. The engine died and the headlights were turned out. Duffy had arrived.

His new owner let down the tailgate and invited him to jump from the truck bed. As soon as he felt solid ground under his feet, and before the man could untie the dangling rope around his neck, he began to run, relieving himself at every upright, shaking out his coat from head to tail, trotting into such total darkness that only his ruff was visible. But he needed water badly, so in time he returned to the man waiting outside the house. His trailing rope was caught and he was led through the screen door to the porch, where a water bowl waited just outside the front door.

While Duffy gulped water, the man unlocked the door and stepped inside to turn on a light. As he did, a dark shape joined Duffy at the water bowl, a nose began to examine him, and, as the light inside the front room brightened the porch floor, it revealed the black and white body of a dog greeting Duffy so silently that it might have been his foreshortened shadow dancing at his side.

"Hey, Shuba. Bring him inside."

The dog beside Duffy circled him, then ran into the house, then returned to the doorway. As Duffy approached to examine her, she circled again, wagging invitingly. They entered the house together.

"I've brought you a helper, Shuba. How you like him?"

The smaller dog looked at the man. She stood in the center of the front room and, although she was half Duffy's size, in many ways she resembled him. Her head was shaped like his with full muzzle and half-pricked ears, dark gentle eyes set aslant in a smooth mask and wreathed by a white ruff. Her straight forelegs and half-cocked hindlegs gave her Duffy's ready stance, and even her white-tipped tail curled upward and was feathered like his.

Their more obvious differences were in size and coloring. Shuba stood a full six inches below Duffy, and her shorter coat was almost entirely black, except for her white collar and tail tip and white stars on each paw. Also, flecks the color of Duffy's sable flanks were sprinkled at her eyebrows, eartips and elbows. Standing side by side as they faced the man, the smaller dog still looked like Duffy's shadow, except that shadows have no eyes and Shuba's eyes were hypnotizing. Her gaze at the man was unwavering. "We'll have to find a name for him, eh, Shuba?"

Shuba stepped toward the man, attentive and wagging with pleasure.

"We'll think of one tomorrow." The man left the dogs to themselves.

Duffy and Shuba, collie and border collie, shared a common heritage which enabled each dog to deal gracefully with its own and the other's bewilderment that first night. It was their collie nature to accept the circumstances of their meeting because obviously each enjoyed the approval of the man who had brought it about. To Shuba he was the center of life, his small house hers, his purposes her motivation. Their life together was all she knew or cared about. They were partners at work, companions at rest, and never had she shared him with another being, animal or human. It was not her nature, however, to resent Duffy. The man in her life had brought him to her, so she accepted him. And perhaps there was something more; he was a male, larger and stronger than she, and the only other dog in her world was a female German shepherd belonging to the owners of the ranch, a dog she seldom saw. Moreover, while Duffy was a stranger who did not belong, his manner toward her, both deferential and interested, pleased her.

Duffy too was true to his breed. Where he was, and why, he had no idea, only that once again he had been removed from one life and carried to another. In the voice of the man who had brought him here he heard strength and kindness. He liked a human who talked to him. That it was a different man and a different house didn't concern him. He recognized the prior right of the dog beside him, just as he had recognized those of the Lhasas in his former family, but it was not submission so much as the gentle and generous nature of a collie which governed his response to Shuba. The hierarchy of the pack, the subordination of the newcomer, traits buried in his feral past, had been so modified by millennia of human social order that he felt no uneasiness in Shuba's house. Besides, Shuba was the first real female he had ever met.

When the lights in the small house had been turned off and all was silent and dark, Duffy followed Shuba back through a short hallway to a small bedroom. He heard the man stirring in the bed. He saw Shuba moving to a place beneath the open window where she curled on a mat to sleep. He found a place near her and sat down, lowering his front legs slowly to the floor, still alert for some signal from the man or the dog, but when there was none he turned on his side, stretched his legs stiffly before him, relaxed and closed his eyes.

Chapter Seven

Duffy's first day on the remote cattle ranch began with a guided tour conducted so subtly by Shuba that Duffy never realized he was being allowed to see only what she permitted. The tour started at sunrise when both dogs were let out of the house while the ranch foreman went back to bed. It was a holiday morning after a rare night out for him and he didn't want to be disturbed by the dogs. And if he didn't know his new dog well enough to close the door behind him, he knew Shuba would never let him out of her sight.

Duffy was delighted with his early-morning freedom and the opportunity it offered to explore the world he had only sniffed at the night before. With Shuba at his side he set off around the circle of buildings which formed the headquarters of the ranch. He came first to a three-story Victorian house as tall as a castle, sprouting cupolas and dormer windows from its slanting roof. The front yard, shaded by an arm of the bay tree, was laden with the scents of a spice garden, of the resident German shepherd, and of years of layered traces of the ranch owner's large and varied family. Duffy trotted up the sidewalk toward the steep porch steps. The house was silent. The couple inside, and their dog, were still asleep. As he paused at the foot of the steps to leave notice of his visit, Shuba moved close against his shoulder, turning him back from the forbidden steps.

The dogs continued, Duffy leading the way as he always did on his morning rounds, except that now instead of following behind as the Lhasas had, Shuba stayed close beside him. His nose led him past a row of small cottages like the foreman's but closed and stripped of even the faintest hints of animal or human life toward a huge old-fashioned barn facing the owner's house at the opposite side of the clearing. Even the air around the barn hung heavily with a rich mixture of manure and oil and rotting wood, and as Duffy entered its dark interior his nose filled with an almost suffocating smell of feathers and hay. In stalls and hayloft, even beneath his feet he heard strange noises, flutterings and nibblings and drippings. The great dark barn excited him and he wanted to explore it, but again Shuba nudged him back into the sunlight. Duffy went along good naturedly, looking over his shoulder at his companion, as if he were showing her how tempting the world could be.

Their path led next down a long driveway between eucalyptus trunks toward corrals and a feedlot dank even at this dry time of year. Everywhere Duffy's nose filled with the sweet and sour smell of cattle, but cattle were familiar, immovable, uninteresting animals. Just at the point where the road wound upwards away from the ranch buildings a wide gate blocked his progress. He stopped and looked through the pipe bars. For as far as he could see the road led off into barren hills where nothing moved except a redtail hawk riding a thermal carpet above the scattered mushroom domes of live oaks.

Duffy went along, catching up with Shuba to nip her neck, growling playfully as they ran together. When they arrived at the cottage panting and excited, Duffy never realized he had been led all the way. After all, hadn't he taken her with him? Hadn't he left his proprietary marker at every tree and post? If Shuba wanted to return to the porch to rest and drink, he was willing. For the first time in his life, he had found a four-legged companion.

Duffy and Shuba were greeted and let in by the foreman.

"I wasn't asleep, girl," he explained to her, "just wallerin' in the bed."

Shuba stood before him while he enclosed her head in his great hands, lifting her nose toward his face as she writhed with pleasure.

"Shall we take ol' what's-his-name along and show him around?"

Duffy moved in to feel the hands on his head and Shuba stepped back to allow it. The foreman was surprised by her willingness to let a strange dog share his affection.

They went to the pickup, Shuba dancing with delight, then leaping into the truck bed ahead of Duffy. He tried to follow, failed to clear the tailgate and fell back scrambling on his back. He wasn't hurt, but he refused to try again until the foreman placed a hand under his rump to boost him up beside the smaller dog.

"What's the matter, ol' what's-his-name? Cain't jump?" The foreman laughed. "Round here you better learn."

They drove down the driveway to the gate where the foreman stopped, swung the gate open, then drove through and stopped to close it again after them. The powerful engine carried them fast up the two-track road toward the top of the nearest hill. As the truck bed rolled on the uneven slope Duffy braced himself, afraid of slipping out across the open tailgate. Shuba raised her muzzle to the breeze and rode the tilting truck like a sailor on a rolling deck.

The track they followed took them along the crest of the hill, then down into a deep ravine where a dozen cattle rested in the deep shade of live oaks, their search for food suspended until sunset. On both sides of the track and stretching to the horizon the desiccated landscape baked in relentless sunlight, its groundcover so overgrazed that the brassy surface of the hills revealed every subcutaneous fold and crevice. The spring carpet of grasses and wildflowers had sustained the herds since the last spring rains, but all that was left in early September was stubble intermixed with dusted stalks of buttonweed and the wild mustard that even hungry cattle would not eat. For the cattle, as for the foreman and his dog, this was a waiting time when only nibblings were left, a time to thin the herd and hope for early rain.

As the pickup and its dust plume rose and fell along the miles of track, moving always westward, plunging through sluggish animals barely willing to step out of the way, Shuba watched and waited. She stood at the forward corner of the truck bed, ears alert, eyes searching the landscape. Finally, the pickup slowed and stopped. Before the driver opened his door the border collie was out of the bed and waiting beside it.

Duffy jumped down and trotted off to explore what appeared to be a way station, a great yard leveled and fenced. At one end was a cattle chute. The graveled bed of a dry stream bordered the yard and a circular concrete cistern had been sunk deep into the streambed to catch the runoff from winter rains. Duffy found an open gate, ran across the empty yard and lapped thirstily at a trough half-filled with brackish water.

"Hey, get back here," the foreman shouted. "Go get him, Shuba."

Once again Shuba was at Duffy's side, leading him back across the yard to the pickup. And again Duffy went along, wagging and nipping Shuba's ruff, willing always to play the game. Both dogs followed the foreman as he carried slatted panels into the yard to set up a pen around the chute, then opened a wide gate leading into the yard. When he was satisfied he returned to the truck and started the engine. Immediately, Shuba jumped nimbly into the bed as the truck pulled away, leaving Duffy standing behind. The truck jerked to a stop, the foreman got out and came around to boost Duffy over the tailgate.

"What kind of dog are you?" he asked, his eyes squinting and hard. "No collie dog, that's for sure."

Away they went, slurring up the track to the next hilltop, taking out the foreman's disgust with his ten-dollar dog in a burst of spinning wheels. Twice more they stopped at fenced enclosures on the far perimeters of the ranch, each with its pens and chute and access road leading to the highway. At each stop Shuba leaped from the truck, followed by Duffy to accompany the foreman in his preparations, and after each stop Duffy waited to be helped back into the truck bed. The pain of one failure was enough to convince him that he needed help.

But after the third stop the foreman refused to help him. Off went the truck without Duffy. He started to run, his paws collecting the thick dust kicked up by the truck tires, racing up and down the hills as he tried to keep Shuba in sight. And soon he fell so far behind that only at the top of each hill could he see the dust trail. On he ran until he saw the truck pull off the road and stop. He reached it just as the foreman and Shuba headed into a grove of oaks.

Despite the vastness of the ranch and the wild state of its rolling hills it had been divided years before into sections of undulating miles of barbed-wire fencing intended to separate the cattle population into manageable herds. Newly purchased lots were thus isolated from older residents; Angus from Hereford, calving females from breed bulls. And at roundup time these fenced segments made collecting easier. It was at the fenceline between two of these sections that the foreman had stopped. On one side of the three-strand fence a group of cows with nursing calves had gathered to wait out the midday heat, while just beyond the fence a white-faced calf bawled its desperate need to return to its mother. Like many a wandering yearling, the calf had found an easy way to slip through the fence, then discovered a basic bovine truth: all fence holes are one-way, big enough when the grass looks greener on the other side, impenetrable barriers when return is all that matters.

The foreman and his dog went into action. While the man widened the gap with wire clippers, Shuba darted under the fence, made a wide circle behind the calf, then crept silently toward it from the rear, her eyes never leaving the animal.

The foreman backed off, then called softly, “Move him, girl.”

Shuba closed in, lifting and dropping each paw in slow motion.

Aware of the man, facing the barrier of the fence, the calf sensed the dog moving in behind. Frozen by its dilemma, the calf hesitated, nosing the wider opening.

Just as the frightened animal was about to choose return through the fence, a great, bounding, barking bundle shot out of the trees straight at the fence opening. The calf leaped to one side in terror and ran along the fenceline to avoid the oncoming attacker. Shuba moved with the animal, darting in to head off its escape. The foreman yelled at Duffy to get back, but Duffy kept on under the fence and away to join Shuba and the bolting calf. He had never seen one of these great nonchalant beasts react before to his bark. Now that one had he would make the most of it.

While Duffy chased the calf, the foreman chased Duffy, and far ahead Shuba tried to reverse the calf's flight. But Shuba was small and silent, far less a threat than the barking dog and the shouting man. The calf plunged on.

"Shuba!" It was a command.

Immediately, the border collie gave up the chase and returned to the foreman's side. Duffy also gave up and trotted back happily to his companions. The calf, abandoned by his pursuers, also stopped and began to bawl again for its mother.

Duffy was grabbed by the ruff and dragged back to the pickup, where he was tossed into the cab. Then, as he watched from the truck window, Shuba brought the calf back along the fence and through the gap to join the herd. While Shuba stood guard outside the circle of nervous cattle, the foreman repaired the fence, then returned to the pickup.

He drove back to the ranch headquarters without another word to Duffy, but the atmosphere in the front seat of the pickup was all too familiar to its passenger. Duffy felt the smothering anger of another human and shrank down under the dashboard. Fearing him, feeling his wrath as acutely as if struck by his callused hand, afraid to meet his eyes, he raised his own in a beseeching plea for forgiveness.

Chapter Eight

Duffy's day began not with the sun but with daytime sounds, as if outside the foreman's dark cottage the day had begun. Arriving vehicles, soft greetings, car doors slamming, sudden soft laughter, all just beyond the front windows, all before the faintest morning light.

Then behind him he heard the heavy footsteps of the foreman and felt the light brush of Shuba's nose across his flank. Still in disgrace, he had been banished from the bedroom to sleep stretched out on the floor of the front room, halfway between his new family and escape from their rejection, unable to understand why both were denied. Now before morning he was at the center of activity as the foreman opened the door and two young men stepped past him. He followed Shuba and the men into the kitchen to wait while the men ate breakfast, their voices low, their boots and jeans thick with the odors of dogs and horses.

As if the sun had waited for the men, its first gray light arrived just as they stepped outside. Duffy followed Shuba to the parked pickups in front of the cottage while the young men transferred saddles, lunch pails and Thermos bottles to the bed of the foreman's truck. In each of the pickups he caught sight of a small dog's head watching him, the excited anticipation of the silent dogs telling him that something important was about to happen, something so rare in all their lives that dogs and men could barely contain their voices.

The foreman and the young hands scooped up the last of the equipment and carried it to the foreman's truck. When all was packed the two dogs leaped from the pickup cabs, ran past Duffy and joined Shuba in the truck bed. Duffy ran behind, leaped and cleared the tailgate just as the foreman tried to head him off.

"Get outta there. You ain't agoin' with us."

The foreman's rejection struck Duffy like a blow. He stood among the other dogs, facing the dark shape of the man he had tried to please, asking with his whole body to be allowed to go along.

The foreman turned back to the other men to explain his outburst. "Rogue dog'll scare more cattle than he'll drive."

"Let him come, Jake," one man called good humoredly.

"Yeah, Jake. You can't leave one dog behind. He don't understand."

The foreman capped Duffy's head with his hand.

"Awright. You come. We'll see what you can do, rogue dog."

The three men climbed into the front seat of the truck, and men and dogs rode slowly toward the barn. There another saddle and hay bale were loaded, crowding the four dogs together between hay and saddles. Duffy turned his attention to his fellow passengers.

The two strange dogs were Shuba's size, but neither bore her collie features. The male wore a smoother coat of mottled black and white, his shorter muzzle spattered with flecks as small as snowflakes, his tail thin and white tipped. An Australian cattle dog, his remote ancestors had been a blue merle collie and a stripped-down wild dog of the outback, but as he stood warily under Duffy's scrutiny his dingo blood raised the hairs at the nape of his neck and curled his upper lip. Duffy had never met warning signals before, but he instantly backed off and wagged.

The second dog, a female, was a Queensland heeler, another Australian workdog, younger and smaller than her counterpart and with even less ancestral sheepdog showing. Under Duffy's careful examination her grizzled coat, patched with russet circles, quivered, but she raised her muzzle to meet his nose and welcomed his wag with her own. She, like her fellow Australian, was a recent import, preferred by many western cattleman to the border collie for single-minded purpose and the stamina her wild forebears had passed to her.

All three of the smaller dogs were silent, expectant riders, more interested in what lay ahead than in each other, parts of a task force moving into action. As he stood among them, Duffy caught their tense air of readiness. It was still too early to be awake and already too late to yawn.

The foreman's pickup continued slowly along the dirt road to a corral where three horses stood already haltered at the fence. The pickup was backed around to an open-topped cattle trailer. One of the young men got out to hitch the trailer to a coupling at the rear of the pickup, then truck and trailer pulled to the corral gate where the horses were loaded. They moved to the pipe-bar gate and through it toward the hills, a caravan of men and dogs and horses climbing the winding track ahead of the sun, the outer limits of the September day theirs to make the most of. No longer did Duffy feel rejected. He was a part of a great adventure, accepted, and he asked nothing more.

The procession rattled and clanked across the hilltop track toward the first collection area, where horses were unloaded and saddled. The three men would work the southwest sector of the ranch, some three thousand acres, locating, sorting, and driving cattle to the enclosure. It was a long day's work, made more difficult because the cattle, scattered throughout almost inaccessible terrain, were not all to be collected. Only steers and cows past calving were to be sold off, and these must be separated from the rest, then driven across the hills.

The timing of the drive was critical. Cattle prices, predictably low when the time to sell approached, would drop as feed grew scarcer and the first rains held off. To wait even a week or two could mean selling thinner animals at prices forced lower by panic selling. To hold out for higher prices without renewing rain meant buying feed or losing many of the youngest calves.

Three teams, each made up of a horse, rider, and dog, would work from three directions, locating cattle, separating those to be taken and working each group across the hills to the yard before settling off to the next. Each man, a veteran cowboy protected from the early-morning chill by a sheepskin jacket and shielded from the noon sun by a western hat brim, carried his essentials: a coiled rope on his saddle and a packet of chewing tobacco in his shirt pocket. Each horse, a range-toughened mixture of quarter horse, appaloosa or palomino, bore its scars like brands and its rider like a familiar appendage. And each dog waited close to horse and rider for the signal to move out as if a great race was to begin.

Except Duffy.

To him three horses carrying three humans meant action and reaction. He circled the standing horses, barking his encouragement, bewildered when neither horse nor dogs paid him any attention. Even when he darted dangerously close to the animals' hindquarters, the horses never moved and the dogs ignored him.

But the foreman didn't.

"I better put that dog in the truck," he grumbled, about to dismount.

"Let him wear himself out," a rider called.

"He thinks it's a damned game," his partner said.

"He'll learn then," the foreman shrugged.

The riders parted. Each dog ran ahead, choosing a path out of the clearing through dry brush toward the slope of a ragged foothill. Duffy followed Shuba, stopping every few yards to look back at the following horse, then plunging on, his high-pitched bark faltering as he fought his way through sage clumps behind Shuba's waving tail.

The foreman had chosen the most difficult segment for himself, the middle slice of an arc of rangeland without a level acre. Cattle were spread through its crevices in small bunches, the herd's instinct subordinate to the need to find the last dry mouthful before the sun drove them to shade. The search for these animals was not haphazard, however; both the foreman and his dog knew every gulch and gully, every grove of oaks likely to harbor a hungry cow. And Shuba needed no urging. She knew where to go and what to find. She was a born collector.

At the top of a ridge she found her targets, cattle grazing in a deep ravine not yet touched by sunlight. She waited above them for the rider to catch up, and as she gazed down on the cattle Duffy joined her. He greeted her, tried to get her attention, barked once and lay down beside her to catch his breath. Why did she stare down at the backs of sluggish cattle instead of responding to him? Why had they run so far for nothing more exciting than this? He knew only that he had been included. That was enough.

The rider joined them, then led the way down a crumbling path to the floor of the mini-canyon. The cattle continued to pull at the dry stalks under the oaks. Only when the horse moved into their midst did they raise their heads to wonder at the silent intruders. Shuba waited outside the circle, so Duffy waited too. Until he saw some reason to pay attention to these boring beasts he would enjoy her company.

While the dogs watched, the foreman made three decisions. Out of the dozen animals he selected four, three steers and a cow so drained by age and calving that flesh and sinew had sagged away from her back and flanks, leaving only the hide-covered knobs of her frame for the flies to suck. His second decision was a way out of the canyon, a narrow draw the cattle had used to enter this last oasis. The foreman's final decision was made only after turning in his saddle to look back at the waiting dogs. Having made up his mind, he dismounted, uncoiled the rope at his saddle and walked back to Duffy.

He slipped the loop of rope around Duffy's neck, then led him to the base of an oak.

"You're gonna wait right here, rogue dog, till we get this job done. And maybe, just maybe, you'll learn somethin'."

Duffy raised his nose to the foreman's face and flicked his tongue in answer. Maybe, he agreed.

Mounted, the foreman turned his horse in to the cattle. With only the slightest pressure of heels and knees the horse understood which of the cattle had been selected. Horse and rider cut a steer from his companions, drove him gently toward the draw, then returned for another.

As soon as the first animal was isolated, Shuba moved to block his return, holding him off with fixed gaze and half crouch. Horse and dog worked in tandem with so little sudden motion that hardly a dust plume rose. And as the old cow jostled off to join the steers, Shuba crept forward ahead of the horse, sending the four animals off along the path out of the canyon.

The four cattle had been separated and driven from the rest before Duffy, watching from the base of the tree, realized that the game was over, before he could even stand to cheer. He saw Shuba, then the horse and rider, disappearing around a bend without a backward glance. Again, he was left behind, a rope around his neck, to wonder why.

As if struck by the deception, as the last faint sounds of hooves and saddle leather died away, he got to his feet, strained against the rope and sent a high, reminding sort of bark after them. This time he would not be left behind. This time he would follow somehow.

He lunged against the rope, only to be lifted and twisted until he sprawled on his back as the noose caught his throat. He turned then, facing the tree, to pull backward against the rope. The noose tightened, choking him until he gave up, coughing. He shook himself violently, a way he had of changing his mind. The noose loosened. He felt the rope rise out of his ruff to hang above his ears. He raised a forepaw to brush at it. It fell away and he was free.

Duffy didn't know he had not been abandoned. It was the foreman's intention to return for him on the way out again to locate the next cattle, to take him along, tying him only during the cutting and driving. The collie would learn by watching, kept out of the way until he did. Meanwhile, Shuba and her partner would deliver the selected cattle to the pens, repeating their searching and culling until sundown. And, if the new dog caught on, if Shuba and he could work together, all the better, especially later when the animals must be driven a mile or more, when even Shuba would have all she could handle and the shadow of a hawk could panic a nervous stray.

The first group was delivered to the collection pens quickly and easily. Shuba saw them through the wide gate as the foreman dismounted to close it behind them. The other riders had not yet appeared with their first bunches, so the foreman called his dog and led his horse to the truck for a coffee break. He had just poured steaming coffee into the thermos cap, tossed a biscuit to Shuba and settled against the truck when Shuba pricked her ears. Then the horse looked up from the hay bale. Finally, the wild medley of sounds reached the foreman.

Pounding hooves somewhere beyond the hilltop.

Bronchial bellowing above the treetops.

Crackling underbrush as heavy bodies crushed a way through.

And above it all, joyous barking.

The uproar became more frenzied as it rolled toward the clearing, then burst through the last fringe of underbrush. Eight bucking, twisting cattle, tassel tails streaming, plunged past the foreman followed by a darting, dodging collie just out of reach of flying hooves and seesawing hips.

As the cattle reached open space and level ground they ran toward their companions, coming to a swirling halt at the fence. Duffy circled them once, his bark reduced to a breathless yip, then squeezed through the gate bars and ran across the enclosure to the water trough. There he stopped, dipped his muzzle into the water and, as always when he was very thirsty, drank in repeated triplets.

Glp glp glp. Glp, glp, glp.

Refreshed, delighted with his accomplishment, certain of his welcome back, he trotted happily across the yard toward Shuba and the foreman.

Chapter Nine

Duffy's first roundup received mixed and confusing reactions. The arrival of the unwanted cattle at the pens enraged the foreman.

"Damn dog. Nothin' but trouble," he shouted as Duffy trotted toward him.

The harsh words thrown at him so unexpectedly stopped him in his tracks. He veered off and away as if trying to dodge them. If there were words in the human vocabulary he understood, words other than his name, they were oaths, excoriating syllables always hurled in anger. "Damn dog" he understood too well.

But that was not the only surprising response to his deed. As he hesitated between the foreman and the milling cattle, new groups of animals were pushed toward the gate from each side of the clearing, followed by the other dogs and riders. And as soon as the cattle had been driven through the gate and the cowboys had joined the foreman to hear the explanation for the loose cattle scattered on the edges of the yard, Duffy heard wild laughter.

"Come 'ere, you crazy dog," one of the young men called. "Brought in your own bunch by yourself, did you? He's some cattle dog, Jake."

Duffy turned appreciative eyes toward the young man, wanting to step forward to feel the praise, still wary of the foreman. Praise from one direction, blame from the other, immobilized him.

"Come on, Jake," the other cowboy said. "What harm'd he do?"

And it was true. The cattle delivered by Duffy would wander off into the hills unharmed.

But it was the foreman's pride which held man and dog at bay. He could still bring cattle home faster than the younger hands. His dog and horse worked better than theirs, always had. This dog had made a fool of him, a dog he'd brought along and wished now he could disown. He'd be hearing the story retold at The Cutting Horse Café on Saturday night, how old Jake's new dog rounded up the wrong cattle, and the laughs would be on him. Old Jake and his ten-dollar dog. You get what you pay for, Jake.

He stepped toward Duffy. "Come here, dog," he ordered.

Duffy cringed, crept forward, lowered himself at the foreman's feet. A leadrope was tied around his neck and he was pulled off to the truck, tossed into the bed and the other end of the rope tied to a cleat.

The foreman turned to the two grinning men. "Come on. We're wastin' time."

Suddenly Shuba ran between the cowboys, past the foreman and leaped into the truck bed. Wagging a greeting to Duffy, she sat beside him, waiting.

"Get outta there, Shuba," the foreman snapped.

But Shuba remained beside Duffy, facing the man but refusing to leave the dog.

The foreman returned to the truck, grabbed Shuba by the neck and pulled her to the ground. He picked up his horse's reins and climbed into the saddle, turned the horse and rode out of the clearing. Shuba watched him go, then jumped back to join Duffy in the truck bed.

Still enjoying the foreman's embarrassment, the young cowboys called after him.

"Hey, Jake. She won't leave her boyfriend."

"She's gone to the dog, Jake."

The foreman rode on, refusing to look back or call his dog. The young men's taunts were too much for him. He'd ride alone. With or without Shuba he'd get the job done. With or without the damn fool hands he'd pen the cattle to be sold. And for sure he'd get rid of the collie. Even if he had to shoot him.

The foreman's humiliation left its wake of silence behind. The joke had gone too far, the men realized. The foreman and his dog were more than a team; they were a matched pair who needed each other. They had never been separated before and had better not be now.

The men remounted. One untied Duffy's rope from the cleat, coaxed him out of the truck and led him off on the long lead. Shuba jumped after him, started to follow and was headed off by the second rider. She hesitated, then chased after the foreman's horse, apparently satisfied that Duffy would join her. Only when she reached the top of the rise above the clearing did she turn to watch Duffy being led away in the opposite direction. She continued on, catching up with the foreman on the other side of the hill, dog and rider together again.

But the great day all had anticipated had turned into a different day. Each of the teams worked the cattle back to the pens without meeting the others. No one stopped for coffee or conversation. Duffy was kept on a rope, out of the way during the cutting and out of the clearing before the foreman saw him. Only when well away from the drive was he freed to run behind the cattle dog, and by then he had lost interest in the game.

The young cowboys drove in the last bunches of cattle in the half light of the setting sun, unsaddled and loaded the horses, and sat waiting under an oak for the foreman. Nearly one hundred cattle had been driven behind the fences to be loaded the next day. Hay bales had been dumped and broken open to sustain them through the night, and the work was finished. Men and dogs sat near each other, Duffy just outside the group, his tongue pulsing with every quick breath, the rich colors of his coat scumbled by layers of pale adobe dust.

The ride back to the ranch headquarters was a weary, jolting ride for men and dogs. In the truck cab no one spoke as cigarettes were lighted and hats pushed back from sweating foreheads. In the truck bed Duffy lay beside Shuba, both dogs reflecting the mood of the men. There had been no words, no reassuring hands as they loaded to go home. The gestures, the gentle renewal of the bond so necessary to their collie natures had been withheld, and somehow the withholding lay between them, the pleasure in each other's company diminished.

Duffy's numbered days on the cattle ranch were among the most perplexing in his life. He was fed and allowed to stretch out on the front room floor at night where Shuba always joined him, both seeking each other's company as refuge from the foreman's heavy silence. For Shuba was also shunned, victim as much as Duffy, blamed as he was, and the sullen resentment was more threatening to her than the flaring anger she always knew would pass.

The week's work schedule continued. Each morning before sunrise the young men arrived. One day would be devoted to rounding up a shipment, the next to loading cattle into large vans to be shipped off to the sales yard. And as the men and dogs and horses set off each morning, Duffy was always included, not as part of the work teams, not certainly for his sake or Shuba's, but for reasons no one understood. If it was a day to round up the cattle he was taken along by one of the cowboys. If it was loading day he was allowed to roam the perimeters of the yards while the other dogs assisted in pushing cattle into the chutes. His reunions with Shuba were brief, usually while the men rested or ate lunch. Not once did the foreman acknowledge him, and Duffy, who felt the chill, stayed out of his way. Even the cowboys avoided any gesture or reference to him around the foreman. He was an outcast, a homewrecker, a dog who somehow was bad news.

The collie was very much on the foreman's mind that week, however, and, although he had made his decision he continued to try to justify it to himself, never quite successfully. He'd bought the dog as much for Shuba as for himself. Collies were work dogs and there was work enough for two, especially now that extra hands were hired only for roundups and calf brandings. He was a solitary man without close friends in the valley, whose only relative was a married daughter back in Texas. He was satisfied to live out the few working years he had left managing the cattle operation for an owner he respected, a man too old to lend a hand most of the time. He spent his days riding the miles of empty country he thought the most beautiful in the world on horseback or in his pickup, accompanied only by his dog. And she was all the company he needed, the best kind, he thought. A friend who never complained, never asked where he'd been when he came home late on Saturday nights, never held a grudge or asked a favor. If a collie could fill all the empty places in his life, maybe another would make things that much better.

But the dog he'd bought from the Mexican had not lived up to his breed. That much was true, but it was more than that, he knew. Because the other reason for the new dog was to please Shuba. And she *was* pleased. She'd been willing to share him with the collie. It was he who had been unwilling to share her. He knew it but could not admit it. He'd told himself the rogue dog would ruin Shuba, turn her into trouble like he was. But she'd worked all week as well as ever, and the worst thing was, now that he'd made his mind up, the collie was learning after all. No, he couldn't make excuses. He just hated the new dog.

Willing or not to face the reason, he was going to get rid of the collie before Shuba got to like him too much. That meant the coming Saturday. He left the ranch only twice each week, once on Saturday morning when he drove to the valley's only large town for a pancake breakfast with a group of cattlemen before restocking his supplies at the supermarket, and again on Saturday night when he drove to The Cutting Horse Café for a night of socializing, his only drinking night and all he wanted. The past Sunday night, when he bought the collie from the Mexican, had been a rare exception, the night before a holiday when no extra hands would be available to begin the roundup.

The oversupply of cattle were collected and shipped by Friday, the men paid off and the foreman was again alone. He slept late Saturday morning and set off, for town at eight, Shuba as usual riding beside him. Duffy was left shut in the cottage until they returned, then let out with Shuba to spend the day together around the ranch buildings. At five o'clock he was fed, then both dogs lay in the kitchen corner while the foreman cooked his own dinner. As always, he tossed the last steak scraps to his dog. And then to Duffy. This was done not out of guilty feelings but was simply fair sharing, he told himself, the same as he'd do for any dog in his house.

To Duffy, however, the gesture meant something else. It was the first time that week that he had been rewarded, even noticed by the man. He responded, laying back his ears, stepping forward to place his head on the foreman's knee, allowing his tail to sway slowly back and forth. To Duffy the steak scraps, the hand he felt briefly resting on his head meant forgiveness, acceptance, the reestablishment of his place in the household. He turned to Shuba, barked softly and nipped her ear.

The foreman set off for The Cutting Horse Café just after dark, Duffy riding beside him in the front seat of the pickup. Shuba was left behind in the cottage, a Saturday-night rule she accepted, although she may have wondered why Duffy was taken along. Only the foreman knew as he separated them that neither would see the other again. Perhaps that knowledge accounted for his hurried departure, his brusque command to Duffy to follow him, and the slamming of the door.

He drove fast across the valley floor along the back roads curving toward the small town, dark country roads where only an occasional gate light marked his way and the lighted windows of hilltop houses twinkled like far-off star clusters. It was along a stretch of blacktop between open fields that he passed the small printed signs stapled at eye level on every telephone pole.

Reward $100
For Information Leading to The Return of
COLLIE
Name: Duffy
Color: Mahogany and White
Sex: Male
Age: 3 years
Weight: 70 lbs.
Missing since Sunday, September 2
Please call 886-5424 Day or Night

The black-and-white signs flashed by for half a mile before the foreman turned onto the town road, but he never noticed them. His daylight trips took him in the opposite direction. He never came this way except at night on his way to the western bar.

He parked in a dark corner of the parking lot, left a half-open window for Duffy to breathe the soft night air and entered through the swinging bar gates. As usual, every barstool was occupied, the tables around the small dance floor taken by couples dancing to the two-piece band. The greetings he received as he walked to the bar were louder than necessary, even allowing for the pounding music.

"Hey, Jake."

"You need a drink, Jake."

He knew each voice well enough to sense immediately, even before he spotted the two young cowboys at the bar, that the collie story had preceded him, that every man there had heard it and was still enjoying it. That, as much as the drinks, was the reason they came to the bar each Saturday night. In the valley without a movie house or even a bowling alley, the entertainment was self generated, an exchange of the week's experiences, repeated for every new arrival. The foreman's collie was this week's feature, and it was already a hit.

He wasn't surprised. He didn't even mind too much, although if he hadn't had good reason he might have skipped this particular Saturday. He grinned and poured his beer and spotted the Mexican kid at the end of the bar. He too would have heard the story, but at least he wasn't laughing with the rest. It would take a few more beers and another hour or two for the collie to be forgotten. He'd wait, then make his move.

And when he did he was surprised.

He joined the Mexican, bought a round and came out with it. "Listen, kid. That dog of yours, he ain't no cattle dog."

The boy grinned and shook his head. "I never said he was. You did."

The foreman leaned closer. "You take him back, see?"

"You had him for a week. I spent the money."

"I don't want the money back, kid. Just take the dog."

The boy looked up. "Okay," he agreed. "Where is he?"

The foreman had not expected that. He knew the boy was afraid of the dog and didn't want him, couldn't keep him. He had come prepared to talk him into it, maybe hint that it wasn't smart to sell a dog under false pretenses, especially for an "illegal." What he didn't know was that for the past three days the Mexican had seen the reward signs posted all around the horse ranch. Not only was the dog worth one hundred dollars; if he didn't return it and claim the reward somehow the collie might be traced back to him. He had worried about that every day.

"He's out in my pickup," the foreman told him.

The thought of the big dog in his car, of taking him back to his sister's house for the night, of feeling the breath on the back of his neck as he drove home still frightened him. He had to do it; he knew that. And it would be worth it. He tried to think of that. But still, he was afraid.

"You put him in my car and tie him tight," he insisted.

"Sure, kid. But he won't bite. He's friendly. You should keep him."

The bargain made, they ordered beers. There was no hurry now. Each man for his own reason felt relieved about the collie, and it was Saturday night after a long week's work. But just in case the Mexican changed his mind, the foreman stayed beside him. One wrong word about the dog from anyone at the bar could scare him out of taking him back. The foreman paid for the round.

It was closing time when they stepped outside. Shouts of "'Night" and "See you" crisscrossed the parking lot as they walked to the foreman's truck, both men hurrying away from the light to avoid explanation. There was no sign of Duffy at the window, but that didn't surprise the foreman. After all this time the dog would have gone to sleep on the floor of the cab.

He opened the door. Duffy was gone.

Chapter Ten

When Duffy heard the voices he stopped in his tracks. The men spoke softly to each other, but he was not far off and he recognized them both. He waited, ears pricked, eyes probing the pocket of darkness which had fallen across the parking lot the moment the bar lights were turned off. He expected to be called. He expected to hear anger in the voices, the inevitable reproach and summons which seemed to seek him out at such confusing moments. Never in his life had he been beyond the reach of a voice he knew, a commanding voice whose call could pull him toward it as forcefully as a rope around his neck. He had been tied at birth to a human voice. He could not have severed the rope if he wanted to, and no such rebellious urge had ever come over him. The call must be obeyed whether its inflection carried the promise of reward or punishment. Duffy waited, held by the invisible rope, listening for the call.

But while he recognized the voices and felt immediately the twitch of the rope, it was a slender strand. Its pull lacked the power of trust and the mutual connection between man and dog established over a lifetime relationship, the kind of bond Duffy needed. In spite of his uncertainty, however, and the tentacles of fear gripping him, he was ready to respond. The stronger tie to the man and his girls and the circle of cats and dogs he knew so well still held him, but where was the call? He had changed families too often to know where he belonged. He needed to hear the summoning voice to indicate the way back. He needed to hear the sound of his name.

But the men who searched for him in the parking lot could not call him by name. To the foreman he had no name. The Mexican now knew that his name was Duffy, but to have revealed his knowledge might cause him to lose the reward. It certainly would if the foreman had seen the posters.

As Duffy watched from the path beside a shallow streambed just beyond the fence, his body screened by its bank and the enveloping darkness of the hillside behind him, he saw them part. He heard the motors start, saw the headlights flash on, and remained where he was as the pickup and the white Chevrolet moved slowly out of the lot and up the road toward the town. For the first time in his life he had been disconnected from humans.

A dog is never free. Lost, set loose, abandoned or forgotten, he trails the invisible rope, an object of concern, pity, or even fear. Like a runaway child he stands out against every background, obviously out of place anywhere. Legally he becomes a stray, an outlaw whose approach turns would-be rescuers nervously aside. A disconnected dog is a social anomaly, the more so because nothing in his genetic past remains to prepare him for the role. His resourcefulness is muted; his survival instinct vestigial. And no dog wants to be free.

When a group of men from the bar had approached the foreman's pickup earlier in the evening, talking softly to each other, looking through the window at him, Duffy had risen to their voices as he always did, his muzzle thrust through the open window to acknowledge their greeting. People often stopped to speak to him while he waited for the return of the man he belonged to. But this time the strangers had opened the door and urged him out. When he jumped to the ground, one of the men had tried to grab him, the hand twisting so painfully in his ruff that Duffy had cried out, causing the man to let him go. As he dodged away, the men had laughed and called him to follow them back to the bar. Perhaps they meant no harm. There was no anger, only laughter in the voices, but they were strangers and Duffy was afraid. Eventually the men had returned to the lighted doorway without him.

Alone, he had wandered across the lot, pausing to lift a leg against aromatic truck tires. The scents were not familiar, nor was this end of the town. The only sounds he heard came from the noisy bar, and none of them beckoned. He had slipped under the rail of the fence to explore the path beside the streambed, neither consciously moving away from the pickup nor toward a destination of his own. That much was evident from his leisurely exploration of the path and his frequent stops to look back.

Duffy continued along the streambed path until it dwindled to a crease in the flatland of the central valley. There was no moon, but the country sky was strewn with stars whose light silvered the empty landscape. The cattle trail he followed led him at first across open rangeland behind the low-lying roofs of the town. Then, as the trail ended, he slipped under a three-strand barbed-wire fence into a sugar-beet field. He was moving northwest. To his right was the river bed winding toward the mountains. To his left was the valley's major subdivision, expensive ranch houses framed by white rail fences, their starlit squares and rectangles forming a vast mosaic along the eastern outskirts of the largest town. Ahead he could see the dark centers of farms under canopies of cottonwood and pepper trees. He avoided these clusters of farm buildings, where crop farmers eked out a living on land worth more than the lifetime earnings of their owners. He also skirted the forbidding fences of the subdivision. Although he moved through unfamiliar countryside, he was within three miles of his home and heading directly for it.

Halfway across a corner field he stopped to listen. What he heard was faint and very familiar, the deep thudding of cushioned pads on sun-baked ground accompanied by the tinkling sound of metal tags, the sound of running dogs. As he stood listening in the center of the field, the sounds grew louder. The dogs were coming from the subdivision and heading directly toward him. Before he saw them he knew that there were several, that they were large and running hard, oblivious of all but themselves.

He stood stiffly prepared, curious to meet the oncoming dogs, aware that they would come upon him at any moment. He saw the dark shapes as they reached the open ground and it was then that they saw him. Suddenly he was at the center of a sniffing circle, wagging dogs all crowding him and none looking like any dog he had ever met before. The boldest of the pack was a giant German shepherd, taller and broader than Duffy with a black mask, sagging dewlaps, and a heavy chain loosely hanging across his massive chest. As the shepherd examined him from head to tail, Duffy swiveled to face him, wary of the dog's intentions. He had never confronted an older male before and he was half-expecting challenge.

Only after the shepherd was satisfied did Duffy turn to meet the other three. The largest of these was a standard poodle, a shaggy black shadow whose bobbed tail twitched as his fox face nudged Duffy's. The poodle was young and eager, floppy as a great stuffed toy and overcome with the excitement of his mad escapade. The third dog, a Rhodesian ridgeback, was the opposite of the poodle. Smooth-haired and compact, marked by the ridge of standing hair along his spine, the ridgeback seemed nervous and reserved. His coppery body trembled at Duffy's touch and he withdrew to stand his distance as Duffy found the fourth dog. This was a young Doberman three-quarters grown, a slender tubelike body balanced on long, graceful legs, ears newly trimmed and taped. The Doberman's freshman status in the group caused him to sit patiently while Duffy nosed him over, but, having passed the test, he rose and seemed to float away into the darkness.

Under Duffy's careful scrutiny it became clear that the four dogs were friendly and shared several things in common. All were males, magnificent specimens of their breeds. All wore collars and identification tags and coats carefully cared for. And all were well acquainted with each other. None showed the characteristic behavior of a stray: tentative acceptance, indecisive circling and backtracking. Instead, each dog seemed self assured, excited, like a swaggering boy off on a midnight adventure. They seemed to know where they were going, what mischief lay ahead and what fun it was going to be. They were certainly not disconnected dogs.

Then what were they doing at three o'clock in the morning in this farmer's field? Duffy decided to go along to find out. The shepherd was the obvious leader, and, having satisfied himself that Duffy was one of them, he set off along the fencelines dividing field from pasture, row crop from grazer. He seemed to know his way, choosing traveled paths, slipping under rail and wire as if he had done it all before. The other dogs followed behind the leader when his destination took them through fences or close to houses, running wide of him when he crossed open ground. Duffy kept up, neither wasting energy to romp with the poodle and the Doberman nor allowing the shepherd's curving tail to vanish up ahead. They crossed a broad enclosure thick with the scent of sheep, the irrigated ground so closely cropped that weed clumps stood out against the starlit terrain like shadowed tombstones. But sheep were not the shepherd's target. Lacking the predator's need to hunt, or perhaps for reasons associated with his domestic life, he led the others around the soft bleating sounds coming from a corner of the enclosure.

The five dogs crossed a road, ran along its shoulder, then turned down a long dirt driveway between fields of ripening tomatoes. Ahead were the glinting aluminum roofs of outbuildings within a fringe of trees and the Mesozoic silhouettes of tomato-picking machines. As the dogs approached the clustered buildings, the shepherd slowed and the rest fell into line behind him, Duffy bringing up the rear. They crept ahead, hunched below the walls of dry mustard on each side of the driveway until they reached the shadow of a long barn.

As they followed the sheltering barnside, Duffy heard murmuring coming from a small pen surrounded by chicken wire. At first, only restless mumbling rose from the pen as its occupants awoke, but as the dogs drew nearer, keeping within the shadow of the barn and stepping ahead a paw at a time, the sounds changed to a rising grind.

For a bird so well greased, the cry of a startled goose is among the most unlubricated of animal alarms. It wrenches and shreds and tears until throats constrict, ears sing, and escape from its gear-stripping clamor is all that matters. Duffy froze in terror as the white necks of five geese stretched absurdly above the wire. Never had he heard such noise. Compared to these doom-ridden voices even the expletives of courting peacocks were soothing sounds of love.

The shepherd ignored the racket as he crept toward the pen, but the rest of the dogs hung back within the barn shadow, waiting for their leader to solve the problem of the pen. This the shepherd did by pawing his way over it. His weight crushed the flimsy wire to the ground. It was never intended to repel such an intruder, perhaps because this well-settled center of the valley offered too many human traces and was too far from the wild cover of the hills for coyotes and bobcats to venture into it. No one expected family pets to turn into night raiders.

Domestic geese lack the defensive ferocity of their wild brethren. Instead of facing the giant dog, necks aimed, hisses challenging, the geese raised their bills to heaven, shrieked their plight and waddled around the pen. The shepherd ran behind each goose, nosed its twitching tail feathers and boosted it over the wire toward the waiting dogs. In no time the five geese were rushing straight into open jaws which quickly clamped around their tubular necks. First one goose gurgled, then the next, as white feathers fluttered over the dogs.

The barnyard bedlam could have been heard half a mile away. Even as one goose after another was silenced, one goose remained to alert the countryside. It was Duffy's goose. Each of the other dogs was too well occupied with a flapping bird to bother with the fifth, and it nearly collided with the bewildered collie before goose and dog realized they were face to face.

The poodle and doberman had easily overtaken their birds, tearing into tail feathers, snapping jaws on outstretched necks. The ridgeback had his goose limp at his feet with no more than a twist of his head. In seconds each dog had killed while Duffy stood frozen near the pen. And, as he watched the slaughter, he saw the light come on in an upper window of a house hidden behind a curtain of branches.

The shepherd bounded past him, followed by the others. Duffy was the last to run, and the slowest. He was still confused by the raid, the killing and the getaway, but the man's shout near him convinced him to flee behind the rest. As the dogs ran in a single line up the long driveway, he was the easiest target, the only dog wearing a white fur collar. The shot made a flat sound, no sharper than the breaking of a small branch under his paw. The sting he felt along his stifle as the pellet penetrated, however, was unlike any pain he had felt before. It nicked the curving bone just deep enough to send a hot flash up and down his leg. He yelped once as his leg twisted under him, then ran on faster to catch up with the rest. When he reached the paved road he scooted up the center of the blacktop, his tail tucked protectively between his legs.

He caught up with the others at the edge of the field. All four dogs were panting and interested in Duffy. The poodle sniffed at the blood trickle along his hock. The shepherd stood close, his head above Duffy's ruff. Even the ridgeback examined him. His escape, his slight wound, and his return seemed to confirm his membership. He was one of them.

But one of what? The episode left Duffy with no sense of the excitement it seemed to have given the others. And what was its purpose? None of the dogs had carried off a goose. The only souvenirs were the white tail feathers sticking to the poodle's chin, just one more ragged fringe on a dog already a blur of fuzz. Duffy loved a game and found one whenever a cat scrambled for a tree or a horse kicked up its heels, but this was a game he couldn't understand. He had seen large birds before. The couple who owned Princess kept peacocks who often wandered into Duffy's territory showing no fear of cats or dogs. He had decided long ago that birds, large or small, were not worth the bother.

And never had he killed. The smell of goose blood was strong on the dogs and faintly familiar. Duffy loved the taste of chicken and turkey, especially chicken livers sautéed in butter, or the juice of a stewed chicken poured over his dinner. But he could not associate the pungent smell of the goose pen with those special dinners, nor the flapping, grinding bird with the pleasure of the chase. The only killing he had ever witnessed was the occasional gopher carried in a cat's mouth, and even the half-eaten carcass he later came across had never tempted him.

Death as it is taking place frightened Duffy. The shriek of a rabbit under an owl's claws, the squeak of a kitten as its life is snuffed, these night sounds startled and silenced him. He had no urge to bark or investigate. He wanted to hide from them, as if he sensed that something that should be alive forever no longer was. He had heard death again just now, and its sounds were more terrifying than the farmer's shout, more painful than the sting in his leg.

And yet, the dogs around him were now his companions. He was one of them, and while their company in no way replaced his need to belong at a human's side, their high spirits had distracted him and given direction to his journey. For a moment, at least, he had been a part of something in which decisions were made for him, and this had seemed natural and reassuring.

The shepherd took the lead once more, but this time he trotted confidently toward the white rail barriers of the subdivision. The other dogs followed, and as they entered an elaborate gateway, brick pillars supporting a wrought-iron arch, the road divided and the dogs separated, each choosing his own way home.

Duffy stopped under the arch to watch the others disappear. Once past the entrance and within the safe confines of their compound none looked back. For them the night's adventure was over and they sought the security of their own backyards. At sunrise each would be welcomed and fed by an owner who would deny, if ever asked, that any dog of his would leave his yard for the joy of killing. Only Duffy was left outside, the disconnected renegade, to be hunted as a killer.

He stood between the pillars, his chest and circling ruff whitened by the glow from the ornate lamp at the center of the archway, aware that he was not welcome to follow the other dogs into the nests of sleeping humans. Then, shaking out his coat, shedding the night's adventures, he turned away.

He headed east toward the brightening sky above the distant mountains, as if by traveling toward it he could reach the morning sooner.

Chapter Eleven

The valley is bisected by a single highway running diagonally from northwest to southeast. It is a throughway connecting the north-central and south-central coasts and also a shortcut for traffic moving between northern and southern California cities. As such, it is newly paved and contoured, patrolled and fenced. It is also a battleground, the scene of nightly slaughter of cats and dogs, skunks and possum and deer. Although the annual count of human fatalities along its course is usually lower than any of the other animals except deer, the highway is avoided by the local population whenever possible. Few who travel on it stop and fewer slow down as they race each other to the freeway junctions at either end.

Duffy and the blue Dodge van reached the same point on this highway at exactly the same moment, just after sunrise that Sunday morning, he moving east across it, the van speeding south toward the coastal mountains. It was a clear September morning and the collie was very visible as he crossed the highway. Also, although the pellet in his left hind leg caused him to favor it and to move at a three-quarter trot, he saw the van and allowed himself time enough to cross in front of it. The driver also saw the collie in time to slow as necessary. Their paths would simply have crossed each other as each continued his separate way if each, having avoided the other, had not stopped.

It is difficult to guess what prompted Duffy to pause on the opposite side of the road, to turn and watch intently as the van pulled off onto the verge. Does a dog sense that he is the subject of excited conversation? More likely he was intrigued by the appearance of the vehicle at that early hour on the empty highway and by the popping sound its tires made as they spun in the loose gravel. It was an ordinary dark-blue van, neither old nor new, its slab sides concealing its contents so completely that only the driver's elbow at the open window could be seen. Its rear license plate, issued in the Canadian province of Alberta, might have drawn a second human glance, but not a dog's.

Duffy's curiosity was rewarded. From the opposite side of the van a door opened and a young girl appeared at the roadside. She wore a long, unironed cotton skirt reaching almost to her sandled bare feet and held a heavy cardigan sweater together at her throat, and, as she skipped quickly across the road, her dark straight hair swung out behind her head to reveal a deeply tanned and slender face. As she walked back toward him, Duffy stepped forward to meet her with a single tail swing, a collie's noncommittal greeting to a stranger. She showed no fear at all as she approached him. She ran her hand along his muzzle, over his head and down the center of his back until she reached his wounded leg. There she found the patch of dried blood, stooped to probe it with long, wide-tipped fingers, then, still squatting beside him, worked her hand back to dig her fingers into his ruff.

Duffy stood patiently while the girl examined him, the dry, clean smell of her hair and the strong dog smell in her sweater filling his nostrils. Her voice as she questioned him was light and soft, the high, sweet sound he loved, and as she lowered her face to his, he extended his greeting, wagging and raising his nose to her cheek.

To the girl the discovery that Duffy was not badly hurt was a great relief. As soon as she had seen him limping across the highway she had called to her companion to stop, certain that he had been struck by a passing car. Duffy was not the first dog she had attended at the roadside. In fact, she was always watching for wounded animals, as pleased to find a patient as she was sorry for its plight. She carried a variety of medical supplies with her, and if she could not provide what was necessary she delivered the animal to the nearest veterinary clinic.

Until that morning.

Her second discovery, that the collie had no collar, was far more significant. Indeed, a sign from God. She had been thinking about just such a dog. That he should have appeared at that particular time and place wearing no identifying tags, needing her and obviously grateful for her help, she accepted as a divine intervention. She did not believe in coincidence.

The one family member she missed ever since she and her companion had left friends and families behind was her dog, but until that very day owning a dog had made no sense, as her companion had pointed out, and she had contented herself with his promise that as soon as they had a place for a dog she could have one. To her a dog represented stability, the difference between a nomadic couple and a traveling family, the evidence she needed to tell herself and the world that in leaving home she had made the right decision. But the dog must not be a small, personal dog. The dog to make this difference in her status must be large enough to share. A collie was the perfect family dog.

The weirdest thing of all was that she and her companion were on their way to a house of their own. For the first time since they had hitchhiked west they were about to live under the real roof of a real house. In fact, when she had seen the beautiful dog crossing their path they were practically at the very doorstep of that house. She hadn't the slightest doubt; he was God's gift.

Walking beside him with her hand on his back she led him across the highway to the van and around it to the open door. When Duffy hung back, reluctant to jump in, she assumed it was because of the wound in his leg and helped him by lifting hindquarters over the doorsill. Once inside, he faced the driver, who, like the girl, was young. His shirt and jeans were scented with the traces of evergreens and smoke.

Like her, his hair fell around his face, but its color was lighter and streaked by the sun. His face was almost completely hidden by a beard which bushed out from his cheeks and jawline. His voice, however, belied his fierce face; it was high for a boy, and friendly. Duffy felt no disapproval in it as he was pushed between the two front seats into the rear of the van.

The girl assisted him and followed to settle him on one of the mattresses. Around him were blankets, boxes of utensils and two back-packs lashed to aluminum strips. It was a small, dark room lighted only by two square windows at the rear and by the sun slanting through the windshield. As Duffy felt the van begin to move, he tried to make his way to the front, but the motion of the vehicle and the ache in his leg as he balanced himself between the mattresses caused him to sit down again. It felt good to be riding, to hear voices, to be included once more in the exciting cycle of human affairs. That he was moving in the wrong direction he had no way of knowing.

The van continued across the valley toward the sun above the crestline of the coastal range. Beyond the last rangeland, the road began the long ascent to the summit within sloping clay banks, then high above deep canyons overgrown with chapparal. As the van reached the highest point on the pass, it slowed, then turned off to climb still farther along a track leading to a clearing which sat like a bald spot at the crown of the clustered peaks. In the center of the clearing was a low-roofed, sprawling building. Across its roof edge were a succession of signs: Ice, Firewood, Fishing Tackle, Kerosene, Butane, Sandwiches. The largest sign above the doorway: The Cielo Store.

While the girl waited with Duffy in the van, her companion went into the store. From his place behind the girl's seat, Duffy could see the adobe-brick front and iron-barred windows under an overhanging eave, but somewhere beyond the building he could hear barking and the drone of music. The driver returned, carrying a bag of groceries which he placed between the two front seats. He then backed up and turned out of the clearing. The van moved slowly along a winding path no wider than a fire break between walls of twisted live oaks. At intervals along this crestline trail were openings through which Duffy caught glimpses of small cottages and occasionally the tops of teepees, each isolated in its own small clearing.

A mile from the store the van pulled through an opening between the trees, bounced over half-buried boulders, and came to a stop next to a boxlike little house resting on a level shelf overlooking the coastal slope. Beyond that was the glistening silver surface of the ocean. As Duffy was helped out of the van, the man used the key he had picked up at the store to open the door. The girl and Duffy followed him into the house.

They entered a square front room whose unpainted plywood walls were hung with Indian blankets and serapes. Its furnishings—a table and two chairs, beanbag pillow, and assorted homemade shelves and ashtrays—were the accumulated contributions of past tenants. Beyond the front room were kitchen and bathroom cubicles as well as a smaller room on the ocean side of the house which contained a double bed with stained mattress and several posters of rock-music stars. As soon as the girl found the kitchen, she carried a bowl of water to Duffy, then opened a can of dog food from the grocery bag. She spooned the mass onto an aluminum pie plate she found on a burner of the kerosene stove and placed the food beside the water bowl.

Duffy drank thirstily, but he turned away from the food. His hunger had reached the stage of rumbling emptiness in his stomach, a signal that he could not eat. Always his appetite depended upon his sense of the atmosphere around him. If he felt uneasy, insecure, or threatened he walked away from food, and the strangeness of his new surroundings, the stinging smell of kerosene in his nostrils, even the creaking of the floorboards beneath his feet, upset him.

His failure to eat worried the girl. She expected all animals she rescued to eat gratefully, especially such a large dog. Big dogs were always hungry, she was convinced, although she had never owned a collie. Were collies that sensitive? Could it be his wounded leg? She led Duffy into the bedroom where she dug in her backpack until she found the ointment a Salinas veterinarian had given her. It was Panalog, in a tube with a long nozzle. She clipped away the fur around the small hole where the pellet had penetrated, inserted the tip of the nozzle and filled the wound. Duffy's leg trembled and once he gave a sharp cry as the tube point went too deep, but the girl soothed him and he had never snapped at a human hand.

She led him back to his dinner. He took a bite to please her, then walked away. Memory in dogs is selective, as it is in humans, and as arbitrary. Its patterns depend as often upon repetition of the uneventful as upon reward and punishment. For seven days and nights Duffy had lived through a series of unexpected events. No element of his life was where it belonged. Where were his girls? Where was the familiar voice calling his name? Where was the food taste he expected, the pan he knew? Where was Shuba?

He listened to the girl whispering to him. She was sitting at his side in the center of the floor, telling him how beautiful he was. He liked her voice and the touch of her hand behind his ears. When she withdrew it he lifted a paw to her thigh. He wanted more of her gentleness. He wanted to believe in her. Perhaps he asked for her patience. Was this now where he belonged? When at last she placed the food pan under his nose he began to eat.

On his first evening in the mountaintop house, Duffy went to a square dance. The Cielo Store was more than a supplier of essentials to the summit settlement it served; it was also the social center. The central building was divided at the cash register, separating a general store offering groceries, drugs, dairy products, wine, beer, and gardening supplies from a café complete with kitchen and sandwich bar, tables and benches, and an open area for dancing. On Sunday evening, couples assembled in the café, young girls in gingham dresses, young men in boots and jeans, to dance to the reels and schottisches of another century. On these evenings, the rock music pouring from the cabins and teepees was turned off, sequestered independence foresaken as the mountain population gathered to link arms, point toes, and do-si-do to the sound of a fiddle.

Now that she lived in a house of her own with a dog of her own, the girl insisted they go to the dance as a family. After a dinner eaten by candlelight because they had forgotten to buy lightbulbs, the couple loaded Duffy into the van and drove back to the store. From the parking area they could hear the music, the voice of the caller, and the stamping feet. They knew no one in this latest stopping place, but they were used to that, and friendships blossom easily among those who share a common alienation.

But were dogs allowed?

"I won't go in if they aren't," she told Duffy, reaching behind her to reassure her collie.

"I'll take a look," her companion said, cooperative because whether they went in or not really didn't matter much to him.

Soon he was back. "There's no sign, and there's a Benji-looking dog wandering around the dance floor."

They slipped through the door with Duffy between them, found room on a bench at the back of the room, and sat down to watch.

During the intermission they were joined at the picnic table by another couple, who introduced themselves as old-timers who had lived on the mountain all summer. Duffy, hidden under the table between the facing couples, was caressed and admired. Were dogs welcome? Why, their new friends assured them, this was dog heaven. Right across the street was the county pet cemetery and a shepherd kennel. New puppies came into the world on their mountain and old dogs went out. Dogs were everywhere, even in the air.

The girl was very moved. Heaven, she knew, included every creature who had ever lived. She confidently expected to rejoin all her childhood pets in Paradise. But to learn that the earthly remains of animals deeply loved rested on this cloud-capped summit, high above the traffic and the pounds, was the final confirmation she needed to rid herself of the occasional tug on her conscience. In bringing him along, making him their dog, she had lifted him halfway to Heaven. How could that be wrong?

She reached down to lift Duffy's head above the table edge.

"I'm Thana,"' she told the couple.

"I'm Mike," her companion added, reaching across the table to shake hands.

"And this," the girl announced, "is our dog Sky."

Chapter Twelve

A collie is a morning dog, and Duffy was no exception. A new morning sharpens a collie's senses. Its light spreads under his haunches, between his toes and down his spine. It is as if he were rewound. His first yawn has a squeak in it. There is a satisfied grunt in his stretch, and his voice is plugged in to his tail. In the early morning a collie can't wag without barking; he can't bark without wagging.

Which made Duffy's behavior on his first morning in the mountaintop cabin strange indeed. He knew that it was morning. Above his head the open window was a square of translucent iron, not a morning light but not the soft black of night either. He heard morning noises, the creak of pliant floorboards and the bathroom and kitchen sounds he associated with a human beginning his day. He raised his head toward the sounds, but all he could see was a gray curtain between him and the girl making breakfast. As he stretched, his wounded leg felt stiff, but also a penetrating dampness crept along his flank. His coat was wet and he was cold. He brought all four legs together and curled tighter into the warm circle of his body heat.

Duffy lay inside a cloud. A fog bank a thousand feet thick had been sucked ashore well after midnight. Drawn inland by the heated land mass, compressed by the high pressure of a summer day, it had crept over coastal foothills, filling canyon troughs, then climbed to summit peaks. There it met the sun, its edges curling and shredding along the inland downslope. But it covered the mountaintop, filling every receptacle, wrapping its occupants in folds of icy droplets.

"Sky," she called, pleased with the name she had thought of on the spur of the moment the night before. "Good morning, Sky."

Duffy felt her footsteps coming toward him. He raised his head, then shifted to his haunches as she stooped to stroke his head. She placed a slice of buttered toast between his paws. He licked the melted butter while she knelt beside him, but the toast was cold. He heard the man entering the room behind her, a misted figure who never spoke to him directly. He remained where he was while the couple ate breakfast at the table, the candle flame between them wreathed in an aureole of pale gray fog.

The man opened the front door. Still Duffy would not stir. He saw no path to the morning, no way through the wall beyond the doorway.

"Come, Sky," she called.

He walked stiffly to the opening, following the figures into the clearing, nosing his way toward the sound of their footsteps. He shook himself until his coat stood out from his body in pointed blades of wet hair. He heard the door of the van being opened before he saw its dark shape. Again he was summoned. He walked toward the girl's voice, his only reference point, but at the door he hung back, reluctant to enter a more confining space than the one he had just occupied. She boosted him into the rear of the van. He heard the slam of the cabin door, felt the man's weight as he sat beside the girl. Duffy stood precariously inside the black box as it bounced behind its headlights into a numinous tunnel through the cloud.

They followed the winding crestline path by staying midway between the tree walls until they reached the highway. There they waited until the headlights of a car appeared, then moved in behind it and trailed its twin taillights over the top of the pass. As the highway wound down into the valley, they drove through the tattered edges of the fog bank, the road stripes appearing and disappearing until suddenly they were in bright sunlight. Ahead, the valley spread under the white sun. Behind them the cloud gripped the mountaintop.

As the van gathered speed, Duffy lay down to ride blindly back the way he had come the previous morning. The young couple carried on an animated conversation, but Duffy was no longer its subject and he accepted his status as passenger on his way to whatever destination his human carriers chose. They followed the highway to a turnoff leading north between fenced pastures. At the first utility pole the girl saw the poster: REWARD $100 for Information Leading to The Return of COLLIE. She saw the lines of posters on both sides of the road and by the time they had reached the stop sign and turned northwest again she had read every word. Her companion read them, too. "Perhaps we should call?" he asked.

She turned in her seat. "Sky," she said. "You're our dog now, aren't you?"

Duffy looked up from the floor behind her seat, aware that he was being questioned. He tried to wag his answer, but a collie answer needs to be seen. If he were riding in the truck so that he could taste the wind and see the countryside she saw, he might have responded.

"But Thana...."

"Look, I'll call, but I don't believe anyone who abandons their dog deserves to have him back." She scribbled the phone number onto her open palm. "But I'll call, Mike. I promise."

They drove to the center of a small settlement, where they stopped for gas and directions. The girl hopped out of the car and trotted to a pay phone. There she pretended to dial the number on her hand.

"What'd they say?" Mike asked hopefully.

"They said they found the dog," she lied. "Sky is ours."

Duffy stood and tried to move to the front of the van while the driver talked to the station attendant. He always greeted a face at an open window and was usually rewarded with an admiring comment, but this time the girl barred his way with her arm. He was to stay behind her, out of sight.

Then they were on their way again, moving north into the rolling rangeland along the fencelines of the cattle ranch where Duffy and Shuba had met. The road they traveled skirted the range, winding down at last into a broad basin, its floor as level as a riverbed, its gentle slopes terraced to the rim of protecting hills. On either side of the road through this hidden valley were ranks of vines staked and spilling over guide wires, stretching from east to west across each tier, their tendrils heavy with ripened grapes. Midway through the vineyard they came to a driveway leading to a hilltop winery, its steep roof almost touching the ground. From the road below it resembled a great nesting bird whose folded wings covered the vats of fermenting grape juice.

They drove to a parking lot already filled with vehicles, vans, campers, pickups, and an ancient school bus. While Duffy waited in the van, the couple walked into the winery. They were gone nearly half an hour, and when they returned to the van they walked with an arm around each other's waist, each carrying a plastic bucket. Inside the van they took off outer sweaters and jackets. The girl pinned her hair in a loose bun at her neck while the young man tied a bandanna around his head. They opened the windows of the van halfway. Then the girl filled a shallow bowl with water from an outside tap and placed it near Duffy.

As they walked off toward a section of the vineyard behind the winery, the girl called to Duffy at the window of the van to wait, to be a good dog, to remember how much she loved him. The sun was already high, promising one of the hottest days of the summer, a perfect day to begin the harvest.

The migratory farm workers who harvest the crops in California follow the sun, moving from the tomato fields in Mexico and San Diego County in early spring, to the strawberry beds along the central coast, to the melons ripening in the Imperial Valley and finally to the lettuce crop in northern coastal counties where fog and sea breeze mitigate dry August heat. Except for the late-fall planting season, there is not a month in the year when those willing to stoop to the rows of fruits and vegetables cannot find work. So constant is the harvest in many areas, in fact, that field workers find no need to follow the seasons. There's a crop to pick wherever they choose to settle.

The young couple who had adopted Duffy, however, were neither typical farm workers nor settlers. When they met both were third-year students at the University of Connecticut, he from West Hartford, she from Rye, New York, and neither had ever picked more than a single rose or a backyard apple. By the mid-year break they had made up their minds to leave college, to reject family support, and to hitchhike to the West Coast. Refusing even to cash their latest allowance checks, they set out to prove what they were already convinced of, that they could live happily without exploiting either the earth or its population. Youth, health, and a Christian respect for all living things were all they needed. They would learn more about life by humble labor than by attending classes.

"What does education often do?" their hero Thoreau had asked. "It makes a straight-cut ditch of a free, meandering stream."

There was one Harvard man, they agreed, who knew what he was talking about.

Their route across the country did meander, but insofar as possible it stayed below the snowline, and their progress toward the southwest desert in bloom was steady. Not until they joined another traveling couple west of Flagstaff, Arizona, did they hear about the tree planting in western Canada and decide to head for Vancouver and points north to begin their honest labor. Workers, they were told, were paid ten cents a tree to restock the northwest timberlands, and it was possible to earn as much as one hundred dollars a day during early spring planting. This was welcome news. Ardent conservationists, they could imagine no greater contribution to the biosphere than creating a new forest. The possibility of making two hundred dollars a day between them, more than either of their fathers made, they also considered a meaningful contribution.

And it was true. Between early March and mid-May they worked their way through the manmade forests planting cuttings and often earning nearly a thousand dollars in a single week. Even though they were not Canadian citizens, they were an attractive couple who had no difficulty finding work. Within a month they had earned enough to buy the van, which they used to sleep in. The rest of their earnings they saved in travelers' checks for winter plans they hadn't made. By the time they turned south they were almost rich, their hands were soil-hardened and their minds were set. They would become field workers, stoop laborers for the rest of the summer. After that they would decide about the rest of their lives.

They spent the summer chopping lettuce in Monterey County. There they joined the United Farm Workers' union in order to be hired by Salinas labor contractors. Usually they were the only North Americans in the field force, their tall figures noticeable among the shorter Mexican workers, their backs and knees the aching price of their height. But they camped in the Big Sur and averaged nearly one hundred dollars a day in union wages and learned to speak Mexican Spanish.

Toward the end of August when they were working to feed the fruit stands along the highway south of San Jose, they met a couple on their way to San Francisco who told them about the fall grape harvest and the cabin on the mountaintop. The cabin was owned by a friend who rented it to his friends in a revolving arrangement, one tenant couple passing it on to the next, the rent paid into a local bank account, the key left at the Cielo Store. Their new friends arranged it. They could move into the cabin in September.

Although they could afford the rent, they hadn't slept under a house roof since leaving Connecticut. The girl accepted life in the back of the van because they never knew where they would be even a week ahead, but she longed for a house of her own. As soon as she heard about the cabin it became her destination, the place to give their relationship a foundation. A house was better than the back of a van to accumulate the evidence of permanence she needed. She wasn't homesick; she only wanted a home.

As they drove south on the weekend before the beginning of the grape harvest she was making plans. She would be able to write letters with a return address instead of sending postcards whose spectacular western scenes allowed only enough message space to tell her family she was having a wonderful time. A house of their own implied a life of their own, resourceful and responsible. A house turned them both into adults. There was a future built into a house.

It was while she was thinking about this future that she had seen the collie at the roadside waiting to go home with her. What better evidence could there be that their partnership, their love, and the cabin awaiting them were blessed?

The couple worked in the vineyard all morning, filling their buckets with warm grapes, dumping the buckets into large baskets which were carried by tractor to the winery before the sun could suck out the precious juices. At noon the vineyard foreman called a lunch break, and the grape gatherers returned to their vehicles to eat their sandwiches and drink their colas in what shade there was.

The girl opened the rear doors of the van, where she kept the portable cooler. Beyond it she saw her collie stretched across the metal floor, his flank heaving, his tongue falling from his half-open jaws. She crawled toward him, feeling the heated air within the walls. There was still water in the bowl, but it was as warm as soup. Even with the back open no breeze ventilated the ovenlike interior of the van. Duffy's life had been slowly baking away within the hot steel walls. Only the faint dampness left in his coat from the morning fog had slowed the acute hyperthermia that was about to boil his blood.

"Help me," she cried to the young man outside. "We've got to get him into the building."

They carried Duffy between them into the winery and laid him on the concrete floor. The high roof and windowless walls held in the night air. The floor was cool, but not cool enough. She sent her companion for towels soaked in the coldest water he could find, then dug a rectal thermometer from the bottom of her supply pouch and took his temperature. It was 107.

By the time the young man returned with dripping towels the prostrate collie in the center of the floor had drawn a circle of silent onlookers. The winemaker and his secretary had appeared from the office area. The vineyard foreman and tractor driver came from the rear of the building. The cold towels were applied and more were sent for as Duffy lay in a widening pool of water. His lolling tongue found the liquid under his head, and as water permeated his coat his breathing slowed, but his eyes stared vacantly and he could not control his tongue to carry water drops to his throat.

"You should take him to a vet," the secretary told the girl. "Want me to call?"

"No. Just give him air and more cold water," the girl replied.

"She knows as much as any vet," her companion added.

Although this, of course, was not true, and the girl had never seen a case of heat stroke in a dog before, she had seen field workers drop in their tracks. She knew that the temperature must be brought down. Another degree could kill. Cooling him fast was the only hope.

And gradually the treatment worked. Duffy's breathing slowed. His panting stopped and his eyes focused on the circle of legs around him. He was moved to a cooler spot and a wet towel was laid under him. As the staff and the couple watched, he raised his head to the faces above him. Then, with a soft sigh, he closed his eyes to rest.

Satisfied that he would recover and assured by the winemaker that the dog could stay inside the building, the couple went back to the vineyard to work until three, when picking stopped for the day. When they returned they found Duffy lying in an outer office beside the secretary's desk. A bowl of water was beside him and an opened box of dog biscuits was on the desk. Duffy had found a friend.

"He's such a beautiful dog," the secretary told them. "Collies are very rare, aren't they?"

"Very," the girl agreed. "They're wonderful family dogs."

"Funny," the secretary added, looking down at Duffy, "there's been an announcement on our local radio station all weekend about a lost collie. I just heard it again. His name is Duffy."

At the sound of his name, Duffy raised his head to her, his ears cupped forward, his dark eyes shining on hers.

"Our dog's name is Sky," the girl told her.

"Well, he's welcome to stay with me tomorrow. He's company."

But Duffy's new owner thanked her and refused. He was led from the winery across the parking lot to the van and helped inside. In the doorway the secretary stood to wave goodbye, but Duffy had no chance to turn back toward her.

He had heard his name.

Chapter Thirteen

Duffy shared with his breed three annual aggravations, each mitigated to some extent by his partnership with humans, but none eliminated from his calendar. The first, known to collie owners as "flipping," occurred when his undercoat of dense, soft fur loosened to be replaced in time by a new one. This metamorphic season, a natural and beneficial exchange resulting in a thicker, glossier coat, lasted many weeks with or without regular combing to hasten the shedding process, and tufts of dead wool, caught between tender skin and his permanent outer coat, itched. It became imperative to rid himself of this irritating excess in the only way he could, by digging it out with claws and teeth.

In California the dog days are delayed. Instead of arriving at the height of summer, they fall invariably between the seasons, extending and intensifying the hot dry summer at a time in late September when summer is supposed to end. Temperatures climb as humidity drops. Tongues drip. Skin cracks. Even noses are warm and dry. Dogs of every coating suffer through this fifth season when even cats pant, but collies are among the worst sufferers. Coated for all weather, they have adapted to no extreme, and like the humans they follow they have settled in climates no sensible dog would choose.

Finally, there is the flea season. In Duffy's valley the uneven contest between dogs and fleas is not quite year-long. The nightly frosts which coat the landscape between late November and early March bring temporary relief, or at least make a fair fight possible. The rest of the year, the flea forces are active, well supplied with replacements, and dogs are kept busy despite whatever help they receive from their human protectors. But during the blazing days of autumn, overheated grasses and sun-warmed fur produce a flea explosion. Settling into their favorite feeding grounds, the almost unreachable area just north of the tail, they turn long-haired dogs into maddened contortionists as each dog lays siege to its own hindquarters.

Any one of these three crisis times in a collie's year is an ordeal. In Duffy's case the combination of all three was enough to change his personality. From late September to early November, he became a different dog. Driven nearly crazy by the flaming hot spots, the crawling itches over his body, he was no longer the responsive reflection of his human partner. While afflicted he had to be called several times before he heard his name. Even on the walks he loved, the cats who ran before him became distractions he barely had time for. The surface turmoil under way from nose to tail demanded his complete attention, and the more he gave it the louder were its demands.

The onset of Duffy's triple curse coincided with his arrival at the mountain cabin. He began to shed wisps of soft beige fur along his back and hips. White clumps were dug out of his ruff. As the weeks passed, he shrank, the noble mane which characterized the rough-coated collie fell away, and even the feathers on his forelegs and tail dropped off in matted strands. All that remained of his coat were the overlay of coarse dark hairs and the remnants of its deep foundation.

At first, the tidal fog bank which overflowed the summit in the early morning hours before retreating under the noon sun dampened his coat, but in late September the Santa Ana winds arrived, gusting down to the sea from the deserts with hot fury. The skies were swept clean, leaving the mountaintop to simmer. The dog days had arrived.

Nor had Duffy risen above the fleas. A new collar was buckled around his neck, a heavy leather strap no rough-coated dog should wear, and a flea collar was added, but its effective range fell far short of the fleas' favorite camping grounds, serving only to add a ring of viscous tangles to what remained of his ruff.

Between six in the morning, when the young couple left for the vineyard, and four in the afternoon when they returned, Duffy lived at the end of a long chain, fastened to a ring bolt set into the corner of the cabin. The chain was anchored in such a way that its radius allowed him only an arc of bare ground in the front yard and shade before noon within the shadow of the west wall. The chain not only tightened the leather band around his neck; it also prevented his retreat to cooler ground in the hottest part of the day and, particularly frustrating, it held him just short of the lookout post above the seaward canyons where he could watch the world he couldn't reach.

After the near-fatal morning in the back of the van when it became obvious that her family dog could not accompany them to the vineyards, the girl had worked out Duffy's daytime schedule. She had anticipated all his needs, provided for his comfort and safety in a way that left her free of guilty feelings. The long chain would allow him ample freedom. It stationed him in the cabin's front yard as guardian of her home and symbol of its occupancy. A collie in the front yard was a statement that told more about the family who lived there than did curtains in the windows or a border of pansies outside the door.

Her final provision for his comfort she considered her most ingenious. Water for the mountain population was supplied by private wells. One well served the Cielo Store, but the rest were shared, each well serving several residents through a network of underground pipes to the clearings. Each house was connected to a well source, and at intervals a riser capped with valve and faucet supplied an outdoor water source. The high fire danger in this heavily overgrown area bordering a national forest was of year-round concern to forest rangers and the county fire department. The standing pipe outside the cabin lay just within the radius of Duffy's chain so that he could reach it without winding himself around it. The girl placed a shallow pan under the tap and opened the valve enough to allow a constant trickle into the pan. Duffy would never lack cool, fresh well water, no matter how much he drank during the long hot days when she was gone.

It was on just such a day when he was lying close to the side of the cabin in the last strip of shade, exhausted by his morning's assault on his saliva-ridden rear quarters, that he received a visitor. Cabins and campsites on the mountaintop were arranged in clusters to take advantage of the wells and the narrow shelves that offered both level ground and, if possible, an ocean or valley view. But so thick were the walls of live-oak limbs and clumps of greasewood and wild lilac between each clearing that, although Duffy often heard his neighbors, he had never seen one. Suddenly through the leafy wall east of the cabin a huge dark animal appeared.

As it paused half hidden by the undergrowth, Duffy rose stiffly, his itches forgotten, to stare. Some visceral whisper deep within him seemed to freeze his response mechanisms. It was not the surface chill of fear; he had never known fear of another animal. Nor had he developed an assertive territorial-defense response instinctive in many dogs. Visitors had always been welcome in his own backyard. But something about this visitor held him motionless. His tail remained down. Only his eyes and erect ears indicated his complete attention.

As the dog that was not a dog stepped into the yard, it met Duffy's stare with wide-spaced amber eyes like his, set in a black triangular face, its broad flat head and cupped ears nestled in a bulging ruff of muscled chest and shoulders. It was nearly six feet long and twice Duffy's weight, and as it stood revealed before him, its coat, which at first had looked pitch black, changed color. Single silver hairs shone along its back and flank, and as the noon sun played along its haunches and chest, its undercoat gave off a lazuline light, black outer coat penetrated to soft fur of shadowed azure.

After the first instant of eye contact, the animal raised its long plumed tail high over its back. Duffy caught a strange, sweet odor, a scent unlike any he had ever tasted before. Then the tail fell and the animal walked slowly to the water pan. As Duffy watched, it drank in deep, quick gulps until most of the water in the pan was gone. Then with a flick of its muzzle it overturned the pan, nuzzling it out from under the tap. The constant trickle overflowing the pan had formed a patch of saturated ground around the water pipe, a circle of mud spreading out from the pipe in all directions. The animal lay down in the soft mud and rolled on its back, long legs waving and kicking the air. It rolled from side to side, burying back and flanks, neck and shoulders, even its swishing tail in the ooze.

It stood then in the center of the mud hole, its paws sinking into the cool slime, to snake off the water drops from nose and ears. As it made its way back across the yard it continued to watch Duffy, but it made no move to narrow the space between them. It seemed almost shy, as if it understood that it had intruded without permission, that it half expected challenge and hoped to be excused.

As it headed for the opening through the trees Duffy made another startling discovery. The huge animal was a female. No female he had ever met behaved or looked like this. She neither welcomed his advance nor warned him off. Only her pause at the edge of the clearing to leave her mark behind offered evidence of her sex. She didn't linger after that. Carrying her coat of drying mud like a carapace, she disappeared through the leaves as silently as she had arrived.

Chapter Fourteen

Her name was Liana, a rough approximation of the Zuni Indian designation for the Blue Wolf of the West, a mediating prey god the color of the western sea. She was a two-year-old timber wolf raised from early puppyhood by humans.

It is said that no wolf pup is ever an orphan, that it is always adopted by foster parents who raise it as their own. That may be true in a wolf society whose population is threatened only by nature's survival ratios, but in the decimated ranks of animals that are in the way of man—trophy animals, bounty animals, and so-called pests—orphans are common. And wolf orphans are destroyed with their parents before they grow into killers. Liana survived alone of her litter because an Eskimo guide brought her home to his wife as a present. There were no nursing females among the dogs that spring, and Liana was too young to eat solid food, so she was fed at the wife's breast next to her infant son.

As the pup grew, the Eskimo family fell into deep poverty. The money offered to them for the young wolf was exorbitant, and they accepted it out of need rather than desire. The young couple who bought the pup were from Taos, New Mexico, temporary residents of Alaska, where the man worked as a welder in the North Slope oil fields. Liana was by then a three-month-old puppy, large even for a wolf, but playful and gentle. The couple were told that she was a wolf, which was why they bought her. They had no difficulty bringing her home as a husky. In fact, according to her registration certificate, she was still a husky, a native Alaskan sled dog now just another transplanted Californian.

Except that to everyone who saw her, she looked like a wolf. It was not her wolfish behavior but her size that frightened people and caused their dogs to act strangely whenever they met her. Liana's enormous dark presence in the community made everyone nervous, and there was always someone who reported her to the sheriff's office or the animal control agency. The only thing that had saved her from being destroyed was her gentle nature. Whenever a sheriff's deputy or an animal-control officer came to investigate a complaint, Liana greeted him by licking his face. Then she lay docilely at his feet while her mistress produced her husky certificate.

Still, the couple took few chances. Their small house in the mountain community was an ideal place to keep a wolf passing for a dog. Few of their neighbors knew of her and fewer ever saw her. She was trained to a leash and free only when one of her owners was at home. Wolves are not indiscriminate wanderers, even in the wild, and Liana's house and yard were sufficient because they contained all she knew and needed: food and love and someone big enough to romp with her, to explore the mountains, and swim in the ocean. She had never gone visiting before and had no canine friends.

But for Liana it was also a difficult time of year. Wolves molt like dogs in late summer and early fall. Wolves itch, and because they are wolves, instinct drives them toward solutions more readily than their dependent cousins. Liana felt the torchlike heat, the fleas, and the irritating change of undercoat. She also heard the trickle of water beyond the trees. The water sound, the relief so close, had been too much to resist. She had slipped through the barrier branches to solve her problem.

Her first visit to Duffy's water hole went undetected. She was back in her yard before her mistress missed her, and the only noticeable evidence in Duffy's yard was the tipped-over water pan. Liana's huge paw prints were left behind in the mud, but the girl who kept Duffy displayed in her yard was too quick to assume he had overturned his drinking pan to notice them. Liana's mud coat was brushed away while she wriggled with pleasure that evening, and the musk scent from her caudal gland, usually too delicate for human noses to detect, had long since disappeared on the hot afternoon wind.

Only Liana remembered the wash of cooling mud over her irritated body, but that was enough to send her back at noon the following day for another bath.

And Duffy remembered well the great silent animal who had come to call. When she reappeared, wafting her perfume toward him before she crossed to his therapeutic fountain, he was ready. No matter how large she was, she was a female, a trespasser, and if her high tail and her sweet scent meant what he thought it did, she would receive him.

Their first nose-to-nose meeting came about on her second visit. There was much tail wagging, hip swinging and curious examination as they touched, then quickly parted to sneeze their approval of each other. There were also many strange sounds. Duffy offered his series of short, high whines. Liana replied with a variety of soft sings and hums, wolf smalltalk. Only when she lay prone in the mud bath did Duffy stand above her to bark as furiously as he could. His excitement ended their interlude.

"Liana!" a woman's voice called from beyond the trees, and Liana hurried home.

Her visits to Duffy's yard continued, however, and became the high point of his long hot days. They played like giant puppies in the dusty yard, taking turns at rolling on their backs while the other stood above in growling triumph. Liana's paws landing on Duffy's shoulders often knocked him down but just as quickly she would sink beneath his embrace, snarling her delight. Liana's mistress heard their noisy conversation, but only after they had played together long enough did she call.

Their only inhibition was Duffy's chain. Each time Liana challenged him to chase her, the chain caught him up and ended the game. And because it had been carefully measured to allow him to reach the water pan without entangling himself in the pipe, he could never join her under the tap to feel the dripping water on his back. Duffy had to watch the wolf roll rapturously in the mud at the breathless conclusions of their play. He could never follow her back through the trees, and the long hot afternoons became longer as he panted without water, to wait for her return.

Was their illicit affair a secret? Neither knew or cared. On weekends, when their owners were at home, they never met. Duffy was entertained on weekends, taken in the van on errands and to the store on Saturday nights to make up for the loneliness of his weekdays. Liana too was kept occupied on weekends, when she was taken on hikes in the mountains and to a deserted beach to swim. The humans in their lives groomed and fed them and provided affection and variety in their next-door houses. Only Duffy and Liana waited patiently for the weekends to end and the humans to leave them to each other.

Duffy's behavior while the girl was away at work worried her. She understood his loneliness, his need to express his frustration without her at his side. She knew many well-behaved dogs often turned into vandals when left behind. His way of showing his need for her, the hurt he felt when she drove way every weekday morning, was to overturn his water pan. She never scolded him. She blamed herself. Still, to destroy his water source in such hot weather was dangerous.

Her solution, reached after careful thought, addressed both the cause and the symptom of Duffy's weekday anguish. On a Saturday shopping trip she bought a large galvanized washtub. She placed it under the running tap and was pleased to see Duffy drinking from the brimming tub that afternoon. She was also satisfied that he could never overturn it. Filled, it was too heavy for her to tip. When she chained him in the yard early Monday morning before driving away, she also made a bed outside the cabin window out of her old cardigan sweater. Leaving him something of hers would reassure him. After all, how could he know when she and her companion drove off that they were ever coming back? The sweater she had been wearing the morning she rescued him would tell him that a part of her was always there, never to be separated from him. As she left him standing in the center of the front yard that Monday morning, she felt much better.

Liana paid her daily call that morning. By then her mistress knew where she went and whom she visited. She could hear their noisy games and saw no harm in allowing the wolf to make a friend. Her only concern about keeping a wolf in a wolfless world had been Liana's isolation. Wolves, she knew, were very sociable animals. As Liana approached full adulthood, her first estrus and the instinctive urge to find a mate, the unnatural life she led might so frustrate her that her personality would change. Liana's owners worried always that one day she might live down to her reputation. They had spent many hours discussing what to do if that should happen, but had never accepted any of the alternatives. Her visits to the collie next door, innocent and so far undetected by his owners, were good for the wolf. Liana came home after each visit happy and affectionate. The woman was still reluctant to allow her wolf to visit the collie when the couple were at home. For one thing, she often heard the couple fighting. But by filling the weekends with diversions Liana loved, she and her husband had managed so far to avoid both ending the friendship and risking discovery.

It took Liana and Duffy nearly five minutes to destroy the sweater. Each grabbed a sleeve to pull. When the sleeves parted at the shoulder seams, Duffy held the other end of Liana's sleeve to tear it to shreds, then they tugged apart Duffy's sleeve. After that, with hind legs braced, growling through mouthsful of yarn, heads shaking to rip more effectively, they reduced the sweater to pieces too small to share. Not since Duffy had discovered one afternoon that it was more fun to hold a ball in his mouth than to drop it at his girls' feet, forcing a tug of war, had he enjoyed himself so much. He sank down before Liana breathless, his ears tucked back, his tongue pulsing with each pant, waiting for her to think of something else to do.

She walked to the water tub to drink. Duffy followed, standing beside her to gulp. She lifted a front paw to the rim of the tub, but the tub would not tip. She stepped into the water, standing half in, half out, but this only spilled off an inch or two. She climbed into the tub and sat down. More water spilled, spreading over the ground in a great circular wave. She stepped out, shook herself, flinging water drops over Duffy's coat, then nosed the side of the tub. It tipped slightly. She placed her front paws on the rim again and stood above it. Her weight tipped the half-filled tub toward her, sending water far across the yard.

Liana pushed the empty water tub out of the way and lay on her back in the middle of the puddle. Duffy watched, feeling the water between his toes as Liana rolled toward him. When she stood to shake herself she left a wide mud bed within reach of Duffy's chain. With a growl he flung himself on his back, wiggled his hips, kicked his paws in the air and used his swishing tail as a rudder to push himself deeper into the mud. The nearly bald spot at the base of his tail where he had chewed himself raw felt suddenly cool. A mud poultice spread over the hot skin in the middle of his back, a place he had been trying vainly to reach. He turned on his side to lie in Liana's shadow. She reached down to lick the water drops from his muzzle, wagging her pleasure.

The sudden silence next door brought Liana's mistress to the edge of the trees.

"Liana," she cried, seeing the collie on his back under the wolf's jaws.

Liana raised her head, then obediently trotted off across the yard.

At the hole in the tree wall she paused just long enough to look back at Duffy still lying in the mud. He saw her and lifted his mud-soaked tail once before letting it fall back.

Satisfied, Liana dove into the leaves and disappeared.

Late that afternoon Duffy received his first bath since his kennel days. Standing in the tub under the water tap, he was lathered with baby shampoo and rinsed until what coat remained hung from his body in dripping shreds. The mud cake was washed away with the memory of its soothing shield. He submitted to the scrubbing, accepting it as punishment because the girl was very angry. He could feel the anger in her fingers, in the way she pushed him under the tap, and especially in her silence as she bent over the tub.

Before the bath it had been her cry as she picked up the remains of her sweater. How could he do such a thing? How could he hate her after all she'd done for him? Where would he be now if it hadn't been for her? Duffy had heard those questions flung like stones at him before. He hung back before the shrill voice, back raised, head and tail down, afraid to look into her eyes, ready to dodge her lifted hand. She had to drag him to the tub and grip his trembling body with one hand while she scrubbed with the other.

Afterward, he was chained to dry, but the sun heated his coat, spinning it into stiff spears. His body flamed again. He wanted to roll in the mud circle, but the short chain held him close to the cabin. He wanted to escape the anger in the dry, hot air, to hide beyond the trees.

That night he refused to eat his dinner. Much later, when the cabin was dark and silent, his bowels gave way. Diarrhea covered the floor when the girl found him in the morning.

That day the girl stayed home. She told her companion she had to spend the day with their dog. He was obviously sick, and she had never abandoned a sick dog before. Duffy was given two tablespoons of Kaopectate and chained outside while she cleaned the cabin. She had just sat down beside the open window to drink a cup of coffee when she saw the wolf.

Liana stood at the edge of the clearing, half in, half out of the trees, hesitating for the first time since the morning they met to come forward toward Duffy. Perhaps she sensed the presence of the girl. Perhaps it was Duffy's strange behavior. He didn't move to greet her. Instead, he watched her, tail down, eyes widened at the expected reaction from the girl just above his head.

Liana walked slowly toward him, her tail shifting shyly from side to side, wary but needing to touch him.

The girl in the window screamed.

Liana fled.

Chapter Fifteen

The grape harvest along the central coast of California begins in the second week of September when the tenderest of the wine grapes, the Pinot Noir, is ripe and ready to pick. The pickers, a labor force made up of local and itinerant farm workers, are usually hired by the vineyard foremen and are paid from five to ten dollars an hour, depending upon the amount of fruit each gathers in the course of an eight-hour day. In a good grape year, a year when late spring frost is kept at bay in the budding vineyards and the long, rainless summer culminates in an even hotter, rainless autumn, the grape pickers move from Pinot Noir to Riesling, from Colombard to Chardonnay, working through October and into the first days of November, when the final crop, the Cabernet Sauvignon, is ripe.

This last variety, the robust finale of the harvest, can be gathered by machine, stilted tractors that ride above the vines shaking the fruit onto conveyor belts where it is washed and carried to a central bin. The Cabernet Sauvignon harvest usually marks the end of the season for the hourly workers in the larger vineyards. Most are laid off to move on to winter planting in the inland valleys or to unemployment lines or to the rewards their weeks in the vineyards have earned for them. November is a limbo month when the earth and all it sustains wait day by day for the promised winter rains. For the restless, the rootless, and those who follow the sun it is a time to move on.

The vineyards where the young couple went to work in early September, one of the largest in the valley, produced enough grape varieties to provide them with steady employment through September and October. In one of the driest and warmest late-harvest seasons on record, without a single day of rain, they each earned as much as seventy-five dollars for a day's work, and although they returned to the cabin hot and exhausted in the late afternoons, the cool nights on the mountaintop, the weekends spent along the coast, and their growing fund of traveler's checks were more than enough to refresh them and to feed their separate dreams. When in early November they were thanked and paid a final bonus for being among the most productive workers, they drove home to their dog to talk about the future.

After nearly two months as members of the isolated population made up for the most part of couples like themselves, young men and women newly self-sufficient who had already seen more of the world than their parents would ever see and for whom all dreams were possible, they had made friends. They had a home as permanent as any, a congenial social life, and enough money to last them at least until the following spring.

To the girl, these assets were enough to settle her immediate future. She would furnish the cabin with the comforts and conveniences of home because the more of themselves it contained the greater its importance would be in both their lives. She would continue her education at the local campus of the University of California. Her failure to complete college continued to gnaw at her conscience because it was, after all, an undeniable failure. She also intended to work part-time for the local Humane Society. Now that she owned a dog, alive because of her, the precarious existence of dependent cats and dogs and the careless disregard for their welfare by self-indulgent owners haunted her. She owed a debt to all creatures for her own good fortune.

She also dared to look beyond the months ahead. Their community was just about self-contained, but its high place between two worlds offered the advantages of both. County services were provided. A school bus climbed the mountain twice each day. One of the most beautiful cities in California spread below their mountain shelf on one side. A country valley lay just beyond the crest on the other. A national forest surrounded their aerie, ensuring years of privacy and safety for her family.

As she thought about past and future, her place in this heavenly outpost, she thanked her Maker and the circumstances that had prevented her from reporting the wolf. She had been sure it was a wolf and that she should report it, but there was no telephone in the cabin and no transportation that morning to the phone at the Cielo Store. And because she could take no immediate action she'd had time to reconsider. Her report would surely have brought an official to her door. Her dog was still unlicensed and might still be recognized.

Besides, the wolf had never returned. No one else she met had mentioned seeing it. Why stir up trouble for herself at the expense of an animal whose survival chances were already nonexistent? Her companion had vehemently agreed. To have called the attention of any authority to themselves for any reason would have been to become involved with a system they both rejected. Let somebody else report the wolf.

The subject of the wolf had been closed weeks ago. The subject of their collie, however, had not. After all these weeks he was still her dog, not theirs, and this continued to bother the girl. It was not that her young man objected to keeping the dog; he just didn't seem to care one way or the other. He never spoke to Sky unless she insisted. He never patted or praised or played with him. When she pointed this out he assured her that, of course, he liked dogs. They'd always had one at home. He acted, however, as if the collie wasn't there and the collie, she knew, sensed this indifference. Dogs are very sensitive to people who don't like them. Sometimes the girl wondered if, after all, their family dog might come between them instead of serving to bring them closer. She refused to think about having to choose between one and the other; that was unthinkable. But as she made her plans for the months ahead, the dog she had counted upon to provide shared responsibility and, therefore, a binding influence in their lives had instead become the cause for unspoken doubts.

Duffy's life changed with the weather in the second week of November. As the nights grew longer and colder and the cloud cap returned to sit astride the summit long after sunrise, his days became more disturbing. He faced the coldest month of the year, December, with the thinnest of protective coats, while the rains held off and every surface wore a layer of summer dust. Also, he faced the confusing and often contradictory behavior of the humans in his life, without the security of familiar routine and the collie's necessary accumulation of reassuring pet names, passing pats, and an ordered schedule. He didn't understand his keepers. They didn't seem to understand him.

Contributing to his own bewilderment was the couple's inconsistent behavior toward each other. Now that they were at home most of every day or off shopping with Duffy riding in the back of the van, they hardly noticed him. They were too busy arguing with each other. Some days he was chained in the yard while they remained inside the cabin. That was worse than being alone. They were there, but not with him. He could hear them shouting angrily at each other, and anger, however directed, Duffy always took personally.

The fights were becoming ferocious. The couple shouted across the inside of the cabin, their voices shrill as their doubts about each other grew, until one or the other slammed a kitchen pan or pounded a table. The sudden crash sent Duffy running from the room. Only humans punctuated their voices with such terrifying explosions. Once the boy threw Duffy's full dinner pan through the open window. What had he done to cause such violence? Often when a fight ended, the girl took Duffy for a long walk along the crestline road, but it was not the kind of walk he liked. She tugged him along without stopping anywhere and never said a word.

He missed Liana. At first, he had watched for her appearance every morning, but she never came. The water tub was filled and waiting, although the tap had been turned off and the mud circle had dried, but the wolf stayed somewhere beyond the trees. One Sunday morning Duffy was let out alone while the girl made breakfast. Quickly he found the passage Liana had used and made his way through the branches to the edge of the next clearing. Liana's spoor led into the yard and toward a small house with a wide screened porch overlooking the ocean. Liana was everywhere around him as he trotted forward, his tail rising to wave the tidings his nose received.

"Sky! Here, Sky!" came the frantic voice behind him.

He knew he was being called, that the girl was angry, but he ignored her. Liana's summons was all he heard. He reached the porch door just as a woman appeared. Behind her Liana's great dark head was framed in an inside doorway. Duffy's wag began at the white tip of his thinned-out tail. As his tail gathered momentum, his hindquarters swayed, then his whole body writhed in welcome. He began to bark, a volley of high puppy sounds, while the woman stood in front of Liana, barring their meeting.

He had found her, but his celebration was short lived. Behind him the girl's voice rose to a shriek, while the woman at the door came out. Duffy was led back to the path between the trees, told gently, then sternly to go home. He left, tail down, turning every few steps to look back until he felt the hand on his collar. He was scolded for annoying their neighbors, and for the rest of the day he was kept inside.

That night, long after sunset he heard a strange song floating above the trees beyond his window. He had never heard anything quite like it. The only night music he had ever heard before had been the wild rejoicing of coyotes in the distant hills, gleeful barking so far away and so unlikely at that hour of the night that he had listened only for a moment before going back to sleep. The call he heard now seemed to come from close by, yet somehow the canyon vaults and facing peaks removed it from its source, swelling it, melting its notes as they carried toward the half moon at Duffy's window. He listened in silence as the five-note wolf song ended in a series of soft yips. Then silence. It was Liana's farewell.

The din of dispute followed by periods of crackling silence between the couple culminated, during the final week of November, in a decision. The boy wanted to spend the winter in Mexico where their hard-earned money would buy them months of tropic idleness. The girl at first resisted. What about their house, their future together? But her companion was adamant. He was going. She could go or stay.

What about their dog?

They couldn't take him with them. That was obvious. You couldn't smuggle a collie across the border. He would be quarantined, caged for weeks or months. One thing the Mexicans didn't need was a Yankee dog. And one thing the boy didn't need was a hassle with immigration officials. They could always get another dog when they returned in the spring.

The ultimatum was followed by several days during which the space separating the three occupants of the cabin widened while the girl made up her mind. During these uneasy days she avoided both man and dog, as if approaching either would commit her to one or the other. She couldn't touch her dog. In fact, the sight of him chained outside or watching her from his bed under the window filled her with intolerable remorse. Perhaps she knew all along the choice she would make. Or, perhaps, justifying it to a perplexed collie would force her to justify it to herself, something she couldn't do. Worst of all, what was she to do with him? He was there in front of her. He was everywhere she turned. She wished she had never seen him because now she could never not see him. His eyes would follow her for the rest of her life.

She thought of the posters that lined the highway, offering a reward for the return of the collie. But how could she call now? Surely she would be accused of purposely stealing the dog, and her relationship with her companion would be further compromised because she would have to admit that she never did attempt to telephone the sign's author, even though she had told the boy otherwise.

Then, once again she was shown the answer. Once again He took her problem upon Himself and solved it. On the morning before they were to leave the cabin she greeted Duffy with lavish hugs and bright assurances. She served him a special breakfast of kibble soaked in a leftover can of beef broth and sprinkled with tuna scraps. She accompanied him on his last exploration of the clearing, then brushed his coat, all the while explaining what was about to happen to him, what a wonderful life he was about to begin. They would miss each other, of course, and never forget each other, but he was going on a great adventure, an adventure she had arranged because she loved him and wanted only what was best for him.

Duffy stood quivering under the brush while her promises fell around him like the loose hairs of his coat.

During the couple's weekend excursions to the beaches and outlying residential areas of the city they had discovered one of the world's last enclaves of the very rich. Located just south of the city and within its official boundaries, lying low behind walls of bougainvillea and high above coastal traffic, was a colony of wealthy refugees driven from the playgrounds of Europe by confiscatory tax laws, from Newport and East Hampton by the insensitive young, from Bel-Air and Pasadena by the smog. Protected by a network of impenetrable private lanes and cul-de-sacs, by patrolling police and the nearly vertical peaks of the coastal range were mansions so artfully situated that from patio or poolhouse, sundeck or tennis court each had an unobstructed view of the sea and the channel islands. Yet these hideaways were so well screened by curving driveways behind self-locking gates, by the treetop carpet sloping to the shore that no Sunday surfer, no freeway traveler, no curious sightseer ever caught a glimpse of pillared facade or rose garden.

The names and the lives of the residents were known only to the interlocking circles of their friends and neighbors, who gathered by engraved invitation every night at a different address to dine and agree once more on the sorry state of the rest of the world. The only outsiders admitted within these private grounds were caterers and valet-parking squads. The only insiders excluded were ex-husbands with new, very young wives—these, and the rare show-business millionaire willing to overpay for a property available in an estate settlement.

But even those who have everything around them must buy food and books and hostess gifts, and so a small shopping center had been provided in the center of this haven next to the fire station and convenient to two country clubs. The shops were small and clustered around a circular mall. Parking was limited and signs discreet. Customers were local and well known. It was not a commercial area likely to be discovered by outsiders, but one Saturday morning the couple had come upon it, parked the van and window-shopped while waiting for the only restaurant to open. When it finally did they were turned away because he was without a jacket and her thonged sandals revealed dirty feet, but she had remembered the area well. If her collie was to move to a new home, what better place to find it than in this wealthy compound where every dog she saw wore its bangs tied in a ribbon that matched its owner's Hermés scarf?

On the day before they were to leave for Mexico the couple drove Duffy to the shopping center. They circled slowly around the parking area until the girl saw a Rolls Royce Silver Cloud parked outside the market at the rear of the mall. They pulled in next to the Rolls, waited to be sure its owner was out of sight, then quickly transferred Duffy from the back of the van to the back seat of the splendid car.

Without looking back, they drove quickly out of the shopping center, turned at the traffic light and headed back to the freeway.

Duffy sat in the soft leather of the back seat. Its rich smell made him sneeze and he raised his nose to leave a damp spot on the polished window.

On his collar a note was tied with a Christmas ribbon.

"My name is Sky," it said. "Please love me."

Chapter Sixteen

It is exactly one mile from Aramanth House, a pink and white villa at the top of a narrow hillside lane, to the shopping center at near–sea level, but it is a gentle downhill grade under a canopy of ancient oaks and redwoods, and the morning air is scented the year round with the perfume of jasmine or hibiscus or camellias, depending upon the season. It was the custom of the master of Aramanth House to set off after breakfast and the *Times* (the *New York*, of course, not the *Los Angeles*) down the hill on foot. He was accompanied on these morning constitutionals by three Yorkshire terriers who followed him down the center of the road like rats behind the Pied Piper until they reached the main artery leading to the shopping center. There they paused while he connected leashes to the Yorkies' jeweled collars and led them safely along the side of the busy street to the entrance of the parking area. By this time all were breathing faster, but they knew they would not have to walk back up the hill, so they hurried through the center toward the Rolls Royce waiting outside the market.

Like every activity involved in the smooth running of Aramanth House, the daily marketing was integrated into the morning schedule of staff and owners for maximum efficiency of the former and maximum convenience of the latter. As the master of the house took up his *Times* with his second cup of tea, the young Scot who served as butler and chauffeur picked up the shopping list from his wife, who was the cook. Previously, she had consulted the mistress of the house about the dinner menu while a maid served the mistress's breakfast tray in the master bedroom. The chauffeur then set off in the Rolls down the hill to the market, his departure timed so that he would have completed his shopping as the master and the Yorkies arrived to be driven home.

Only the periodic fires in the hills above the villa and the resulting runoff which occasionally turned the narrow lane into a raging torrent during heavy winter rains had ever cancelled this morning rendezvous. As master and Yorkies reached the car, the chauffeur had already stowed the groceries in the trunk and was waiting to open the back door for the man, then the front door for the dogs before returning home.

Until, that is, the morning the chauffeur returned behind his shopping cart to find a collie sitting in the master's place in the backseat. He had just discovered the dog and read the note through the window when his passengers arrived. His face was flushed under his chauffeur's cap and his hand was on the door handle, but he could not open the door, not because he was afraid of the collie, his favorite breed of dog, but because for the first time in his employment he had no idea what was expected of him.

"Look what we've got here, sir," he announced as the walkers joined him.

The master of Aramanth House was a native of Devonshire and a naturalized American citizen. Shortly after distinguished service in World War II, during a diplomatic posting to the British Embassy in Washington, he and his wife had decided they preferred post-war America to post-war England. Like his father and grandfather, who had served the Empire in various uncivilized outposts, he carried English habit and custom with him, at least insofar as possible, and one of these was his way of speaking. The English have a curious way of concluding every observation with a question that assumes agreement. Conversation is often lopsided, requiring of the second party only a nod or a mumble. To Duffy the discussion that took place that morning just outside his window in the Rolls sounded like the series of gentle questions his owner used to ask on their morning walks. He always enjoyed such consultations, so he listened attentively in his usual way, by moving his ears forward during the statement, then backward at its final rising inflection, and answering each question with a soft click of his tongue.

"Handsome dog, isn't it? Someone's way of leaving the unwanted child at the rich man's doorstep, wouldn't you say, Charles? Chose us, I suppose, because of the car, wouldn't you think?"

Collie and chauffeur answered each comment with synchronized nods and tongue clicks.

"But Sky?" Here the master leaned closer to read the note on Duffy's collar. "No sort of name for a collie, is it? Either it ought to be spelled with a final 'e' as in Skye terrier, which of course he isn't, or he should be called Lad or Laddie, wouldn't you agree?"

The questions were directed not at Duffy but at the chauffeur, who still waited beside the car, his hand on the door handle. Meanwhile the three Yorkies were dancing and barking, but because a Yorkie bark is almost as small as a Yorkie, no one, including Duffy, seemed to notice them. Only when they stood on their hind legs to paw at their master's shins did he realize that action was demanded and that the decision was his to make.

"Well, I suppose we must take him along," the master decided. "We just can't leave him here, can we? You'll call the S.P.C.A. or whatever they call it, won't you? They'll know what to do, or will they? I see he has no license. What do you think, Charles?"

At last, the question the chauffeur had been waiting for, the one he could answer with an opinion of his own.

"Let's take him home, sir. Unless someone adopts him quickly he'll be destroyed, and that would be a shame, sir. He can live with me and Mary, at least for a while. Would you mind the larger dog, sir?"

"Willing to give it a try, are you, Charles? Well, all right then.

Let's be on our way. Mary will agree, will she?"

Assured that she would, the morning routine resumed, except that the master rode home in the front seat, while Duffy remained in the rear with the Yorkies tucked around him. As the Rolls glided out of the shopping center, the collie felt the noses of the tiny dogs poking into the fur around his tail. He wanted to scratch them away, but they were obviously dogs, not fleas, and it was such a pleasure to be riding once again at a window he could look out of.

The business of Aramanth House, its purpose and its mandate, were the conscientious manufacture and distribution of happiness. The aphorism repeated most often by maids and houseman, gardeners and cooks, on this island of privilege was: Money can't buy happiness. And there was ample evidence in the colony that it was true. But as all who occasionally augmented the regular staff at the villa agreed, Aramanth House was the exception. Master and mistress were still deeply in love, or so it seemed to all who observed them holding hands in public, exchanging gentle compliments and courtesies. Always their behavior toward everyone around them exemplified civility, polite deference and impeccably good manners. Orders to servants were suggested, always with allowance for a difference of opinion which, of course, was never expressed. Voices were never raised, birthdays never forgotten, and the state of everyone's health was of daily concern.

But the riches with which Aramanth House was blessed were intended to be shared with friends and neighbors, as well. It was not enough to set the example; it was the obligation of master and mistress to convert. Guests were celebrated with the finest crystal and English china, even at an informal luncheon in the garden. Formal dress was mandatory at dinner, and gentlemen were offered brandy and cigars while their ladies enjoyed cordials in the mistress' boudoir. Evenings were carefully arranged. A string quartet or an uplifting talk by a distinguished visitor reduced the opportunity for gossip and family disagreement, allowing just enough time for fond farewells before sending each couple home, drowsy with rich food and edifying entertainment. If their guests were not happier after such an evening, they were ashamed to admit it.

No such ideal household would have been complete without pets, of course, and especially one where there were no grandchildren to display. In addition to a kitchen cat and a garden strung with bird feeders, the three Yorkshire terriers had been carefully selected to add just the right touch to the carefully managed happiness at Aramanth House. They were given the run of the house and grounds. Weekly shampoos and pedicures kept them as odorless and flealess as stuffed dogs. They were too small to jump into human laps. Their cropped tails never brushed a priceless porcelain figurine from its pedestal, and their clipped and buffed toenails never tore a stocking. They were dogs, all right, as their small, alert faces and tiny barks attested, but, like the measured proportions of all ingredients that went into the production of happiness at Aramanth House, they were not too doggy.

The group of humans and animals that surrounded Duffy as he stepped out of the Rolls that morning to stretch his legs in the parking circle was almost too good to be true. The immediate well-wishers consisted of master and mistress, chauffeur and cook, each taking turns at patting and praising him. A bowl of water was provided, then a handful of tea biscuits were fed to him, while the three Yorkies dodged between his legs and a large tiger cat viewed him with loathing from the top of a wall. The air he sniffed was cool and moist from garden sprinklers. The voices were soft, the questions floating around him congenial. Not since he had arrived at the ranch to join his third family had he felt so immediately welcome, so tantalized by the possibilities of his new home, so reassured by his human benefactors.

Almost immediately, however, his presence in this haven of orderly good fellowship was felt by every member. He began his explorations of the three-acre property by following the gardener off to the formal gardens. There, under the stricken stare of the Mexican horticulturist, he relieved himself, then proceeded as he always did to fling topsoil into the air while raising his nose to the sky. The gardener couldn't understand why a dog should choose the newest bed of seedlings, then insist on trying to cover up his indiscretion by digging up the plants, especially since his aim was poor and the gardener had quickly removed the evidence with a shovel.

As Duffy trotted happily back to the driveway, he noticed the cat on the wall. He dashed toward it and leaped high as the cat reached down to bat him across the nose. No cat had ever attacked. No cat, chaseable or not, had mistaken his good-natured pursuit before. Next, he discovered an enclosure outside the kitchen door filled with tall containers of delicious-smelling food. He had nosed the cover off the nearest, which happened to contain scraps of beef Wellington mixed with morsels of coquille St. Jacques, before he was chased away by the cook.

On his first day at Aramanth House he was invited to sit decoratively beside master and mistress during their late-morning discussion of the evening plans under an umbrella on the patio. He was ordered away from a small pool of swirling hot water in which the mistress floated. He was urged to accompany the chauffeur down the driveway to the mailbox, but gently reprimanded later when he entered the library through open French doors while master and mistress were enjoying high tea. A maid led him back to the kitchen where he was fed a tasty mixture of puppy chow and prime rib.

He discovered a wooded acre near the gates where he ran through tall trees until he sank exhausted in the driveway, but when he plunged through a circle of cedars to drink from a bird bath, he was chased away by the gardener.

It would take time, everyone tolerantly agreed, for the collie to learn the ways of Aramanth House. Once he did, however, he would be an asset. The chauffeur was particularly pleased with this assessment because not only was the dog his responsibility, he had always wanted a collie. He and his wife lived in a spacious apartment above the four-car garage. There the dog would spend nights and evenings when he and his wife were on duty in the main house. He could be trained to observe the rules everyone followed, and during the many weeks in the year when master and mistress were traveling abroad, the chauffeur and his wife could devote every day to their new dog.

Judging by Duffy's enjoyment of his first day, his ravenous appetite, and his willingness to put up with the imperious dispositions of the Yorkies, he had found a home he liked. And one of the things he liked best was the constant presence of humans around him. There seemed always to be someone he could follow, someone always doing something interesting. When master and mistress disappeared to dress for dinner, he was allowed to lie under a kitchen table while the cook and chauffeur ate. When a maid was driven to the bus stop, he rode along in the back of the station wagon. When at last the Scottish couple retired to their apartment to watch television, he joined them. His first wonderful day ended when he was allowed to stretch out on a bench at a window overlooking the gardens.

To the couple who watched him it was apparent that another unhappy soul had come under the spell of this magic place. Their new dog was responding to the therapeutic potion dispensed within the gates of the estate.

As Duffy shifted to lie on his back on the bench, he sighed his satisfied sigh. Wherever he was, however he got here, he felt secure.

Chapter Seventeen

The following morning Duffy was prepared for his happy life and his important role at Aramanth House. As soon as the master and the Yorkies were driven home from their downhill walk, the chauffeur was sent off in the station wagon to attend to the business of making the collie legitimate and presentable. He was taken first to the veterinary clinic, where he was given a rabies vaccination, his second in less than a year, but there was no way the chauffeur or the veterinarian could have known that. Having obtained the verifying tag and certificate, they then drove to the pet parlor.

Like the rest of his breed, Duffy seldom appeared to need a bath. His coat, even his broad white ruff, remained free from obvious dirt and debris that dogs with shorter legs and woollier fur accumulate. Loose particles were easily shaken out of his long, straight hair, leaving only a film of summer dust at the roots along with an occasional foxtail or burr he was unable to pull out himself. But the weeks of shedding, the days of lying in the mountaintop clearing, and the poor condition of his ravaged skin had left him less than the picture-book collie he was expected to be. Appearance, particularly in so obvious a dog, was important, and so Duffy was lifted into a tub, lathered and rinsed and blown dry, combed and trimmed until he stood shining and miserable in the holding pan.

While Duffy was being groomed, the chauffeur drove to the county clerk's office to purchase a dog license. Unlike race horses and cattle, who wear their owners' marks for life, dogs have no permanent identity. Their legal existence is annually reestablished with the payment of a fee and the filing of a few statistics: name, breed, sex and whether or not the dog has been spayed or neutered, and the name and address of owner. No cross-check is made or even possible. No zealous filing clerk would ever discover that the male collie named Laddie was also the male collie named Duffy reported missing at a north-county office since Labor Day. To almost everyone's satisfaction, Duffy became a different dog that morning.

All dogs experience a post-bath euphoria. Whether this is the result of invigorating cleanliness or relief that the ordeal is over, or a combination of both, they shed years with final release from soap and water. The moment Duffy jumped from the station wagon wearing his new tags on a new choke collar and feeling the soft air on his scrubbed skin, a wild exuberance overcame him. He began to run. He raced across the lawn and through the gardens, running up and down the narrow turfed paths until he came to the gardener crouching over a pansy bed. He leaped over the gardener and ran through a citrus grove, scattering a basket of lemons as he went.

He charged around the poolhouse and onto the paved terrace where the mistress had chosen a deck chair to take the sun. She lay stretched in the chair, a reflector strapped under her chin, while the three Yorkies slept in the shade beneath the chair. As Duffy bounced over to lick the cream from her nose, the Yorkies flew out from their hiding place to defend their mistress. Duffy withdrew, barking and wagging, delighted to be chased even by three snarling midgets. He ran along the side of the pool and turned at the deep end to make another circuit. The little dogs pursued him, but at the corner the oldest, whose eyesight was failing, decided to take a shortcut across the water. In she went as her mistress struggled to remove the reflector to see what was happening.

"Boodles!" she screamed as the little dog sank, than reappeared paddling toward the center of the pool.

The master and a maid came running. Although it was the warmest hour of a warm December day, no one ever used the pool at that time of year. It was clear, however, that the Yorkie, swimming away from the side, would never reach the opposite side. Hesitating only to remove his reading glasses, the master dove in, swam to the Yorkie and bore her dripping above his head to the ladder. There the mistress clasped the dog, wrapping it in a towel, and hurried toward the house.

The master followed, then the maid. Bringing up the rear was Duffy, still barking at the excitement he had caused. Humans running and dripping, little dogs squeaking, the sun warm on his polished skin—it was the happiest moment he had enjoyed since he and Liana had rolled in the mud bath.

Games take on a vital importance in the lives of those who only play. Accordingly, two golf courses, tennis courts, a polo field, and a beach club were provided to members of the colony who preferred formal competition or a larger social arena. Most of the estates, however, included areas for private games, and in a community of aging exiles, the games tended to be non-aerobic. Jacuzzis were popular. So were putting greens. The owners of Aramanth House had converted a tennis court left behind by previous and more vigorous owners into a croquet court and had introduced the game to their friends.

Croquet, as it was played at Aramanth House, was a mixture of the English and American versions of the game. The higher and wider hoops of English croquet were used, as were wooden-headed mallets. The plastic balls used in roque, the American refinement of the game, were preferred, however, because the mistress found them easier to aim. Both versions of the ancient game require strategy, as well as skill, and often become fiercely competitive, even quite sadistic as the will to win races like a spreading blaze through hot-blooded contestants. To control this threat to the tranquility and purpose of all diversions at Aramanth House, English croquet manners were enforced. Visitors were expected to attribute their victories to lucky shots; the vanquished were promised quick revenge. Arguments over foul strokes were avoided by leaving all decisions to the vulnerable. Lavish praise for an opponent's devilish marksmanship and temper-melting second chances were enough to muffle the killer instinct aroused between competing couples. Money, needless to say, never changed hands.

Of courses the Yorkies enjoyed the afternoon croquet tournaments. There were so many busy legs to sniff, so many soft-spoken giants to bark at. And through the years they had learned to stay out of the way of the huge bounding balls that rolled in all directions. They remained near their mistress during the crowded matches, never tempted to join the game. The addition of a collie to the furnishings of Aramanth House demanded his presence at the edge of the court. How picturesquely English, after all. And so, he was brought to a match on his first Sunday by the chauffeur, who was warned to keep him leashed.

"Until he understands the game, wouldn't you think Charles?" was the master's way of putting it.

Happy as Duffy was with every day, his first Sunday of croquet was the highlight of his week. He stood and sat and lay by turn beside the chauffeur, patted and admired by one and all and obviously a member of the family. Because the games were slow and involved only two couples at a time, there were always humans around to ask him gentle questions. They called him Laddie, a name he didn't recognize, but it sounded friendly and Duffy loved to be liked.

Although he was content beside the chauffeur and pleasantly distracted, it didn't take him long to notice what was happening on the grass court. Balls were rolling back and forth. Sometimes one rolled slowly toward him, sometimes away. And every now and then a player shot a ball far across the court to the edge of the citrus grove. No one noticed Duffy's soft whine and only the chauffeur felt the occasional tug on the leash as the collie concentrated on the balls, but by the end of the game his full attention was devoted to the whereabouts of every croquet ball. He could hardly wait to take his turn.

That Sunday evening when master and mistress had left for dinner, and Duffy was free to roam the grounds before being called to bed, he returned to the croquet court. Mallets and balls were kept in a large wooden box in the corner of a gazebo used by the players and other guests on hot afternoons for shade and late-afternoon tea. The box, of course, was open, so Duffy chose one of the balls and carried it back to the main house looking for someone to roll it for him. The chauffeur and his wife were enjoying a quiet dinner in the kitchen when Duffy arrived with the ball, so he left it outside the kitchen door and returned for another.

By the time the chauffeur called him to bed Duffy had delivered all four croquet balls to the doorstep, but in the darkness no one noticed them until the cook stepped on one and fell heavily against the kitchen door. She was helped across the driveway to the apartment, uncertain whether her ankle was broken or merely sprained, while Duffy followed, still waiting for one of them to play with him. The chauffeur wisely decided not to mention the incident to the master. His wife's ankle was swollen the next morning, but she could walk on it, and the croquet balls were returned to the box. When the chauffeur drove to the market that Monday morning, he stopped at the sports shop and bought a can of tennis balls for his collie. No dog should have to steal croquet balls at Aramanth House. He would have his own.

Mild December weather continued, as it often does in the pre-Christmas weeks when shop windows are artificially frosted on the inside and sleigh bells jangle as customers enter a wonderland of wreaths and tinsel. To the residents of the wealthy colony too old to ski and sick of snow, the warm days allowed them to continue their games, while the cool nights gave the ladies the chance to wear their furs. It was a festive season when the number of parties doubled and everyone was in residence. One of the popular holiday events was the annual croquet tournament at Aramanth House. This was more than the usual Sunday-afternoon contest. Like the World Series, it was intended as the climax of the croquet season, which began in September with the return of the players from summer cruises and ended before everyone departed for winter vacations.

The games were played every afternoon of Croquet Week. Couples were eliminated or rematched in semifinals until two couples faced each other for the championship. There were expensive prizes for everyone invited to participate, and all other games were suspended. Even Christmas shopping was rescheduled so that flights of competing couples could be present for the toss and the choice of colored balls. No one who had ever played at Aramanth House was overlooked, and no one missed his turn. In fact, so popular was Croquet Week that there was always a gallery of onlookers on hand for every match.

For Duffy, Croquet Week was the most exciting week of his life. He was busy all day long keeping track of growing numbers of humans. Early every morning he ran beside the chauffeur and gardener to the court where they renewed chalk lines, reset hoops and pegs, and rolled the lawn. He carried one of his tennis balls along and obligingly the chauffeur threw the ball every time Duffy presented it. He played his own game while the court was being prepared, but as soon as the day's contestants and supporters began arriving, he was in the parking circle to greet every car. He was a familiar sight, the first member of the gracious household to welcome its guests.

As the game began, the chauffeur became the bartender, serving cool drinks at a portable bar in the gazebo. Duffy was led by the master to the edge of the court where he joined the gallery to watch the game. Only the chauffeur knew that Duffy was really watching as he wagged and wriggled among the guests. His amber eyes followed every stroke, especially when a croquet was made and a ball went out of the court. Always there seemed to be a hand on his head. Always someone was patiently explaining the reasons he was not allowed to join the match.

The championship match was held on the Saturday before the Christmas weekend. Of the twenty couples who had competed during the week, eighteen had been eliminated, each consoled by a special gift custom-made by Tiffany. That year the men received a set of gold croquet-ball studs and mallet cufflinks. The ladies were presented with handsome pins of crossed mallets in gold set with sapphire chips.

Because this was the deciding match, as well as one of the highlights of the holiday social season, everyone who could get an invitation was there. A buffet lunch was served at the poolhouse. Then the guests crossed the lawn to find chairs before the first striker sent his ball into play. Although master and mistress competed each year and were among the best players, they never participated in the final competition for the championship. Instead, they withdrew during the early days of Croquet Week so gracefully and logically that they were applauded for the true champions they were. As the master always explained to the press, "One shouldn't, after all, risk the possibility of awarding the cup to oneself, should one?" As always, his question required no answer.

The final match began slowly. Every shot was discussed. Rules were strictly observed and the master's decisions in all fouls and stroke faults were accepted as final. The large gallery fell silent before each stroke, then applauded a particularly difficult point. Two balls were used, each couple taking turns to complete the course, their chosen colors clipped to each hoop yet to be made.

For the first hour, the game proceeded defensively as each couple played to avoid a croquet, the striking of their ball by the opponents', which entitles the striker to a croquet shot and a serious setback for the vulnerable ball. Duffy, lying beside the master's chair, his leash fastened to the chair leg, soon lost interest. Often the balls hardly rolled at all. No one spoke to him. The Yorkies huddled under the mistress's chair and the chauffeur was behind the bar. The master was refereeing the match. It was all too quiet to be interesting. When one of the guests sat in the master's chair and leaned back, releasing Duffy's leash from the chair leg, he remained where he was, the stately collie asleep at the center of the audience.

It was after four o'clock when the match reached a critical stage of final hoops and close point separation. The sun was low in the sky and the court was in deep shadow. A croquet was made, and a ball was firmly hit across the court and into the crowd where it stopped at Duffy's outstretched paws. He took it delicately into his mouth, rolled it until it was safely locked behind his canines and stood up. As he did he realized that the leash was no longer fastened to the chair leg, so he stepped away to walk toward the court. He intended to present the ball to the master, drop it, and wait for it to be rolled again. That was his version of the game, and he had waited long enough to join it.

Instead of waiting to receive the ball, however, master and players ran toward him shouting "Drop it, drop it" and waving their mallets. Duffy's old fear of humans brandishing broom handles turned him away. He dodged and ran across the court, the ball forgotten but riding in his jaws. The humans followed, croquet mallets swinging above their heads. Duffy was afraid to stop. He ran into the citrus grove, then continued across the garden toward the main house. He could hear the shouts, the master's order to stop, but all he thought of was being struck by a mallet handle. He ran past the house and into the woods beyond. His pursuers were out of sight, so he dropped the ball, then circled back to the house to sit trembling outside the kitchen door, awaiting whatever punishment would come.

Several firsts were established at Aramanth House that afternoon. It was the first time in the history of Croquet Week that a championship match had ever been called off in midplay. Darkness was given as the reason in Monday's issue of "Doings," a society column in the local newspaper. The truth was much more sinister. As soon as the chauffeur found Duffy at the kitchen door and led him to the apartment above the garage, he continued his search for the croquet ball, which was not found until the following January. It was certainly growing dark as players and gallery debated what to do, but it was the female member of the couple whose ball Duffy had carried off who stopped the match. She would not finish the game unless the ball was found. The lost ball was blue, her lucky color, and without it she knew she would not win. No amount of pleading by her partner and the master could change her mind. Either the blue ball was found or the game was over.

It was also the first time in memory that voices had been raised in anger at the villa. As players and spectators joined the discussion, those who sided with the woman who refused to continue play with yellow or green argued with those who thought the game should continue. When the female member of the competing couple accused her counterpart of quitting because she was losing anyway, both couples refused to replay the match, or, for that matter, to be seen in the same company again.

Master and mistress were at the center of the controversy. United as always in the cause of harmony among their guests, they ordered an all-out search of the grounds for the missing ball. As it grew darker, the mistress invited all to return the following afternoon to resume play. When the competing couples refused ever to meet again, adding that no cup, even if it was solid silver, which they doubted, was worth it, the mistress fled in tears toward the house.

It was the first year that no croquet champions were announced, no cup presented, no press photographs allowed.

Much later, after the guests had departed still arguing over who was right and wrong, it was also the first time the staff at Aramanth

House had ever heard master and mistress shouting at each other in the library.

Finally, it was the first time since Duffy had joined the happy household that the cook forgot to serve him his dinner.

Chapter 18

During the first days of the new year when the colony caught its breath after a constant round of holiday parties and life at Aramanth House settled for a moment into the preparations necessary for the winter, the collie in their midst was never mentioned by master or mistress. He was, however, very much on their minds. Neither could think of a reasonable complaint about his behavior, let alone an acceptable solution, and neither cared to admit that their happiness and their celebrated hospitality were so fragile, so rigidly bound and sanitized that the presence of one new dog could threaten either, let alone come between them. But the fact that he had and that each harbored unmentionable thoughts about the other's responsibility for their dilemma was already evident even to the staff. The master and mistress were more than usually polite toward each other and stiffly deferential. There were awkward silences at each end of the dinner table, and shameful evasions. The problem of the dog, each of them realized, was the more embarrassing because he shouldn't have been a problem. They were compassionate people and, above all, fair. How could so handsome, so good-natured a dog seriously affect their lives? What better place for a collie than their fenced estate? That he had adjusted to their ways and was happy was all too obvious. He was well attended by the Scottish couple. Their guests admired him, and them, for giving him such a happy home. He had caused no real damage and he meant so well. Unlike their cat who had simply moved in without an invitation, the collie was a victim and a well-bred victim at that. Perhaps if they had been able to have children of their own, they would have been better able to deal with such boundless enthusiasm and energy.

But, of course, neither was prepared to share these disturbing admissions because they didn't solve the problem; they only signified a failure.

Meanwhile, Duffy thrived. He was up at sunrise making his rounds of the estate as soon as he was let out of the apartment, returning at a call from the chauffeur when the kitchen opened to share the breakfast scraps before his day really began. When the gardener arrived, Duffy was there to meet his truck. He played ball in the driveway while the chauffeur dusted the Rolls, and always he kept an eye out for Monty the cat, as he emerged from the kitchen and raced to the safety of the wall. Duffy had his household in order at last. His humans behaved reliably, aware of him and his appetite for rides, for kitchen handouts, and for back scratching. The cat was chaseable. His world had become once again a satisfying mixture of dependability and surprise.

Somewhere beyond closed doors and patio gates on the other side of the house were two different humans and three small dogs he hardly ever saw and would never understand, but he was rarely aware of those mystifying members of his family, and he had learned when one of them crossed his path to keep his distance.

The chauffeur and cook were all too well aware of the rift between master and mistress and its cause. It was obvious enough to anyone privy as they were to the innermost sancta of the villa where faces fell and sighs escaped. And after talking it over between themselves they were still baffled. How could their collie be the problem? One thing they did know. It was the mistress who didn't like him.

But neither knew exactly why or what more to do about it. He was such a friendly dog, so anxious to please, and so sensitive to the slightest displeasure he caused—the way he hung his head and tail after being scolded for eating three dinners the cook had prepared for the Yorkies before she could call them. His apology was always so genuine, the slow approach, the careful way he had of sitting down before her and lifting a paw to her knee. Why, the only time he barked was when a delivery truck arrived, and that was even helpful. Of course, Monty hated him now that he had the cat on the run, but Monty hated everybody. And he certainly hadn't upset the Yorkies. Those spoiled little beasts were as uppity as ever. What could the mistress possibly find to object to about so grand a dog? They couldn't imagine, but they knew their employers well. "He's so large, isn't he Mary?" and "My Charles, how do you put up with him?" They knew it would not be long before the collie was mentioned again.

It came about almost casually.

As Duffy strutted forward one morning to greet the returning Rolls, the chauffeur slipped his leash on to hold him while the Yorkies dashed off to find their mistress. The master lingered, actually reaching a hand down to pat Duffy's head.

"They have obedience classes for large dogs, don't they, Charles?" he began. "Do you suppose they really do any good?"

Whatever he had expected, the chauffeur was not prepared for this.

"I've heard they do sir. To obey commands. That sort of thing."

"He is handsome isn't he?" the master continued as Duffy sat between them, enjoying being talked about. "Would you think the training might do him good?"

"It couldn't hurt," the chauffeur agreed. "But he's a well-mannered dog already. He only needs to know what's not allowed. To be frank, sir," the chauffeur added, "he'll still be a collie."

"He will, won't he?" the master said sorrowfully before following after the Yorkies.

Later that morning the chauffeur came to the kitchen door.

"It's come," he called to his wife. "They want to send him off to obedience school to train him to be small."

Duffy's keepers heard no further mention of the collie in the days that followed, but both knew well enough that the problem remained unresolved. For the first time since they had come to Aramanth House, in what they considered to be the most congenial situation possible, they were unhappy. For the first time they discussed their employers critically. The mistress, always so soft-spoken, so full of understanding, was really an intolerant hypocrite whose concern for everyone's welfare was nothing else but a rigid defense of her own dull contentment. She sat like a fat hen on her nest of Yorkies, clucking orders as if they were mild opinions, and reading her romantic novels. The master, they agreed, would do whatever he must to keep the peace. He was the executor, the organizer, the placator, but he danced to the mistress's tune. Consult them he would for appearances' sake, but in the end he'd find a way to make wrong seem right.

With Duffy in the seat beside him, the chauffeur drove to the only school for dogs in the area to investigate its methods and results. Perhaps, after all, there was a way of keeping their collie if the master was serious. As he expected, he found that most of the dogs in the training class were hardly more than puppies, and that most belonged to the larger breeds. Floppy Newfoundlands, agile young shepherds, and wriggling setters were being taught not to be annoying. The only older student was an arthritic dachshund who, the trainer explained, was moving from a large estate to a seaside condominium and had never been housebroken.

"What faults need correcting in your collie?" the chauffeur was asked.

For a moment he couldn't think of a single thing he would change about his dog. Finally he said, "He barks."

"Ah," exclaimed the trainer. "The most common complaint about a collie. And there's only one solution. Have him debarked."

The chauffeur was stunned. He had never heard such a terrible word. It was a simple operation, the trainer assured him. Any good vet could perform it. The dog would still bark, but it would be no louder than a bad cough.

The chauffeur drove back to the villa discouraged. Whatever happened, he promised Duffy he would never be debarked.

The master could put off a decision about the collie no longer.

His failure to present his wife with not only his sympathetic recognition of the problem long before it came between them, but an inspired solution, was most untypical. Their happy marriage and its radiating example to all had always depended upon relieving her of both worry and decision. Her confidence in his mastery of their affairs had always been supreme. Because he had not brought a solution to the collie problem to her weeks ago, that confidence was noticeably shaken.

And it was affecting their entire life together. Already she had rejected his late-winter vacation proposal, a tour of the canals of France in a private barge, as sounding too muddy. She was becoming querulous. She was even going back to bed before noon.

But his solution must seem best for the dog, whatever its true purpose, and that nicety had stumped him for weeks. Their consciences must be clear and their explanation of his removal both logical and kind. Cruelty to animals was anathema to them both and contrary to everything English they treasured. He feared not only for his reputation in the community, but for his wife's fragile health if they should be responsible for anything unfortunate happening to the collie. When he made his proposal it must seem like a gift to all concerned.

And then one January morning his mail included a notice of the mid-winter meeting of the Board of Trustees of The Stafford School, and suddenly he had his answer. He left the rest of the day's mail to be handled by his secretary and hurried out of his study to find his wife. He passed the cook, who told him her mistress was on the patio brushing the Yorkies. There he found her with Boodles on her lap.

Pausing to kiss the tip of his wife's nose, he sat down in one of the ice-cream chairs around an umbrella-shaded table.

"What would you say, darling, to my offering Laddie as a gift to the children at Stafford?" he began. "As a sort of mascot, don't you see?" he clarified. "He'd love them, wouldn't he?" he suggested. "And he's the same size they are, isn't he?" he pointed out, laughing nervously.

"At least," the mistress agreed, fervently for her. "Oh, Toddie, I think it's a grand idea, and aren't you smart to have thought of it!"

"He'd have the children to play with during the day and the custodian to take care of him at night. He's not really a guard dog, but he does bark at strangers."

"He does that," she agreed, "and he is so playful, isn't he?"

"Do you suppose Charles and Mary will be very upset? They have grown rather fond of him, haven't they?"

"But it's so near, Toddie. They could visit him often."

"And take him for drives on weekends. We'll be away in March, after all, won't we?"

As she wound Boodles' bangs around her finger, then slipped a small elastic band over the topknot and attached a bright blue bow, she was almost gay. Life would soon be back to the way it had been, and that was really all she ever asked.

"Will you miss him, Toddie?" she patted his hand.

"Of course, won't you?"

"But it's for the best, isn't it? He'll be ever so grateful to have the children." She set the small dog down beneath her chair. "They'll surely accept him, won't they?" she asked, her soft blue eyes widening for a moment.

"You know they will," he answered, standing and taking a deep breath.

And, indeed, she did know.

Chapter Nineteen

In the summer of 1927, a young couple, graduates of a small teacher's college in Montclair, New Jersey, arrived in southern California, where their credentials might prove to be more impressive to found a private elementary school. They had also chosen the West Coast as the location of their school because they believed that the children of that far frontier were in the greatest need of the classical education and moral discipline a school in the tradition of the East Coast private schools could offer. Not the least of their reasons for heading for southern California were the stories they had heard of vast wealth accumulated by the pioneer families. After a cursory inspection of these enclaves of the new West Coast aristocracy within a hundred-mile radius of Los Angeles, they chose to go north rather then south along the Pacific coast because to their surprise, they discovered old money among the descendants of the earliest Spanish and American settlers. Moreover, these land-rich rancheros and railroad tycoons wanted their children to be educated at Harvard and Wellesley, at Andover and Emma Willard. As Easterners, the couple could offer a primary education guaranteed to prepare even the scions of cattle barons and fortune hunters to pass the entrance examinations.

Although inexperienced both as educators and fund raisers, the couple were attractive and convincing. Within a few months they had managed to enlist the support of the best families and were able to purchase twenty acres of level land where they built a small house for themselves and the first one-room unit of The Stafford School. The land they bought lay between the old coast highway and the lowest tier of foothills where already the wealthy were building their castles overlooking the channel. Across the narrow country road leading to the school property was a vast lemon orchard protected by an impenetrable stand of eucalyptus. The undeveloped land on each side was also heavily wooded, and beyond the ten-acre playground site only the highway, the tracks of the Southern Pacific Railroad, and the rocky shoreline lay between the school and the ocean.

The first curriculum offered instruction to sixteen children in grades one through eight in subjects ranging from physiology to Latin. All subjects were taught by the husband or his wife. Later, a kindergarten and ninth grade were added, and still later summer school and preschool classes were held during July and August. As the enrollment grew, so did the physical plant, until grades six through nine were taught in a U-shaped assemblage of one-story classrooms built in what might be described as post-office Spanish, pale cream adobe walls under fireproof shingles, each unit connected by a covered walkway. Also, to separate the lower grades, a line of cottages was built along the west perimeter of the playground. All of these small structures were in place by the early 1930s and remained the only buildings until the mid-1970s, when a handsome new auditorium was added. This towering edifice, facing the classrooms and the inner courtyard, was the couple's crowning achievement, completed only a few weeks before the headmaster died. The principal donor to the fund for its construction had been the master of Aramanth House, who was promptly made a trustee of the school.

With the death of its founding headmaster the hierarchy of the school was rearranged. The headmistress, now in her seventies, became the director. A young headmaster was brought in to head the faculty and staff of twenty, and for the first time in the school's history, instructors were hired to teach upper-class courses in the sciences and mathematics. Despite her age and widowed status, there was no doubt among faculty and students about who ran the school. She still lived next door in the small house she and her husband had built, and she still arrived every weekday morning promptly at nine for the flag raising. To the youngest children she was Missus Director, a feared and awesome presence. To the older students she was known as The Eagle.

This nickname would have been appropriate enough if it had only described her most prominent facial features, an aquiline nose grown longer and sharper with her advancing years and eyes like polished pebbles that seemed to see through walls. There was, however, an even more literal basis for the name. Each school day began with a patriotic ceremony as strictly observed and flawlessly executed as a parade-ground exercise. At five minutes before nine, the entire student body assembled in the courtyard, forming ranks around the flagpole according to class with kindergartners in front. Faculty and students stood at attention as two ninth graders prepared to raise the flag. At the first notes of reveille, reproduced on a small cassette player, the flag went up the pole, after which the school recited the pledge of allegiance, led in the loud, crackling voice of its director. It was her unfailing custom to appear for this ceremony wearing a large medallion on a gold chain around her neck, the symbolic eagle's head on a field of the stars and stripes. As she intoned the well-known phrases, the eagle's head resting on her bosom seemed to shout the words through its half-open beak, and every student watched in fascination.

After the ceremony, the director marched to her private office in the administration cottage where the medallion was removed, but always she wore on the lapel of her suit jacket an American flag pin made of rubies, diamonds, and sapphires, a gift from her late husband on their fiftieth wedding anniversary.

In its sixth decade the school's location, on the threshold of the colony of millionaires, continued to provide benefactors and more than its share of widow's legacies. What was surprising was its increasing enrollment of young children. From the original sixteen it had grown until there were nearly two hundred boys and girls, all of them day students. The sources of this supply lay mostly in the newer suburbs of the city, not in the colony surrounding the school. Two private buses delivered forty children every morning, while the rest were driven to school by parents living as far away as twenty miles. And because of the generous scholarship fund in recent years, there were even a few Black and Hispanic children from the poorest city neighborhoods. Only the high standards of the school remained unchanged, and among its graduates were many of the city's most distinguished citizens. Carved in a walnut panel above the doorway leading to the director's office were the words of her hero, Woodrow Wilson: "...we shall walk with the light all about us..." taken from his second inaugural address, to which she had been taken by her parents.

Although to the Stafford family of parents, graduates, faculty, and students its director seemed immortal, she realized her time was short, and she had a last goal, the capstone of the school she and her husband had built. Until recent years, the broad playground with its softball diamond, volleyball and tennis courts, soccer field, and children's corner equipped with sandbox, monkey bars, and jungle gym, had offered an athletic program for every student. The mild climate and all but rainless winters allowed daily exercise for all. Still, the one facility most public schools provided was lacking: a gymnasium for basketball and indoor track competitions with, perhaps, a basement swimming pool.

The director did not intend to die before this last embellishment was added, and she had already decided upon how to get it. Each member of her board of trustees had been selected according to his or her ability to bring to the school either prestige or money and preferably both. All were well known in the community and most were wealthy, but the wealthiest without question was the master of Aramanth House and, as his contribution to the auditorium fund had demonstrated, the most generous. She had already suggested to him the advantages and rewards of a single donation sufficient to build the new gym, hinting without promising to name it for him and his wife. And, unless she was mistaken, which was rare, he was about to agree. She had chosen an architect and intended to see the new gym completed before the first rainy day of the new fall term.

The morning she received the call about the collie happened to be the first day of rain in the new year. A full-fledged storm broke against the coast from the southeast with unpredicted fury. Such days, however rare, were always trying. Not only were the students confined to classrooms, but they were soaked as they dashed between the cottages and the auditorium, never properly dressed for rain. Neither nature nor man had prepared coastal California for deluge. The land slanted toward the sea without either the capacity to absorb the water or the proper drainage system to shed it. The result in the low-lying areas was indiscriminate runoff, muddy torrents pouring down from barren mountains, from landscaped slopes and hillside streets without storm sewers. Water flooded the school's parking area, dribbled through open hallways and into classrooms. Puddles appeared in every depression, and a pond developed in the children's corner of the playground. And always, to the director's consternation, it was on such days that the toilets overflowed.

In fact, she was on the phone to the plumber when she received the call from Aramanth House.

If there was one individual more important to the school's survival than its principal benefactor, it was the plumber. In spite of strict discipline and severe punishment, including the locking of both boys' and girls' lavatories for an entire day, the director's failure to teach her students not to throw towels and gum wrappers into the toilet bowls had become a paranoid preoccupation. Nothing she did, including storming into the lavatories without warning, prevented the periodic clogging. The toilets overflowed so regularly, in fact, that she was even considering the hiring of a live-in plumber.

She couldn't ask either man to hold the line. The plumber pleaded emergencies all over town. The master of Aramanth House extolled the collie's virtues. The director lost track of which man was on which line.

To the plumber she murmured uncertainly, "We'll be ever so grateful, of course."

To the master of Aramanth House she cried, "Get here as soon as you can."

And so it was that the plumber did not arrive until school was over for the day, while a station wagon driven by the chauffeur with Duffy in the front seat pulled into the visitors' parking area shortly before noon.

Duffy was led by his friend through the downpour to the administration cottage. When confronted by the dripping man leading the dripping dog, the director's secretary asked both to wait while she announced them. Neither, she was sure, was expected, but experience had taught her never to turn away anyone before consulting her employer. And, not entirely to her surprise, she was told to send them in.

Duffy walked obediently beside the chauffeur into the large square room with its oriental rugs and leather sofas and armchairs. With room enough at last he stood in the center of the office and shook himself, sending water drops flying across the director's wide desk. Then, pleased to be included in this strange-smelling human haven, he sat down to face the woman who stared at him from behind the desk. He listened as first the chauffeur, then the director spoke, sensitive as always to voices discussing him. He felt secure enough beside the chauffeur, but he quickly understood the note of caution in the woman's voice and her determination to keep the desk between herself and him. She wasn't glad to see him. That was clear. When the secretary entered to take his leash and lead him into the outer office, he hesitated, looking back. The smell of the room, dogless and acrid, told him that he was not supposed to be there, but he wanted to stay near his friend.

He was relieved when the chauffeur came out of the director's office to join him. They waited in a small anteroom while typewriters clicked and telephones buzzed and the director's secretary received her instructions on the intercom. Duffy grew more uneasy. He had never liked rain, but now he lifted a paw to the chauffeur's knee, a plea to be taken outside to a better-smelling world. Instead, he was patted and softly reassured.

Then the custodian arrived wearing oilskins and rubber boots and leaving a trail of water behind him across the floor. The school's only permanent resident was an old man, weathered and wrinkled, a retired city policeman who lived alone in the end cottage. Heavy work was no longer expected of him, although he was often the only employee on hand when a floor needed mopping or a desk needed quick repairs. His regular duties included locking and unlocking the classroom doors, seeing to it that his young assistant cleaned and put back in order each room in the school after classes ended at three each afternoon and keeping a professional eye on everything movable. His most important responsibilities were the lowering of the flag at sunset and simply being there when no one else was. In return, he was allowed to live undisturbed well beyond the age of retirement in his cottage, and in his nearly twenty years at the school he had never had to deal with vandals or fire his policeman's .38 at an intruder.

The custodian was the only member of the staff who was unafraid of the director. Not that he underestimated her. Indeed, it was his respect for her often devious methods of getting what she wanted that made their adversarial relationship so satisfying. He went about his business without even meeting her most of the time, and when occasionally their paths crossed they hardly spoke, but he prided himself on his ability to see through her means to the end she had in mind.

He knew she was a tyrant and that since the death of her husband she was lonesome, which made her even more demanding, but he had to hand it to her; she ran the school and took no nonsense, and because she did, his job was easy and his life comfortably his own. But now she had really gone off her rocker. What did she need a dog for? At the moment he was feeding and watering a pair of rabbits in the kindergarten on weekends and there was always a frog or a turtle dying in the biology lab when no one else was around to bury it. He liked dogs well enough, but at second hand. He had never owned one. His favorite time of day was the evening when the school was deserted. He was too old to need company, even a dog's, if it meant worrying about anyone after three o'clock.

The thing that puzzled him most as he arrived to meet Duffy was that he knew for a fact that the director was afraid of large dogs. But he had his orders. Let the chauffeur tell him all about the collie's care. The dog was to live at the school, which meant live with him most of the time. Suddenly, his life was to be complicated. The old lady had pulled one on him. Maybe he ought to put in for retirement after all.

This was his mood when he was introduced to Duffy. He led the way out of the cottage and across the parking area with collie and chauffeur following. The rain poured, but the custodian avoided the sheltered hallways, leading them past the auditorium, then down the row of cottages to his. As they passed each lighted classroom filled with rows of small heads, faces turned to the windows to watch the two men and the dog go by, but only the sound of the teachers' voices could be heard, and in the rain, not even Duffy raised his head.

They were let into the custodian's cottage where again Duffy shook his coat, then looked up at the chauffeur to ask the unanswerable question. His leash was removed. Then the chauffeur ran back through the rain to the station wagon to carry a case of Duffy's favorite food to the cottage. His license and vaccination certificates, tucked into an envelope marked Pet Papers, were handed over. Finally the chauffeur opened a box of dog treats he had bought along the way. Stooping to put his cheek against Duffy's, he tucked one of the hot-dog-shaped cookies into the dog's mouth, then quickly turned away and left the cottage. The old man would probably have taken the trickle down his cheeks for raindrops, but the chauffeur couldn't allow him to see him crying.

In a two-column box on the front page of the Sunday edition of the city's only newspaper the headline read: Philanthropist Donates Family Collie to Children at Stafford School. In the classified advertising section of the same edition the small notice under Lost & Found: Pets continued to appear: Collie: male, 3 yrs. Mahogany & White. Pls. call 886-5424 day/night. Reward!

Chapter Twenty

Duffy was introduced to the students and faculty of the Stafford School the following morning. It was one of those windswept days that follow a storm, intense and polished, when little girls' clean hair is spun and little boys' collar tabs are lifted by the breeze as they stand stiffly at attention around the flagpole. Duffy was brought on his leash to the ceremony, and as he stood beside the custodian gusts lifted the hairs on his back and burrowed into the underfur along his flanks. His new coat, thicker and darker than the last, rinsed by the rain and dried in front of the custodian's fireplace, made him look heavier. His tail, once again a thick brush ending in a comma of white strands, swayed gently back and forth. Only his ears and his eyes held steadily upon what, to an informal dog, must have appeared unbelievable human behavior.

There before him stood one hundred eighty-three children. At least, they were children-sized and as they tried to look at him without turning their heads their eyes were children's eyes. But they didn't move. They didn't shout and laugh. And then suddenly they all spoke at once, saying the same words in a meaningless monotone as sinister sounding as the lawn mower Duffy remembered. Then, as suddenly, all were silent, waiting as he was, almost unbearably.

The performance was too odd for Duffy to ignore. He laid back his ears, set his tail to a medium tempo and began to bark. At first, his bark was deep-throated and measured, but when no one responded its pitch and tempo rose. Was he the only one alive in this strange garden where children grew like sunflowers rooted in the grass? Someone had to notice him. Someone had to move.

And just then someone did. Instead of dismissing the students for their first class of the day, the director walked to the base of the flagpole where now and then she made special announcements, a school picnic or a trip to Disneyland or, on rare occasions, the arrival of a new teacher. The children's eyes were on her and the eagle medallion pulsing at her breast. The custodian was summoned to her side pulling Duffy along, silent now that he had attracted attention.

A kind, generous friend of the school, she told them, had given his handsome collie to the boys and girls of Stafford as mascot and playmate. He was to live at the school, where every morning he would be waiting. No, he wasn't Lassie. Perhaps Lassie's brother Laddie. He was gentle and well mannered, a thoroughbred, surely. But remember, she added sternly, her tattered voice rising against the ocean breeze, he belonged to all, not to any one of them, and he could stay only if everyone continued to observe the three A's of Stafford behavior: Altruism, Amicability, and Application. Even the kindergartners understood the meaning of those unpronounceable words.

The moment came. As the director hurried out of the way, the children surged forward, hands reaching out to pat their dog. Their teachers ran to organize the introduction, shouting commands and warnings that went unheard. The custodian was carried backward on a wave of driving little bodies. Duffy's leash was removed, then his collar. Each student had to touch him once. Each had to stake his claim. Duffy was nearly buried by the swirling admirers. There was no escape. All he could see were bobbing faces and thrusting knees.

The teachers waded in, parting bodies as they came, to save him. When finally they cleared a circle around him, one small boy still clung to Duffy's neck, his arms locked so tightly in his ruff that not even his first-grade teacher could pry him loose. Duffy struggled to his feet, but the boy hung on, his face pressed against the collie's, his heels dug into the water-soaked turf. The custodian stepped forward, found Duffy's leash and collar and lifted the little boy into the air under one arm while he held the dog by the neck. Only then did the boy release his hold. When Duffy was once again on the leash, the boy was allowed to lead him toward the first-grade cottage, the teacher and the custodian following.

His name was Robbie, a dog's boy, and no matter what Missus Director had said about the collie's belonging to every student, from that moment Duffy was his.

Only a dog and a child are created equal, a winged pair, the two halves of love, and of all dogs the collie, large and even-tempered and deep coated, seems made for children. At the first pressure of sponge nose against new cheek, the arching muzzle and soft, approving eyes, the endless expanse of handholds, a baby reaches out. And no collie can resist a child. But in any group of children there is always one whose instant love is so unmistakable that from that moment child and dog share a private world. In Robbie, Duffy had found his complement. As they walked together hip to hip toward the first-grade cottage, eyes meeting every few steps, Duffy and Robbie needed no words to express their pledge.

At the classroom door the teacher and custodian caught up with them. One entered the cottage; the other was led off to await the next appearance of the children. Once again Duffy was being manipulated through a bewildering series of disconnections. Instead of his bench in the chauffeur's apartment, he had spent the night in a strange little house with an old man who talked to the television, never to Duffy. Instead of his morning circuit of the familiar estate he was kept inside the cottage. There were no familiar voices, no scents he recognized. Finally, there had been the children, suddenly there, then not there, and the little boy who clung to him, then was pulled away. To Duffy, uncertainty was worse than disapproval, and he sensed that the man who held his leash wanted nothing to do with him.

Although Duffy may have wondered as he waited inside the door of the custodian's cottage why so many children could appear and disappear so quickly, or why his day was over just as it had begun, he didn't have long to wonder. Promptly at ten o'clock a cottage door opened and a flock of kindergartners ran like sandpipers across the grass to their play area. According to his instructions, the custodian sent Duffy off to join them, but also according to the chauffeur's warning, he followed to keep the collie in sight. Whatever he had to do to prevent it, the dog must not run away. Privately, the old man hoped he would, but it would not be his doing. As dogkeeper, he felt put upon. As seasoned observer of his employer, he knew she had a reason for keeping the dog, and it was not to please the children. Until he found out what the reason was and found a way to use it to his own advantage, he'd let her have her way.

And so, as his keeper watched, Duffy joined the children. Or they joined him. As soon as they saw him coming toward them several ran to drag him to the small arena, where for his benefit they performed every trick they knew. To cries of "Watch, Laddie. Watch this," the boys swung on the monkey bars, catapulted through the jungle gym, and ran in crazy circles around him. Little girls arranged his tail and swept past him in their swings. His paw was shaken, his ears were combed, and for a moment he wore a pail on his head. At the end of the half-hour recess there was no doubt that he was popular. Or that he was patient. But when the teacher called the children back to their classroom, Duffy sank to the grass panting and exhausted. He loved to play, but never before had he been the game.

Ten minutes later the elementary grades recess began. Children streamed from cottage doors toward the field where Duffy lay. Robbie was the first to reach him. The little boy dropped at his side and once more locked his arms around Duffy's neck, determined not to be dislodged by anyone. But there were seventy-five other boys and girls who had been told by their teachers that the collie was theirs to play with, and if that was true, well, each intended to have his turn to teach him a trick or to ride on his back. Not only was the crowd larger this time, the children were larger too, and with more imagination. A collie could, for instance, rescue a boy from drowning by pulling him to safety with his tail, so one third-grader hung on Duffy's tail while another pulled with Robbie clinging between them. A collie could hold a wolf pack at bay, so a circle of snarling boys threatened to eat Robbie while Duffy cringed and tried to run.

It took two large fifth-graders to drag Robbie from Duffy's neck, and because Robbie kicked and screamed it took two more to hold him. As Duffy was parted from Robbie, his fur painfully torn, he yelped and snapped his jaws at the nearest hand. He didn't bite, but the click of his teeth frightened the boy, who ran to his teacher to tell her the collie had tried to bite him.

The children backed away. Robbie lay sobbing on the grass. His teacher lifted him to his feet, and as she did, Duffy came forward to lick his face. Once again Robbie knelt and placed his arms around his dog.

For the rest of the twenty-minute recess the children were told to stay away from the collie, which they did, all except for Robbie. And because Duffy seemed to want to stay with the little boy, they were left alone. When it was time to return to their classrooms, Robbie led Duffy back across the grass, while the custodian marched behind giving Robbie's teacher his opinion of the experiment. It didn't make sense to put a dog together with so many kids. Even if he hadn't bitten today, before long he would. Dogs were dogs, not toys.

Duffy had a half hour to rest before the kindergarten lunch period began. His collar had been pulled so hard that his throat ached, and he was grateful to the custodian for a fresh pan of water. The old man felt sorry for him. He had half a mind to keep him inside during the lunch periods, but no, he'd been told to give him the run of the school whenever the children were outside. If he was going to show the Eagle how wrong she was, the only way was to let the dog cause more trouble.

The kindergartners ate their lunch at eleven-thirty, allowing them a half-hour head start before the rest of the school took over the lunch tables set out under the wide eaves around the courtyard. Small cartons of milk were provided by the school; otherwise, each child carried his own lunch from home. But lunch was a brief, noisy affair, taking no more than ten minutes, after which tables were cleaned off, lunchboxes returned to the classrooms and the children sent off to play until twelve-thirty.

Duffy was brought to the courtyard as the smallest children were dumping milk cartons and half-eaten sandwiches and nibbled fruit into large barrels. Peanut-buttered fingers were presented to him to lick as he made his way from table to table, but dogs don't like banana peels and apple cores, the children had been told, nor do dogs eat lunch, so off the children ran to enjoy the swings and teeter-totters before the older classes descended upon the playground.

The lunch period for the rest of the school lasted from noon to one, a segmented picnic which allowed older students to eat in the new auditorium, while the first five grades took over the courtyard. It was also a busy time for the custodian and his assistant, because no matter how often the students were told to leave every lunch area as they found it, tables and floors were littered. Duffy was forgotten by his keeper but not by Robbie. And perhaps because it was Robbie's lunch he shared, Duffy discovered he liked bananas and even raisins. He sat at Robbie's side watching every bite and eating every other. Then they ran to the playground to make the most of their hour together.

The hour between one and two o'clock was a quiet time, when it was the custodian's privilege to rest in his cottage. Just as he was wondering what to do with the collie so that he could nap in peace, the kindergarten teacher found him to explain that the children refused to take their afternoon naps unless their new dog slept with them. He handed over Duffy, relieved to be rid of him, and went off to his cottage.

As Duffy entered the large room, the floor, cleared of tables and chairs, was covered with children lying on mats and whispering to him. He made his way up and down the rows, wagging and sniffing, intrigued by so many tipped-over bodies. Then the teacher led him to a mat of his own under a table and he was told to sleep.

But Duffy couldn't sleep any more than the children could. Not only were all of them wiggling and whispering to him, there was an intriguing odor coming from an enclosure under the window to his right. While the teacher shushed the children and not a pair of eyes closed, Duffy found the rabbit pen. He had never seen a rabbit before. Now and then on his morning rounds at his ranch home he had picked up the sweet scent of cottontail, but the trail was always cold and he had no idea what sort of animal had crossed the yard at night. Now within a wire frame open at the top were two tawny little animals frozen in fear, their flanks heaving, their ears flattened and a single eye on Duffy's side of each small head wide and dark and shining.

Duffy's first reaction to any small animal was cautious curiosity. His tail wagged just enough to signal his friendly intentions, and he made small feints with his nose to provoke reaction without risking it to claw or tooth. He wanted the rabbits to move. Only then could they fulfill their possibilities. His concentration as he stood above the pen was so complete that he was unaware of the stillness behind him, the gasps from the children and the teacher's frightened cry. She had completely forgotten about the rabbits. They had been living in the pen in the corner of the room for so long that even the children had lost interest and had to be reminded to feed them. Now the worst was about to happen, and right in front of their eyes.

Duffy moved closer until his nose was inches from the nearest rabbit. In a quick thrust he poked his nose into the rabbit's fur to nip it into action. The rabbit shrank and shivered but refused to budge. Duffy was mad with frustration. What sort of animal was this? What was the point of anything alive that wouldn't move? He backed away from the pen and looked questioningly at the teacher. He sent her one of his high, baffled barks, a plea for explanation. Maybe she could make them go.

As soon as she saw him turn toward her she grabbed his collar and pulled him away from the pen, across the room to the door. But she didn't dare to leave him while she ran for help. She was also afraid to disturb the custodian in the middle of his nap. Finally, she decided to take him to the administration cottage. Let them decide what to do. The children were too excited to sleep, so she left them to put away their mats and calm the rabbits. As she hurried off with Duffy she reminded herself of the mistake she had known it would be to bring a collie into the classroom. She just hadn't been able to think of a reason logical enough to convince the children. Now she had one and it had been a lesson to them all.

Duffy wasn't welcome in the office, nor had the director's secretary any compunction about waking the custodian. Quickly she hustled the collie off to the cottage, where she pounded on the door until the old man opened it, angry and scratching himself. Duffy was let in and almost congratulated as the custodian imagined the panic he must have caused. One or two more incidents like that would be enough to get rid of him.

But the peaceful hour was over and Duffy was expected to participate in the last of the school activities. At two-fifteen he was sent from the cottage to the athletic fields for physical education. In front of him, the entire ten-acre playground was filling with boys and girls, teachers who doubled as coaches, and every sized ball being bounced or thrown as the teams ran to their afternoon games. Neither Duffy nor the custodian understood just where he belonged in this organized variety of games, but into the field they walked, the old man watching expectantly like a man who has just released a mouse at a tea party.

He was to be disappointed. At the sight of so many children running in all directions Duffy lay down at the edge of the field. He was tired. The shouts and flying balls were not for him. And a friend was waiting. Robbie had come to say goodbye. The little boy sat down beside him to explain that he had to go home, that he must wait for his mother in the driveway. Duffy turned to smile. It was good to hear a soft voice speaking only to him. He didn't want crowds of children. He only wanted one.

The whistles sounded. Children ran. Duffy was led back to the cottage. His first school day was over.

Late that afternoon the custodian set off with Duffy to lower the flag and secure the school for the night. As they crossed the courtyard in the fading light, they met the director on her way to the gate in the fence that separated the school property from the small yard around her house. This meeting was predictable, the only time in each school day when the director and custodian came face to face, and the old man had brought the collie along on purpose. He wanted to remind her of the dog, to force her to bring up the subject.

"Well, Simmons," she said as she saw the man and dog approaching, "how did Laddie enjoy his first school day?"

"He didn't," the old man snapped, the wattles drooping from his broad chin emphasizing his disgust. "And neither did I."

"Oh, I heard about the rabbits. No harm done. Miss Thatcher was foolish to allow him into the classroom against my orders."

"How long is he supposed to stay here?"

Although shorter than the custodian, she had a way of tucking in her chin so that she seemed to be looking down at him. "Until I tell you he's to leave!" she answered.

"It won't work," he growled.

"Yes it will, Simmons. Oh, yes it will. You'll see."

And on she went toward home while Duffy and the custodian looked after her, neither understanding a word she had said.

Duffy spent the evening in a dark corner of the cottage sitting room. He couldn't eat all of his dinner, but the man hadn't noticed. He sat in his chair in front of his television set alternately feeling sorry for himself and vowing to find a way to force the director to get rid of the dog.

Across the small room, Duffy lay on his side. As he slept, his legs began to twitch and his stomach growled and he dreamed a collie dream.

Chapter Twenty-One

On Duffy's first Saturday as the mascot of the Stafford School he had the kind of adventure that had been missing from his life since he had slipped under the fence to follow the sound of children's voices. For the first time in the long months of leaving one life for another, an important part of a life he had left behind caught up with him, and the result was one of the happiest days a dog or a human can have, a day of new experience in the company of familiar and trusted friends.

The day began with a baffling emptiness. The school grounds were deserted and silent. The children were gone and there was only the custodian to follow through the courtyard and down the shadowed hallways between the locked doors of the classrooms. Although Duffy continued to accept the gruff, brooding old man as the necessary human in his new life because he was always near, watching to see that he stayed close, hoarsely shouting "Here, you!" and "Come back!" the moment Duffy strayed too far, he heard no kindness in the voice. He was neither welcome in the old man's life nor chased out of it. Duffy kept a safe distance, his tail low, his eyes on the hunched shoulders, the gray-fringed neck, and the seaman's knitted cap, ready to dodge at the lifting of a hand. His worst times were when he and his keeper were alone, when he wasn't wanted and wasn't free, and on this sparkling January morning when he could see a wide world tempting him to its edges, he and the custodian were captives of each other, neither able to enjoy the day.

Then, just before noon and as sudden as the arrival of his girls at the end of the long dirt road on those almost forgotten Saturdays, the station wagon drove into the visitors' parking area at the front of the school. Duffy heard the approach of the car, the slam of its door and the footsteps on the gravel before the custodian realized they had a visitor. He recognized the car sound before he heard the call and was on his way across the courtyard and through the entrance hallway, ignoring the custodian's command to come back. He met the chauffeur head on, lunging toward him, raising front paws to his shoulders, then dancing a frenzied seesawing dance around the man. He saw the cook stepping out of the car, and he raced toward her. Once around her and he was back barking and spinning like a puppy at a family homecoming.

As the custodian joined them, Duffy ran in wider circles, afraid to be caught, but determined to keep his friends close by. On one of his circuits he passed the station wagon, saw its open door and jumped in. There he waited in the front seat while the humans talked. All were watching him, the cook laughing at his plea not to be called out of the car. Then the couple joined him, squeezing in on each side and shutting the doors. He was safe. He was on his way. He lifted his head and sent a volley of collie barks back at the old man all the way to the road.

They drove to a public beach, a crescent of sandy shoreline between two jutting rock fingers, ectomorphic warnings to protect the private beach properties on either side. There they parked and set off down a narrow path carrying blankets and hampers for their picnic. Duffy ran ahead toward the ribbons of sand and water, drawn toward the empty horizon. Although he had lived his life within a few miles of the ocean, he had never before reached its edge. He had never felt sand beneath his feet or tasted the brine-flavored scents. Now he ran forward across the storm-littered beach toward the hard surface of the tidal flats. Then he raced along the spreading aprons of dying waves, pausing to examine ropes of rotting seaweed and a trunk-sized log.

Behind him, the chauffeur and cook spread their blankets, pinning the corners with the parcels of their lunch, then set off to follow the collie up the beach. Although it was a winter morning the breeze was soft and the sand warm. And it was a Saturday, so there were other beach walkers far ahead, dressed warmly above knees, their bare feet and rolled-up trousers giving them the appearance of large sea birds. Far ahead Duffy saw the racing shapes of dogs circling the walkers and chasing a low-flying pelican as they high-stepped into the surf.

Duffy was the first to reach the beach dogs, a pair of Labradors, a drenched red setter, and a terrier with a small, sandy face who never stopped running. As he trotted in to greet each dog they barely acknowledged him. Soaked with sea water, they all watched a young man with a stick in his hand. Before Duffy understood what was about to happen, the man threw the stick far out into the cresting waves. The four dogs fought their way into the surf, the smallest dog in front. As soon as he reached the floating stick, all four dogs turned to paddle ashore where they raced back to the man.

When the cook and chauffeur caught up, Duffy was barking at the edge of the game. The tireless dogs around him seemed to know where the stick would land before it left the thrower's hand, and time after time it was the smallest dog who retrieved it and returned to place it at the thrower's feet, while the large dogs waited to try again. There was no fighting over the prize. The dogs all wagged their tails, inviting Duffy to join them, but each time the stick sailed over his head he stopped at the water's edge while the other dogs plunged on through the breaking waves. How he wanted to play the game, to be the bearer of the stick, but the waves frightened him.

The chauffeur chose a stick and threw it far across the sand. Duffy raced to catch it, but he was too late. The small dark blur flashed past him, picked up the new stick and returned it politely to the chauffeur, who then threw the stick right at Duffy. Just before the collie could catch it the small dog leaped to take it in mid-air. Finally, the chauffeur chose two sticks. One he tossed far into the water for the beach dogs. The other he threw across the sand for Duffy. A winner at last, Duffy pranced back rolling the magic stick in his jaws. The small dog ran beside him empty-mouthed.

They turned back then, leaving the beach dogs to find another thrower. Duffy raced at the water's edge, the stick in his mouth. He had discovered he could play the new game after all and carry off the prize, but always he skirted the advancing waves.

The chauffeur joined him to hug him close. "Come to lunch," he invited. "Collies were never water dogs."

It was to be Duffy's picnic. Packed in the hampers were all the treats he loved, fried chicken, bite-sized meatballs, cheese cubes, and his favorite biscuits. He sat between the couple on the blanket sampling everything except the chilled Chablis and the blueberry tarts. After lunch while his wife napped in the sun the chauffeur set off with Duffy in the opposite direction, walking at low tide to the end of the beach and back so that Duffy could explore each shell, greet each walker, and feel the approving compliments.

They sat together on the sand as the sun dropped lower and the chill returned. And as the time grew shorter, the couple faced the reddening sun, unable to look down at Duffy asleep between them. Their day with him had served to remind them both of how much they missed him, how sad it would be to leave him at the school. They were resolved somehow to take him back, but neither knew just how. Aramanth House was not the same without him, nor could they ever again respect their employers. But rescuing him would not be easy, the chauffeur thought. And he had to know the collie was safe until they had a plan.

Back at the school, the chauffeur and the cook hugged Duffy, rubbing their tear-stained faces against his ruff. When the chauffeur handed the custodian the leash, the older man emitted what sounded like a dog's growl.

"She's made a mistake," the custodian snarled.

"Who has?"

"The director. She knows the dog don't belong here, but she can't find anyone else to blame for him. If she could, he'd be gone by Monday. As it is, she'll need a better reason to get rid of him than to keep him. So far, he don't seem about to give her one."

As the chauffeur turned to leave the custodian called out. "You'll be here next Saturday? There's a trustees' meeting and I don't want the dog around."

The chauffeur promised.

Hurrying back across the school grounds after being unable to say goodbye, he wondered again why the master had chosen the school as a way to dispose of the collie. Had it anything to do with his being a trustee? If so, the dog might be safe for a while.

He must ask his wife to find out.

Chapter Twenty-Two

At the end of the elementary-school recess period on Monday morning, the first-grade teacher noticed that Robbie was missing from his seat. At first, she went on with the class work, her eyes moving from the empty chair to the classroom door as if she were watching for the door to open and the little boy to tiptoe to his place. But the door remained closed and the empty chair was drawing more attention than she was. She paused in the lesson to send another boy to find Robbie in the boys' lavatory. When he returned to tell her Robbie wasn't there, she sent the boy out to the playground, but by that time she was worried.

Then she remembered the collie. She remembered that the dog had not been with the children during recess. In fact, Robbie had even asked about him. She felt somewhat better. Wherever the collie was, Robbie was with him. Next she became annoyed. Now she would have to interrupt the classwork to go herself. The dog was a nuisance, the cause of disputes and a distraction. He couldn't be a playmate for dozens of children, and how long would it be before he tired of being mauled and bit someone? She knew that several of the elementary teachers agreed with her. Now for the first time in her teaching experience a child was missing from her class. As she put the children to work and ran to the custodian's cottage, once again she promised herself that she would confront the director with the problem of the collie.

She saw the custodian coming toward her on his way to his cottage and hurried across the grass to explain what had happened. The old man was in no mood that morning to listen to another complaint about the collie, especially from a young woman who seemed to be blaming him for the boy's disappearance. He had been called at eight o'clock, in the middle of his breakfast, to come to the director's office. Although he knew the reason well enough, never before had he been called out at that hour, or, for that matter, could he remember seeing his employer at the school before flag raising.

He had almost lost the collie the day before. He seldom left the school grounds anymore, even on weekends, but he did drive his old car to the shopping center every Sunday morning to buy the newspapers. He had left the collie tied to the front-door handle, and while he was gone somehow the dog had managed to slip his collar. The custodian had spent his Sunday morning searching. He had combed the woods around the playground, then visited neighboring yards. Finally, he had driven up and down the road and all the way to the freeway. He had returned just before noon, worried and resigned to calling the director at home, and also his friends on the police force.

And standing in the visitors' parking lot beside a gleaming Rolls Royce was a man holding the collie by the ruff. The dog, the custodian was told, had been found on the fairway of the golf course which had replaced the old lemon groves across the road beyond the eucalyptus grove. He had followed a foursome back to the clubhouse where the master of Aramanth House was sitting on the terrace after finishing his round.

"How very fortunate, wasn't it, that I happened to be sitting above the eighteenth green," he told the custodian, his privet mustache lifting just enough to reveal his polished dentures. "But until he gets used to his new home, you must be more careful to keep an eye on him, mustn't you?" As he looked at the embarrassed custodian from under the bill of his tweed golfing cap, his pale blue eyes showed his annoyance, but the militant red mustache remained lifted.

Of course, the director had been notified that evening of the collie's miraculous return. Mortified and furious with the custodian for his carelessness and awake all night with worry over the effect this might have on her project, she faced him behind her desk to warn him that the next time the collie disappeared so would he, and without his pension.

The custodian had made his rounds as usual to open up the school, then returned to the remains of his breakfast during flag raising. By that time he had decided to quit, and he'd also decided that the dog would stay shut in his cottage. He had been called out during the early recess period to fix a broken swing seat, but he went without the dog. He was not going to let the dog out before he had a chance to tell the director what she could do with her dog-sitter's job.

Now a boy was missing, and again he was being blamed. He told the first-grade teacher to come along to his cottage. There he unlocked the door to show her the collie under a table in his sitting room. Robbie wasn't there. If he had run away, it wasn't with the dog. Report him missing at the office, he told her. Just don't expect him to go looking. He'd had enough for one day of the school and everybody in it.

Alone inside his cottage with Duffy, however, the custodian was uneasy. It was not the first time a child had been reported missing during his years at the school, although such occasions were fortunately rare. Always before it had turned out to be a misunderstanding. A parent had picked up the child early without informing the office, or a new student had gotten lost in the wrong classroom or the perennial school troublemaker was hiding in a lavatory stall. The custodian felt his responsibility in spite of himself. If the boy was really missing, he'd be needed, and wanted to be. He tried to remember what the little boy looked like, but that was too much for him. He did remember pulling a kid off the collie's neck the first day the dog had been introduced to the children.

His eyes drifted to Duffy lying under the table. The dog refused to look at him. By then Duffy was so accustomed to the hostility radiating from his keeper that he tried to remain invisible. He no longer sought forgiveness or came forward to greet the old man. He hadn't raised his head or gone near his dinner since he'd been brought back the day before. He heard the man's voice speaking to him.

"It's got to have something to do with you."

Duffy curled tighter against the silence that followed. Then the voice changed.

"Come here," the old man called, but the summons was gentle and he leaned forward in his chair to hold out his hand to the dog.

Duffy looked up, wanting to believe his ears.

"Come over here. I won't hurt you."

Duffy's ears pricked. Had he heard kindness, even affection?

"Come on, boy."

Slowly Duffy rose to his feet, shook himself, and took a hesitant step toward the outstretched hand. He came forward, stopping just out of reach. He wanted to trust; he was born to trust. The man reached closer, urging him another inch. Duffy took the final step. The man touched his muzzle, then leaned to run his hand over the top of Duffy's head. Duffy's defenses fell. He wanted to feel the fingers in the silken fur behind his ears.

"Nothing you did," the old man whispered. "Still, you're bein' blamed, just like me. We're a pair, all right."

Duffy looked deep into the man's small eyes in their nests of skin folds. He sat down before the man and placed a front paw lightly on his knee.

The old man snorted. "More'n I deserve, at that."

The custodian rose from his battered armchair, looked down at the dog once more, and turned to the door. He had to help in the search for the boy. His conscience, and perhaps the collie, had told him that. In the doorway, he turned as if to call to Duffy to come along, but he changed his mind. With a reassuring grunt, he left.

In the director's office, the custodian joined the circle made up of the headmaster, the first-grade teacher, and the secretary. Already, decisions had been made. For the time being, neither the boy's parents nor the police were to be notified. Spreading the alarm would cause irreparable damage to the school. The little boy could not have gotten far so soon. If he could be found and the crisis contained, no one else need be told. Those were the director's sentiments, and the others agreed. The headmaster, the director, and her secretary would use their cars to cover every road around the school. The custodian would search the woods on foot. If they found no trace by noon, all would meet again to review the strategy.

The searchers set out without a word to the rest of the staff, except for Robbie's teacher, who had to arrange for a young assistant in the kindergarten to take her class.

Although most of the area surrounding the school grounds had long ago been subdivided into one-acre parcels, which now contained houses and cleared yards stretching to the freeway fence, there were infinite places where a boy could hide. There were also paths and narrow lanes crisscrossing the remaining wooded fringes separating the properties. Then, on the opposite side of the road in front of the school the peeling eucalyptus forest rose as densely as a natural fence, screening the fairways of the golf course. Robbie's alternatives, all relatively safe from traffic and natural hazards, were difficult to search because, except for the golf course, there was no open ground and no straight road. Also, there was no obvious destination to attract a little boy.

At noon, the searchers returned to the director's office, each resigned to the inevitability of a public search and each, for personal reasons, dreading the consequences, whether or not the search was successful. At the very least, each had failed the boy and his parents in one way or another and the repercussions of that failure would affect them all. The director, with by far the most to lose, was the first to face the reality of their position and the futility of further delay in calling for help.

"Either Robbie doesn't want to be found, or someone has seen to it that he won't be," she told the rest.

The four people in her office stirred uncomfortably. As usual, all deferred to her analysis of the situation, with the exception of the custodian, who seldom agreed with her on anything and in the past had never failed to say so. But that day the old man had held his tongue throughout the discussions, much to the surprise of everyone except the director. His self-confidence had been badly shaken by the collie's disappearance and the accidental rescue the day before, and the director's threats that morning had left him uncertain. He had decided at the first meeting to organize the search and keep his opinions to himself, to follow orders and to let the old woman squirm. But that had been before they failed to find the boy. His own reputation as a former cop and peacekeeper at the school was now in jeopardy. He had confidently expected to be the one who found the boy. Now he couldn't keep still any longer.

"I say he wants to be found all right, but not by any of us."

The director fixed her black eyes on him. "What do you mean, Simmons?"

"He wants to be found by the collie is what I mean."

"I think he's right," said the headmaster.

"So do I, now that I think about it," the first-grade teacher agreed.

"But collies aren't tracking dogs," the director interrupted. "If they were, I'd say we try it. How would Laddie understand he was to look for one child out of nearly two hundred? The boy may want him to, but the dog can't know that. And I might add," she said, returning her glance to the custodian, "that just yesterday the dog ran away. I don't intend to lose him again."

"You won't," the old man assured her. "I'll be following him."

"What about the parents and the police?" the headmaster asked.

"Give the dog one hour," the director decided. "That will still leave us two hours of school time and two more of daylight."

The custodian left them to their own attempts to find the boy, glad to be rid of them all. He had never in his police career worked with a dog. He didn't know how to begin, or why the collie should cooperate, even if he understood. But he thought he knew something about little boys none of the others did. If the dog came close, Robbie would find himself.

When the custodian came out of his cottage with Duffy on the leash the school lunch hour was nearly over. Children were scattered throughout the grounds, playing or sitting in groups on the grass. The custodian had thought to begin the second search for Robbie in the open school yard where the boy, if he was watching from a nearby hiding place, would see the dog. But so many children outside would only distract the collie and deepen the boy's resolve to stay hidden. The custodian set off instead on a wide circle of the playing fields, well within sight of the school but too far away for the children to catch up. The broad acres of the playground behind the school were enclosed only by a fringe of trees and bushes. No fence had ever been considered necessary or practical and only the oldest students ventured to the farthest edges of the field for team sports.

But there were paths everywhere leading into the trees. Anyone who wanted to leave the school grounds could easily do so simply by walking to the tree-lined borders and making his way through neighboring backyards to the nearest road. As soon as the custodian was beyond the children he unleashed Duffy. He was nervous about setting him loose, but it must be the dog, not the man, who appeared to be hunting for the boy.

Free for the first time that day and sensing a new and welcome tolerance in his keeper, Duffy trotted on ahead. This was inviting new territory for him to investigate, and he always enjoyed a walk in the company of a humans going his way. Now and then he even stopped to make sure the man was following.

They completed the circle of the playground behind the school just as the children were summoned back to afternoon classes. Once again the school grounds were deserted, the nest of school buildings as silent as if every child had suddenly vanished. Duffy ran on far ahead of the man, but always within sight. He seemed more interested in his freedom to cover ground than in wandering into the narrow openings between the trees. His route became suddenly purposeful as he reached an open field on the far side of the administration cottage. This section of school property had never been cleared for use except as a supplementary parking area. In fact, it was the proposed site for the new gymnasium, but now after the first winter rains it was rutted and overgrown with weeds. What made it especially worth exploring to Duffy was the strong cat smell he found wherever he went.

And sure enough, just as he began a zigzag course through the wild mustard, a great calico cat flared up ahead of him. The cat bounded across the field toward the safety of an ancient oak whose elbowed limbs spread so close to the ground that, as the cat leaped to the lowest branch, Duffy almost grabbed its tail. Instead of climbing into the higher branches, the cat ran along the horizontal limb until it ended in a thicket of dark leaves, hissing at Duffy all the way.

Duffy was delighted. He had not only found a cat and treed it, he had it trapped with nowhere to run. He sat down under its perch and barked the good news for everyone to enjoy.

As he barked and waited under the cat for the man to catch up with him, something fell out of the tree at his feet. The soft thud the object made as it landed startled him, but when he looked down between his paws, he saw a large dog biscuit. He picked it up and crunched it, still keeping an eye on the cat. But just as he swallowed the last of the bone-shaped biscuit, another fell beside him. He was too busy eating biscuits and watching the cat to notice the approach of the custodian. To have a fat cat too far out on the limb of a tree that dropped dog biscuits as fast as he could eat them was too good to be true. Somehow the arrival of the man would spoil it all.

And it did. As soon as the custodian reached Duffy under the tree, his face on the level with the cat's, the cat leaped to the ground and ran to the shelter of the bushes marking the boundary of the school property. Caught between his urge to chase the cat, his appetite for the cookie shower and the reprimand he expected because somehow every time he treed a cat someone was there to call him off, Duffy froze. Then, when nothing happened, he barked.

The excited barking after the cat had disappeared puzzled the custodian. He looked up into the tree and there tucked in the notch of a great limb a few feet above his head was Robbie, his bare knees hugging the limb, his face tear-streaked and solemn as he looked down at the man.

The custodian allowed the boy to lead Duffy back to the administration cottage where the director met them outside her office. While Robbie was led off by his teacher to have his face washed, the director and headmaster were told how the collie had found Robbie in the oak tree and barked until the custodian came to the rescue. Everyone was smiling down at the hero of the day, who wagged so appreciatively that even the director dared to reach out a hand to pat his head.

When Robbie was brought back to join them, his gray-flannel short trousers and navy-blue sweater brushed, his face polished and his hair neatly combed, the director told him he could walk with Laddie outside her office until his mother arrived to pick him up. To have his dog all to himself suited Robbie. He was even more pleased to be told by Missus Director that because he had been found unhurt and on school property his mother would not be told about his adventure, providing, of course, that he promised never to do it again.

Promptly at three o'clock, Robbie's mother arrived in a line of cars to pick up her son. In the stream of children running from every door of the school to find their rides home, his mother saw her son walking slowly toward the car beside the custodian. Between them was the collie, with Robbie's hand resting possessively on the dog's head. As they reached her car, she leaned across the seat to open the passenger door and saw her son kiss the collie's nose.

She laughed and called to the custodian.

"Did Laddie enjoy the dog biscuits? Robbie wouldn't leave for school this morning until his pockets were stuffed with them."

Chapter Twenty-three

One of the weekly highlights of the school curriculum was Friday-morning assembly in the new auditorium. Not only did this gathering of the entire school body replace the first hour of classes on the final day of the school week, reason enough for its popularity, it always included some sort of entertainment and concluded with a singalong led by the fifth-grade teacher, an attractive and vivacious young woman who doubled as music and drama coach. The program always began with important announcements by the headmaster, who was careful to reward the children's anticipation by using the occasion to hand out scholastic prizes or award school letters to winning teams. The rest of the program consisted of one-act plays or performances by talented young musicians and singers, or, best of all, faculty skits offering the students the chance to laugh at their teachers.

Only rarely did the director appear at assembly. As she was well aware, her matriarchal role, the unseen but all-seeing presence, tended to subdue and over-solemnize any school function for both faculty and students. Except for her regular attendance at flag raising, the Eagle remained in her aerie while the rest of the school celebrated Friday with unrestrained relief.

On the first Friday morning in February, however, the director sat next to the headmaster on the auditorium stage. As she faced them, her piercing black eyes set like an umlaut atop her beaky nose, her corseted bosom and hips impervious, the students hurried to their seats. Something special was about to happen, that much they knew. The headmaster rose to introduce her. The teachers and students squirmed uneasily. The Eagle was about to pounce.

"I have an announcement of the greatest importance to all of you," she began, as if she were declaring the closure of all plumbing facilities, "and so it is proper that you, the students of Stafford, should be the first to hear our good news." Here she paused as bodies slumped and breathing resumed. "A generous friend of the school, who prefers to remain anonymous until the formal press announcement is made, has given us a magnificent new gymnasium."

As the gist of the director's message was explained up and down the front rows of younger children and its significance spread among the upper classes, the auditorium hummed. No one quite dared to applaud until a teacher did, but everyone was excited.

The director continued. "Plans have already been drawn in anticipation of this day when our dream comes true. Construction in the east field will begin next week. Except for the graduating class, all of you will share our glorious gift next fall. Our architects have promised us a model which will soon be on display here in the auditorium, and I can promise a basketball court, an indoor track and," she cast a slight smile to the front rows, "an Olympic-sized swimming pool."

The headmaster rose, applauding as he came to her side. The audience responded, at first with wild applause, then as she allowed the headmaster to turn her toward the wings, with screams and stamping feet. Either it was the new gymnasium or her disappearance, but for the first time in the memory of the younger teachers, the director was actually whistled off stage.

During the morning meeting of the Board of Trustees on the previous Saturday, the chauffeur sat with Duffy beside him in the custodian's cottage. He was on duty but free until the meeting adjourned, and he not only wanted to visit his collie but to speak confidentially to his keeper. By then his wife had found out about the gift of the gymnasium from the master's secretary, so the chauffeur knew how the dog had come to the school, but he was still shocked by the transaction. The calculation involved and the hypocrisy with which it had been accomplished were beyond his ability to imagine. He felt foolishly naive and even guilty, an unwitting accomplice in the collie's betrayal.

His purpose in speaking to the custodian was to ask for his help in the process of getting the collie back. He and his wife had made up their minds to give notice as soon as possible, but for several reasons that would take time. He had to know the dog was safe and well cared for. He had to be sure the custodian understood his intention to take the dog off his hands as soon as he could so that nothing would happen to him in the meantime.

First, however, as he sat facing the old man, he felt obliged to explain how Laddie had been used for his master's purpose.

"If you want your new gym you'll take my dog. It was as simple as that."

The custodian grinned. He was surprised. He had known all along there had to be a reason, other than the one given for the collie's presence at the school. And he knew something else. Now that the old lady had got her million to build the gym, she'd find a way to get rid of the dog. He liked the young chauffeur and felt sorry for him. There was no way he'd ever get his collie back. Whatever excuse the director found for disposing of the nuisance, she couldn't hand the dog over to the servant of the man she'd made the deal with.

Of course, he couldn't tell the chauffeur that. And he wanted to reassure him.

"You needn't worry. The dog'll be well cared for. He's made a few friends here. I'll see to him all right."

The chauffeur felt better. The collie and the custodian seemed to be friends at last. And he knew something else he couldn't reveal that would resolve the problem. His master and mistress would be leaving soon on their spring cruise. After much discussion, they had settled on a cruise of the Galapagos Islands with an exploration of the coastal desert of Peru. The chauffeur and his wife must stay at Aramanth House while they were gone to take care of the Yorkies and to see to the safety of the villa, but he could visit his dog more often, and he would be looking for the job that would free him to take Laddie back as soon as they returned.

"Come, Laddie," he called. "Let's go for a walk while we're waiting." Duffy came wagging toward him, lifting his front paws in the prancing step he used whenever he heard the word "walk" spoken by a friend.

The same memorable Friday morning that the director announced the gift of the new gymnasium, she located the custodian in the courtyard. She was on her way to lunch at her house next door. He was collecting the usual debris left behind after the children had eaten lunch. Duffy was nearby with Robbie and a group of his classmates, his eyes on Robbie's pocket where there was still the possibility of one more biscuit.

"Ah, Simmons. I've been looking for you," the director announced as she hurried toward him between the tables. "You'll be relieved of dog duty, as you call it, this weekend. Robbie's mother has invited Laddie to spend the weekend at their house. She'll be picking him up after school today and returning him Monday morning."

Once again she had caught him by surprise. She was always doing that lately, making it difficult to handle her as he used to. In order to do things his way, in spite of her ordering him around, he needed to see the way her mind was working, then turn her notions around to suit himself. But ever since the collie had arrived, she had stayed one jump ahead of him. And he hated her for it. Now once again she had tricked him into going along with her decision because he hadn't expected it.

Still, he couldn't just agree. "Can't take the chance he might get loose," he tried. "It's better he stays with me where I can keep an eye on him."

"Oh, you needn't worry. They have a large fenced yard. He'd never leave Robbie anyway. We both know that."

So that was it. She was planning to present the dog to Robbie. Of course, she couldn't do it right away. There would have to be an interval between taking the man's money and dumping his dog. But now he saw how her mind was working. He felt somewhat better. Then he remembered that the dog would be leaving that afternoon, that it was already almost time to send him off until Monday.

"It's not fair to the dog," he told the director, meeting her sharp eyes with a stare of his own. "He feels at home with me. He knows my ways and I know his. How's he to understand it's only for the weekend?"

The director cocked her head, a glitter of amusement flashing from her eyes that seemed to see right into his head.

"My, Simmons. For someone who's been complaining ever since the dog came here, your sudden concern for his feelings surprises me. Anyway," she concluded, "It is all settled. I've told Robbie's mother the dog can go." She turned away. He was dismissed.

He watched her march off toward her house. He was quivering with fury. There was nothing he could do. The boy's mother would be picking the collie up in less than two hours. What was more, if it worked out the way it probably would, he'd be going every weekend until the day came when the old woman could hand the dog over and make it all look as if she was doing everybody a favor. Her scheme was bound to work unless he could think of some way to upset it. So far, she was way ahead of him.

All of this went through his mind. His failure to give as good as he'd been given, the feeling of frustrating helplessness as he watched the woman disappearing into her backyard, were enough to send the blood to his face and the tremor to his hand.

But there was more. He didn't want the dog to go because he would miss him. He had grown to like his company, the way he had of asking to go for a morning walk before the children arrived when they could circle the field alone; the sigh he made as he settled for the evening beside his chair. The best times for dog and man were at the solitary ends of the day and the long peaceful weekends. The cottage would be empty without him. Nothing but television to talk to. Nobody at all to listen.

He turned then to watch the collie waiting for Robbie to dig a dog biscuit out of his pocket.

"Time for you to go along to class," he called to the boy. "I'll take the dog."

He grabbed the collie by the collar and led him off. At least, he'd keep the dog with him for the time they had left.

Chapter Twenty-four

During the next three weekends Duffy's social life became a matter of intense concern to the humans who vied for his company. Each Friday in February Robbie's mother called the director to ask that the collie be allowed to spend the weekend with her son, a request the director was pleased to grant. But there were others not at all pleased to see him go. The chauffeur and his wife looked forward to their Saturdays at the beach with their collie. The only other time they could visit him was their mid-week afternoon off, not at all satisfactory because they had to wait until school was out and return him before dark. And they were worried by the custodian's prediction that Duffy would be given to the boy before they could find a way to take him back themselves. As the chauffeur heard each week that the dog was off again for the weekend, he felt helpless to prevent what he knew would eventually happen, helpless and angry and more determined than ever to see that it didn't.

The custodian's reaction to Duffy's weekend visits was also one of anger and frustration. He considered subterfuge, hiding him or telling the director the dog was sick, but always he realized that his employer would see through any attempt to deceive her. Now that she knew how much he wanted the collie's company himself, she seemed to take special delight in announcing his weekend visits to Robbie.

Early in the first week of March, Robbie's mother called the school office. She needed the home telephone numbers of most of Robbie's classmates so that she could call their mothers to invite the children to Robbie's seventh birthday party on the coming Saturday afternoon. While she was speaking to the secretary she happened to mention that she thought it best that Laddie not come home with her son that weekend. There was a reason, she explained, but she couldn't tell her what it was,

"It's a surprise," she added, laughing.

The following day, the director told the custodian that the dog would not be going away that weekend. She made a point of it, as if she were granting the old man a special favor.

"Just make sure he stays with you," she warned, allowing him to wonder whether she knew about the chauffeur's claim.

When the chauffeur came to take Duffy for a walk on the beach that Thursday afternoon, the custodian told him he could borrow the collie on Saturday. The chauffeur and his wife were delighted. By coincidence their master and mistress had left that morning. The Scottish couple would be alone at Aramanth House for a month. The collie could spend the weekend with no one the wiser. The chauffeur thought it better not to mention this to the custodian, however. He had noticed that the old man was becoming increasingly protective of the dog. Instead, he promised to be back on Saturday morning to pick up Laddie.

Then on Friday morning Robbie's mother called the director with another change of plan. Could Laddie come that weekend after all?

"You see," she explained, "Robbie doesn't know why Laddie was not invited to his party, and I can't tell him. It would spoil his surprise."

Of course, the director would allow the dog to go home with Robbie that afternoon. She couldn't imagine what could have prevented his being invited in the first place, especially for such an occasion, but then, she had never had a little boy or a dog of her own.

She hunted down the custodian during her lunch hour to tell him the dog would be going after all.

The custodian exploded, "But he's going to the beach," he shouted. "It's time he stayed with me one weekend. The dog don't know who he belongs to."

"Oh. Simmons, you delight me. You're as soft as butter, aren't you? You need a dog of your own, and maybe I'll get you one."

Trilling an unbelievably girlish laugh, she left him still protesting. Now that the collie had turned him into such a pussycat, she decided she was really quite fond of him.

Duffy enjoyed his visits to Robbie's house. The house was located on a bluff above the rocky shoreline north of the city, a subdivision of expensive properties, each with an ocean view or hilltop dominance or wooded privacy. Robbie's was a dream house for a little boy and a dog, as congenial inside as out, and Duffy was welcomed as an honored guest. He sat beside Robbie's chair during meals, slept at the foot of his bed, and ran with him down the sloping back lawn to the sea. The family included a tolerant dachshund and a parrot on a perch in Robbie's father's study. Every time Duffy passed by, the parrot whistled, then, as Duffy obeyed the whistle, the parrot pretended not to notice him. Duffy's weekends with Robbie were filled with novelty and laughter, compliment and love, the best of human gifts.

The most exciting weekend of all was to be Duffy's last at Robbie's house. It began like the others with a late-afternoon run to the bottom of the rear lawn and gardens where Duffy and Robbie probed the rock caves and tidal pools, filling their lungs with sea smells and shaking off the long school week. They returned to the house in early darkness to join the rest of the family in the high-ceilinged living room for cocktails before a crackling fire, then dinner served in a spacious dining alcove where Duffy's pan was placed under Robbie's chair. Later, Duffy and Robbie went to Robbie's bedroom in the east wing where, because it was Friday night, Robbie was allowed to stay up an extra hour to play the games he had invented for his friend. He read stories, showing Duffy pictures of animals. He played a cassette of wild-animal calls for

Duffy to identify. After his mother came to tuck him in bed he made up his own story, whispering it to the collie as he dug his toes under the warm body stretched across the narrow bed.

The real excitement began on Saturday morning. While Robbie and Duffy ran to explore their secret places, Robbie's father drove away on his important errand. His mother and the maid began the preparations for the party setting outdoor tables with party favors and tying nests of balloons under umbrella canopies. Robbie's presents were not to be brought out before the children arrived, so the little boy was not expecting any surprises before noon.

Then his father called him. He and Duffy raced each other back to the house where his parents waited at the edge of the grass. Between them a collie puppy sat watching the boy's and the dog's approach. He was eight weeks old, still wrapped in puppy wool and puppy wonder, still unable to sit on his haunches without his rear legs popping out from under him around his taut pink belly. Only his pliant amber ears and eyes the color of burnt sugar animated his expression. The rest of him was a tawny ball supported by four white pylon paws.

The meeting of puppy and little boy was all there was to watch. Even Duffy had to stand back. There was no room between them for an investigative nose. His nostrils filled with long-forgotten odors, warm traces of milk and saliva and musky new body, and the sour, worrying smell of vomit. But the puppy was wrapped in Robbie's arms. All Duffy could see of it was a pointed, white-tipped tail flailing outside the embrace.

If ever a little boy was ready for his first puppy Robbie was, and there had never been a doubt that the puppy must be a collie. But locating a collie litter had not been easy. Unlike kittens, who are usually born in the spring and early summer, puppies can appear throughout the year, but human management controls breeding. January puppies are rare because they are inconvenient, and collie puppies are rarer still because collie popularity has waned. It had taken many calls to locate a pet-shop owner who could promise delivery from a Fresno kennel in time for Robbie's birthday. A puppy barely weaned had traveled by air via Los Angeles to be there on that day. Crated in a box dank with dog smells, shipped in a pressurized hold of a bouncing jet, transferred by luggage cart to a smaller place, then carried still in the box to the pet shop, the puppy had arrived that morning. He had been cleaned and fed, but on the way home to Robbie he had thrown up his breakfast. Now, however, as he felt the boy's body pressed to his, he sensed a return to the caresses of his mother's tongue, the warm folds of his siblings. He wriggled closer and his puppy breath on Robbie's cheek was hot with sweet frenzy.

With the arrival of the birthday guests, Duffy regained attention. Most of the children knew him, and as the long rear yard filled with racing boys and girls, Duffy had his day. Robbie never left the puppy, and of course he was the star attraction, wobbling forward, then sitting breathlessly to watch the figures on the lawn, then reaching clumsily for a first flea. His every action drew cries of surprised delight, as if his admirers could hardly believe that anything so toylike could actually yawn and pant and scratch an ear. Even Duffy was fascinated. A young puppy was as new to him as to the children, certainly like no other dog. Unafraid, with none of a young dog's deference, it seemed to reach out to him as if in this confusing tangle of faces and hands a collie nose was the only familiar thing.

Robbie's party was a great success, but Robbie himself, the center of everyone's good wishes, hardly spoke. He had to be reminded to open his presents. He had to be called to the front door to say goodbye to his friends. When late that afternoon the children had gone and the house was back in order, Robbie sat next to the puppy's blanket bed dipping his finger into a bowl of warm milk for the puppy to lick. Duffy was forgotten, an elderly uncle in the background.

The next day, a Sunday that should have been the beginning of a new life for Robbie and his puppy, was one of agony and tears. The little boy and Duffy were awake at dawn, and so were Robbie's parents. The puppy was sick, very sick. His bed and the floor around it were smeared with vomit and blood-stained diarrhea. The little dog was too weak to walk and unable to eat. The light in his eyes had gone and he lay trembling in his bed. At first, the upset stomach was explained as the inevitable aftermath of plane travel, the strange surroundings, and all the excitement. But the symptoms were too violent, and it was clear to Robbie's parents that the vulnerable little dog would not survive without professional treatment.

Like all professions in a specialized and affluent society, the practice of veterinary medicine has adjusted to the changing importance of animals in human lives. The veterinarian who works on weekends, who treats large animals, and makes house calls is as rare as the carthorse who once supported him. Regular office hours to treat the ailments of poodles and Persians assure the easy life, and who among his patients' owners is to blame him? Except that love, which has replaced the economic importance of family animals, has produced a stronger dependence and an even greater concern for their welfare. No price is too high to save a precious family member; no loss more devastating.

The weekend hiatus, so understandable until a sick animal can't wait until Monday, has created in many populated areas an animal emergency clinic whose services are available on Saturdays and Sundays at desperation prices. After several calls to answering services that morning, Robbie's father reached the clinic, located in a downtown office building and open twenty-four hours a day between Friday night and Monday morning. Robbie carried the blanketed puppy in his arms as the two drove away to seek help. Duffy and Robbie's mother watched them leave, neither able to understand how overnight a family could turn into silent strangers, unable to comfort each other.

Robbie and his father were back within an hour without the puppy. Nor would they hear again from the clinic that day. Duffy sensed the boy's withdrawal. He followed slowly from room to room, sat with him through the waiting hours, seeking the small hand, a softening of the solemn eyes.

Early Monday morning Robbie's father drove Duffy back to the school. There, the collie was met as usual by the custodian and led away, while the father walked to the administration cottage to explain why Robbie would not be in school that day. The boy would not leave home without word about his puppy. His parents understood, although they would rather he had gone along with the collie. Already they feared the worst. How does a parent explain nature's indiscriminate waste, or God's indifference?

Duffy's school week began in a way that had by then become uneventful. Where once the very prospect of an entire day surrounded by children would have seemed the ultimate adventure, the noisy courtyard and crowded playground no longer excited him. One reason for this apparent indifference to his favorite of all humans might have been the children's changing reactions toward their mascot. Like a familiar toy, he was always there. His ability to challenge their imaginations had been tested. His responses were no longer wondrous. The children went back to their games, Duffy's presence accepted but no longer insisted upon. But Duffy's reaction to the children had also undergone alteration. During the days he spent with more of them than he could possibly meet, he had discovered that one little boy was really all he wanted. It was Robbie he looked for, Robbie's welcoming hug he missed, Robbie's pocketful of treats he remembered.

On Monday and Tuesday he searched in vain for the boy. Then on Wednesday Robbie came back to school a different Robbie. Duffy found him sitting on the grass at the edge of the children's play area. The collie greeted the boy as always with nose to cheek and one paw raised in the standing strut he used for special reunions, but Robbie turned away, brushing off Duffy's attentions. He approached the boy again at lunch time, expecting the usual biscuit to be fished from

Robbie's pocket, but the pocket was empty and Robbie brushed him away.

Robbie appeared each day, but he avoided the collie so obviously that Duffy finally stayed out of his way, watching puzzled, ever willing to resume the friendship. On Friday there was no invitation from Robbie's mother for Duffy to spend the weekend. Duffy had become the cruel reminder of tragedy, to be avoided because he was alive.

The custodian awoke earlier than usual on Saturday morning to find his dog standing close to the bed watching him. Although the old man thought he understood the collie's ways, never before had he seen such intensity in the dark eyes. There was pleading. He was asking the man to get up. There was fear, as if punishment was expected when he did. There was also the wild light of desperation in the collie's eyes that held the dog at the bedside, willing the man to open his eyes no matter what the consequences. The moment the custodian met those eyes, the dog turned away toward the bedroom door. There he stopped to look back. When the custodian failed to follow, he turned back to the bed, tail tucked under, then hurried into the front room.

The custodian lay on his back a moment longer, reluctant to begin the day so early, but the dog's strange behavior finally forced him to get up. He shuffled into the front room where he stared in disbelief. The worn carpet was strewn with pale puddles of diarrhea. There was hardly space to walk across the room without stepping in a mess. Not until he had taken in the extent of the explosive droppings did he notice the collie. He was standing at the front door, his head raised, his haunches bent for escape.

Swearing, mumbling the short words Duffy had learned too well, the custodian stepped carefully across the room. With his hand on the doorknob he hesitated, looking down at the upturned muzzle. He wanted to grab the collar, to rub the nose in the nearest pool. The dog had done the damage. He was only to trying to avoid the consequences. Duffy pressed closer to the door, refusing to back away, hardly able to hold his tail down against the pressure in his bowels.

The custodian turned the knob and pulled the door open.

Duffy fled.

He ran across the broad playground. Now that he was away at last, the urge to reach the cover of the trees before stopping again drove him on. Behind him in the cottage doorway the old man called, but Duffy never slowed. The man turned back and the door closed, but Duffy was no longer aware of the man. He was running toward a hiding place where he could rid himself of the pains wracking his lower abdomen. He reached the far edge of the athletic field and found a path into the undergrowth. There he stopped and strained.

The pains did not diminish. The urge returned in waves. He had to go farther. Behind him he heard the faint shout, but no call could turn him now. Perhaps it was fear of punishment. More likely it was the internal eruptions he wanted to escape. He moved through dense thicket and between saplings like a hunted animal, crouching, hardly pausing to choose his direction so long as his path put his pains behind him.

Several times he had to stop to pump his tail, then continue, intent upon reaching relief as if it lay just ahead. He entered a clearing, crossed a shaded yard and ran down a driveway to a narrow road. He slowed then, feeling better. The exercise seemed to have cleansed him. His tail rose to its normal half staff and he began to take an interest in his surroundings. He could no longer hear the call of the man behind him. When he did he would turn back. In the meantime, he would turn flight into a morning of discovery. The road he followed led toward distant sounds of traffic and now and then, the barking of a dog.

He had been trotting along the unpaved shoulder of the road for several miles, catching the cross-scents of exhaust fumes and wood smoke and dog markers, when the sound of an engine behind him caused him to move farther to the side of the road. The vehicle slowed, so close that Duffy stopped and looked back. A small white truck pulled in behind him. Its cargo shell was a square metal box with louvered panels along both sides. It resembled one of the ice-cream trucks that once prowled neighborhood streets, except that its panels bore no advertising, no bells tinkled its approach, and on both doors of the cab were decals of the city seal. In lettering too small to read from any distance were the words Department of Animal Control.

The young man who stepped out of the truck wore shoulder patches and a badge similar to those of the police department, but he wore long blond hair and glasses, and as he approached Duffy, he spoke gently and held out a friendly hand. Duffy's tail began to sway as he decided to respond. The officer stopped closer and ran his hand along Duffy's back, establishing his good intentions. Then he took the collar to lead him back to the truck. While he held the dog with one hand he opened one of the vertical panels on the right side of the truck. Then, still moving slowly and speaking softly, he wrapped both arms around Duffy's legs and lifted him into the narrow compartment. He closed and latched the panel door, and the truck moved off down the deserted road.

Duffy managed to turn around in the narrow space to face the door, but when he looked up from the dark interior of the steel-sided cell the bright, endless morning had shrunk to slits of sunlight, and the pains in his loins were returning.

Chapter Twenty-five

The white truck, its mission accomplished, moved slowly through the downtown city streets, heading always northwest, following the coastline. The young Animal Control officer intended to arrive back at the shelter just before noon so that his half-day Saturday duty would be nearly over by the time he delivered the stray collie. He had been the only city officer available when the complaint came in from a south-coast resident that a large dog was disturbing the peace of the neighborhood by causing properly confined dogs to bark. The caller had not identified the dog as a collie, but the officer had no doubt that the dog he had picked up was the culprit. And even if it wasn't, the collie was loose on a city street and therefore by definition a public nuisance. A county truck would be covering his territory the rest of the weekend. If he timed his return to the shelter properly, he could book the collie and be home for lunch, and while it was still March, the weather was warm enough to spend the afternoon at the beach.

Although the sign outside the new compound at the northern edge of the city labeled it a county shelter, it also served the city and was partially funded out of city revenues. Its staff was also divided between city and county personnel, and county officers often patrolled within city limits on weekends or when the complaints became too numerous for city officers to handle. The complex of low-lying buildings tucked within a screen of trees at the far end of a cul-de-sac included the shelter itself, a discreet, ranch-style headquarters which from the newly-paved turnaround could have been the model for a new housing tract, and rows of garages and service buildings, all as immaculately secured as a Saturday barracks. Nor, except for the bank of steel, self-locking cages at the curb, a depository for the convenience of the public who might want to get rid of a dog or cat anonymously or after the shelter closed, was there any indication from the outside that the residents of this trim dwelling were canine and feline strays.

The white truck parked at the rear of the shelter. It was the custom, even though there were few visitors and no neighbors within sight, to make deliveries at the back door. Only when an animal was rescued by its owner did it use the front entrance. The collie was the only passenger that morning, so the officer tied a leash to the ring of the chain collar to lead the dog into the buildings. What might have served as a family room if the shelter had really been a private house was an office with desks and files and a high front counter. At the counter the officer was met by a young woman and a kennel attendant in coveralls. While the attendant held the leash, the officer read the expired license number and provided the woman with a formal description of the dog and the approximate location of the collection. Then, as the officer headed out the door for home, the collie was led through a sound proof door into a block of cages.

The room Duffy entered was almost as dark as the truck compartment. There was adequate ventilation from small windows near the ceiling, but with the heavy door closed behind him the narrow room remained in half light. Two tiers of cages lined each side of a walkway, scored and slanted to allow drainage. The cement floor was still damp from a recent hosing, and the room smelled strongly of disinfectant. The attendant pulled him along to a lower cage at the center of the righthand block of cages, where he was gently pushed inside and the wire cage door latched. The space was barely large enough to turn around, which immediately Duffy did to watch the attendant leave, closing the door at the end of the passage behind him. The cage was provided with a metal water bowl clamped to the wire and a small metal platform six inches above the floor to permit the occupant to avoid lying on the wet concrete. As he stood waiting behind the cage door for someone to let him out Duffy faced a bank of empty cages opposite. He heard no sound, caught no body scents. Whether it was the shock of being isolated in this place without a sign of life, or some perception of his utter helplessness, he began to shiver.

Although it was a Saturday, a day of minimal activity at the shelter, and nearly noon, the young woman decided to contact the collie's owners before she went to lunch. He was obviously a family dog who would be missed, and she would not be on duty the next day. Her office files contained copies of all license certificates, so it was a simple matter to locate the name and address of the owner and to look up the number in the directory. She let the phone ring for a full five minutes before she gave up and left the office.

At Aramanth House no one heard the phone. When the master and mistress were out of town, calls were answered by the master's secretary on weekdays between ten and five. At other times either the chauffeur or his wife picked up a kitchen extension unless they had retired to their apartment over the garage. When the call was made from the shelter, however, both were out for the afternoon. For reasons of his own, the school custodian had not informed them of the last-minute cancellation of the collie's weekend visit to Robbie, so they had gone to their beach picnic without him.

The young woman at the shelter did try once more late that afternoon, but when she got no answer she decided to wait until Monday. She knew from the address that the collie's owners were members of the wealthy colony and probably away for the weekend, which would explain the dog's being picked up so far from home. She was also unworried about his fate. The seventy-two-hour holding period before he must be destroyed would not begin until Monday morning. Certainly by then she would be in contact with his owners.

Duffy had become the source of concern to another of the shelter's employees. When he returned from lunch, the kennel attendant went back to the cage block to move the dog into one of the outdoor runs, narrow alleys enclosed in chain-link wire leading from the inside cages. He found the cage floor covered with diarrhea and the dog standing on the metal platform, shaking with fear of punishment, unable to escape the fouling of his cage. The attendant quickly moved him outside where again he was the only dog. He then hosed out the cage and placed a bowl of kibble inside it for Duffy's evening meal. It was not that uncommon for new occupants of the shelter's cages to react to their confinement as Duffy had, but there were traces of blood in the loose stool, and that was not at all common. The attendant decided to keep an eye on the dog during the following day and to put no more dogs into his cage block until he was satisfied that the collie had no contagious disease.

Duffy spent the night and the following day in the most miserable isolation of his life. He ate nothing, not only because the kibble was dry and nearly tasteless, but also because he had no appetite. Even his occasional attempts to drink from the water bowl seemed only to bring on another wave of stomach cramps. The long night, black and soundless inside the cage was spent in fitful dozing and straining to hear the slightest reassuring footfall. The following day was hardly better. He was moved outside again where, from the run, he heard occasional barking, the sounds of trucks, and faraway voices. But he saw only the attendant who replenished his water, replaced his untouched food, and moved him from cage to cage and run to run as one after the other was soiled with the contents of his bowels.

It was not until Monday morning that at last the leash was tied to his collar and he was led from his cage, through the doorway, and into the sunlight. By then he was too weak to notice where he was being taken. His shining coat lay dull across his back. His head remained down and he walked beside the attendant like a beaten animal. Fortunately he had not far to walk. He was patiently led to a wire gate which the attendant slid open, then across another paved area to a small white building.

Inside the door the attendant spoke to a girl behind a small counter, then passed around it, urging Duffy along to the open doorway. The scene before them was strange enough to bring Duffy's head up and to send a quiver to the tip of his nose. In the center of the small white-walled room was a long table. Lying on the table was a cat asleep on its back, its four paws pointing limply toward the ceiling. On two stools at each side of the table were a man and a girl dressed in surgical gowns, their heads bent over the cat. More interesting to Duffy as he examined the contents of the room were its other occupants. On counters, on every possible surface, were small cradles of aluminum or cardboard, and in each cradle was a sleeping cat, each on its back, each with shaved abdomen, each totally unaware of the dog in the doorway watching them. The scene was so unimaginable to Duffy that, for the first time since he had been caged in the shelter, his ears stood up and a soft inquisitive whine escaped from his upturned muzzle.

The man and the girl looked up at their visitors, then returned to their patient.

"Whatcha got, Julio?" the white-coated man asked as he recognized the attendant over the rims of his drugstore glasses.

"Bad diarrhea for two days. Won't eat. Looks like parvo to me," the attendant answered.

The veterinary surgeon took a final moment to check the incision in the cat's midsection. Then, leaving the suturing to his assistant, he came to the doorway where he stooped to examine the collie. He pulled down an eyelid, ran his hand along a flank, and probed gently in the groin.

"Let's put him in the ward," he said, leading the way into an adjacent room.

Like the cage block Duffy had just left, the long narrow room was lined with tiers of wire cages, enclosed within cinder-block walls, and ventilated by small windows. At each end of the center aisle was a self-locking steel door giving the room the atmosphere of a crypt. No other animal stood at any of the cage doors to watch as Duffy was pushed into a lower cage and the gate latched behind him.

The veterinarian had noticed the tags on his collar. "You'll inform the owner we've got him?"

The attendant nodded and walked back through the small clinic and out into the open area between buildings. Behind him the veterinarian called to his assistant to prepare the next cat for spaying. In the meantime, he would examine the collie more carefully, but he was inclined to trust the shelter attendant's diagnosis. The young man had spotted the disease before. He was observant and interested, saving his money to enter a veterinary college. If he thought the collie had parvo, he probably did.

<u>Canine Parvovirus Enteritis</u>. As if the timeless balance nature has established among living creatures had been momentarily tipped by the discoveries of vaccines and antibiotics, a new virus appeared in dogs in 1978 and spread throughout the country. Related to the virus that causes distemper in cats, it was still so new that many veterinarians had never seen a case. Those who had, or had read the literature, knew its symptoms: fever, vomiting, and diarrhea. They also knew it to be extremely contagious, the virus remaining highly stable for several years in the stools of afflicted dogs, and deadly, especially to puppies and old dogs. The most frequent sources of contamination were believed to be pet shops, boarding kennels, and dog shows, all places where dogs are brought together.

Only recently had an effective vaccine been developed to provide long-term protection against parvo; so recently that most dog owners were unaware of either the disease or its prevention, so the virus remained rampant. Only the symptoms could be treated once a dog was sick, but in mature dogs the illness usually passed in a few days with rare fatalities reported. As usual, however, with a disease still little understood, statistics were not complete. Only the dog struck down by the virus, and the humans who struggled to save him from the complete destruction of his digestive tract, knew parvo to be the most virulent killer of dogs since distemper had been all but eliminated by vaccine.

Against his accumulating share of misfortunes during the days preceding his arrival in the ward cage, it is perhaps fatuous to describe Duffy's latest predicament as offsetting good fortune. And yet, in several ways it was. The choice of location for the new animal shelter was too propitious to have been made by bureaucrats interested only in seeking the least controversial solution to one of society's embarrassing failures, the ever-increasing number of unwanted pets. Indeed, the location was thrust upon the city and county fathers by an organization dedicated to finding homes for these same animals. It began when a family residence, consisting of a wide-verandaed old house and its surrounding lemon orchards, was donated to become the headquarters of the County Humane Society. And because there was more adjacent land than was required for the Society's purposes, and because the city pound was inadequate and a disgrace, a portion of the bequest was transferred to county and city to become the site of the new animal shelter.

This adjacency of agencies committed on one side of the high dividing fence to collecting strays and on the other to bringing abandoned animals and adoptive owners together, although never quite complementary, often accomplished miracles in lives of those whose luck had run out. A further advantage also worked in Duffy's favor. Although the county employed a veterinarian as a consultant, the shelter had no clinic. Sick and wounded strays brought to the shelter had to be transferred to the Society for treatment, and now that they were next-door neighbors this accommodation was more readily available and therefore more often used.

Duffy was now in capable hands. Moreover, although animals brought to the Society for adoption could be kept no longer than the law allowed, three days not including weekends, the Society's function was to provide second chances. While the process of reuniting the collie with his registered owner continued at the shelter, relief of his parvo symptoms began under the supervision of a veterinarian familiar with the disease who believed the collie's chances for full recovery were good. Most important, he recognized a fine dog when he saw one.

The master's secretary received the call from the shelter on Monday morning. She realized immediately what had happened. Through an oversight, possibly her own, the collie's license had not been renewed, nor his registration papers changed to show his new owners at the school. Rather than explain the transfer to the shelter, she decided to notify the school director herself of the dog's whereabouts. She assured the woman from the shelter that someone would be there to collect the dog.

She called the director immediately and told her that Laddie had been picked up, but he was now at the Humane Society where he was being treated for a serious infection.

For once the director was speechless, totally flabbergasted. When she had discovered earlier that morning that the collie was missing, she had again baffled the custodian by taking the news calmly, almost as if she was relieved. And she was. She had decided the time had come to get rid of the dog, and a way had now been presented. But the call from Aramanth House made it impossible to leave him where he was.

On the other hand, he was sick, undoubtedly with a fatal disease, and probably infectious. No one could expect her to take him back in that condition. He might spread his parvo, whatever that was, to the children.

She called the Humane Society demanding to speak to the veterinarian in charge. When she was told he was busy spaying cats, imperiously she announced her name and made sure that he would call her back.

The veterinarian returned the call before noon. He recognized the name. Two of his children had gone to Stafford, although he decided not to remind her of that.

Managing a note of what she imagined to be dog-owner distress, the director asked a favor. Could Laddie remain at the Society an extra day or two until he was completely well?

"We must think of the children too," she reminded the vet, thus involving him in the responsibility for preventing a possible epidemic.

Parvo could not be contracted by humans, but the veterinarian didn't mention that. Keeping the dog longer than three weekdays, even a dog in need of medical treatment was against the law. Not that it was never done. Both the Society and the shelter made exceptions, particularly for a valuable dog, but the clinic was not supposed to compete with private veterinarians. The collie should be transferred to his own doctor.

But the veterinarian wanted to help. And the dog would probably be well enough to go back to the school by the end of the week. In the end he agreed to keep the collie until Friday morning, and not a day later. And he reminded the director that in addition to the shelter's usual fees for retrieving a stray and the fine for an expired license, there would be extra costs for treatment and board at the Humane Society.

The director thanked him coolly, her distress ratio considerably reduced now that she had gained the favor and been given time to make her plans. She had until Friday to think of a way of turning the incident into an excuse for disposing of the dog. At that moment, that was enough.

Duffy's whereabouts were soon known to both his would-be saviors. The chauffeur heard the story from the secretary. At first, he saw the collie's fate as an opportunity to get him back simply by claiming him, but thinking it over, he realized that the Humane Society would have contacted the school and might refuse him. On the other hand, if somehow he couldn't find a way to take the dog before Duffy was returned to the school, he might never have another chance. He decided to visit the collie and while he was there, to investigate the possibilities of taking him with or without permission.

The custodian arrived at the same decision by an alternative route. He knew where the dog was. He had also been told by the director that the collie was ill and that he was not to pick him up before Friday. His old antagonist was at her schemes again. He knew, from his days on the police force, the procedure involving dogs picked up as strays. If Laddie was left unclaimed for three days he would be destroyed, and the old woman had somehow found out about the rule. All she needed was an excuse for delay. The dog's illness had given her that.

As the custodian thought about it, he began to feel more and more excited. At first, he grunted with satisfaction. After weeks of small defeats, at last he saw through his employer's plot to rid herself of the collie in time to thwart it. Once more he could enjoy the comfortable pleasure of being one jump ahead of her. Then, as he sat in his old armchair hatching his counterplot, the thrill of it warmed him. He felt the heady mixture of anticipation and a tingling fear he had felt before entering a building where a holdup was in progress. It had been years since he had experienced the blood-racing moment of total confidence in himself as he faced a challenge most men would have backed away from.

He would mount a rescue. He would make use of his police training, even perhaps one or two of his police buddies. He would save the collie, and while he was at it, leave the old woman completely defeated.

That his plan might involve danger, certainly some risk to himself, made it all the more exhilarating. He got up to turn off the television. He had to think.

Chapter Twenty-six

On Monday afternoon the chauffeur and his wife visited Duffy in his ward cage at the Humane Society. Their visit was prompted by their concern. How sick was he? Were the veterinarian's assurances to the master's secretary that he would recover to be trusted? But the chauffeur also wanted to learn as much as he could about the place, to establish, if he could, their claim to the collie and to devise a plan legally or illegally of taking the dog back. His wife insisted on accompanying him, and, although he hadn't told her how far he intended to go in his efforts to rescue Laddie, he was glad to have her along. Together they might more easily persuade someone in charge that they were the rightful owners and that returning him to the school would surely doom him.

These were gentle, law-abiding people, grateful still for the opportunity that their guaranteed employment at Aramanth House had offered for them to immigrate, and they were proud of their new American citizenship. Breaking the law and defying authority had never before occurred to either of them. But the collie had been given to them, then taken, only to be used, then discarded. The chauffeur's faith in American justice and the basic kindness that Americans felt for their pets convinced him that, at least in this case, the end would justify whatever means were necessary.

Both were animal-lovers, and their reaction, as they walked into the Society's attractive grounds was, like that of all its visitors, at first one of delight. It was like entering a small zoo where every animal waited to greet them. Beyond the main house, which served as the staff headquarters but which still looked like the comfortable residence of generations of family members, was a puppy shop whose display windows were filled with small faces and wagging tails. Spaced attractively across the shaded yard were islands of runs and cages, each sized for its occupants: large or small dogs, puppy litters, dogs quarantined, or dogs simply waiting to go home.

As the couple walked through the grounds searching for their collie, they came to a poultry yard where geese and ducks and chickens shared the afternoon shade. In adjacent cages were dozing rabbits, fat furry loaves that turned out to be guinea pigs, and a box of white mice. Near the entrance to a classroom where schoolchildren came to learn about animals from the animals themselves was an aviary in which parakeets and pigeons graced the polished branches of a leafless tree. There were puddles for turtles, and beyond the circle of small animals was a corral holding a colt and a pair of burros. Only the Society's collection of cats and kittens was not on view, but these too waited in a special building to be chosen and carried home.

It was even better than a zoo, the couple decided, because these well-cared-for animals were there for the taking. It was all they could do to resist loading the station wagon with one of each, or maybe two of each, or maybe all. How could anyone choose one and leave another when all were there for the taking?

It was then, as they found the small clinic and headed toward it, that they remembered where they were and why these family pets were waiting, watching them, on such attractive display. All had been abandoned, brought to this halfway house to be adopted or destroyed. How many would be given a second chance? What of the old, the less endearing? What about the puppy drooping in the window of the puppy shop, or the scarred hound whose dewlaps dripped? How long would these castoffs be allowed to wait for love before their places would be needed for a new supply of rejected pets? Like any other market, this place depended upon turnover, even if the wards were alive and filled with hope.

When the couple explained to the young veterinary assistant behind the clinic counter that they had come to visit the sick collie, she smiled and led them back to the ward, opened Duffy's cage and allowed him out to welcome his friends. He was definitely thinner and, although his tail told them how pleased he was to see them, his greeting was subdued. In answer to their questions about his condition the girl could tell them that he was recovering. He still refused to eat, but that was not unusual or really harmful. Dogs, she explained, could go for days without food. What was encouraging, indeed vital to his recovery, was that he drank water. Dehydration was one of the dangerous side effects of parvo, so much so that intravenous feeding was often the only way to restore the fluids necessary to keep stricken dogs alive. So far the doctor had not thought it necessary in the collie's case. Kaopectate had controlled his diarrhea, and it was expected that he would begin to take food within a day or two. If not, an I.V. solution containing the necessary minerals and dextrose would be used.

As the chauffeur's wife comforted Duffy, her husband grew more alarmed by what he heard and saw. The veterinary assistant was explaining that the dog could only remain at the clinic for two more days. Then his owners must move him either back home or to a private veterinarian. That was the law. She also could not disturb the vet to allow the chauffeur to speak to him. He was busy in surgery with the day's supply of cats to be spayed. Neither she nor the chauffeur knew of the exception granted to permit the collie an extra two days' grace. Wednesday, she told them, would be his last day at the clinic.

The chauffeur heard the ultimatum, helpless to make his case to anyone in authority, certain that his dog would be lost to him one way or the other after Wednesday. He examined more carefully the blockhouse security of the ward. Only the solid doors at either end of the room permitted entry. The inside door through which he and his wife had entered the ward connected it with the operating room and cat cages, but he had noticed that even during visiting hours, the assistant had used a key to open it. The ward was kept isolated from the other rooms of the clinic, and its lock was new and probably burglarproof.

The opposite door, now open to allow fresh air and sunshine to reach the ward cages, led to the edge of the property where a high chain-link fence rose to tree-branch level, but the chauffeur could see that this was a self-locking exit only, like the fire door in a theatre. The room looked to be escape-proof, and impenetrable from the outside. Still, there might be a way.

The couple returned to the parking lot in silence. Only when they reached the freeway to join the homebound traffic did either speak.

"I'm almost sorry we came, Charles," his wife confessed, a tissue ready in her fist for the tears she felt burning her eyes.

He reached to take her hand. "It had to be done, Mary. And maybe it wasn't in vain."

She looked at him, saw the set of his mouth and didn't dare to ask what he meant.

Now he knew. The collie had only two more days, and he only two more nights. Wednesday night he would take his dog home.

The custodian's reconnaissance of the Humane Society also began that Monday afternoon, but it did not require a personal visit. For one thing, the old man knew the location and the layout. In his days as a city police officer, he and his former partner had participated in the apprehension of two dog thieves who had managed to steal a puppy from the compound. While one of the young men had entered the Society's grounds as a visitor, the other had waited outside the parking-lot wall. The first thief had sauntered to a run filled with a litter of golden retriever puppies, opened the gate, grabbed the nearest one and dashed to the wall, where he tossed his prize to his accomplice. The theft was witnessed by several visitors, the police were called and the kidnappers caught before they left the freeway. The custodian and his partner had had the pleasure of returning the stolen puppy to the Society, where they were received as heroes and urged to adopt the puppy themselves.

The old man remembered the exploit with satisfaction. He also remembered his tour of the Society's facilities to check security and to recommend any measures he thought necessary to prevent a recurrence of the incident. He knew that there were at least three barriers between every dog and the outside world. No animal could escape on his own, first from his cage, then through the locked enclosure surrounding each kennel area and finally over the high fence surrounding the property. But the collie would not be on his own. He would have outside help and that of the best kind.

That thought prompted his call to his former partner, a retired officer now working as the night watchman at a shopping plaza and probably as bored as he was.

At first, his former colleague just laughed. "You? Kidnap a dog? Last time we were there you wouldn't have one for the taking."

The custodian expected this reaction. He didn't try to explain. He needed a man he could trust for the job he had in mind. If it went off as he expected, his friend would never be suspected of complicity, nor would he ever have to know the reason. And yet, because his partner's role was vital to the success of the rescue, they would both share the excitement. They would know that they were still professionals and as sharp as ever.

The custodian had chosen well. Predictably, his former partner was intrigued. The job, as outlined, would have its problems. He would have to hire a substitute to take over his early rounds at the shopping plaza, but he could handle that. He would also have to do some digging himself, make a call or two to set up the necessary diversion. But he had done all that before. He made a point of keeping in touch with members of the force, men like himself, retired from the only career they enjoyed and working, if at all, as private guards and watchmen with no authority, no responsibility except to stay awake. Breaking out the dog might also involve some risk, and it had been years since he had felt the tingling sensation of danger ahead.

The two men agreed on the procedure, promising to keep in touch during the following day as their preparations were made.

They also settled on nine o'clock Wednesday night as the time of the break-in.

Chapter Twenty-seven

As he slipped into northbound traffic along the freeway, the chauffeur became aware of the returning fog bank. From the hill where Aramanth House overlooked the coastal strip, he hadn't noticed it, but now at nearly sea level the taillights of the car he followed were roiled by mists moving shoreward. He considered this a good omen. The incoming fog blanket might work in his favor as he made his way to the rear of the grounds and the cage where the collie waited. But moist air transmits sounds more clearly than dry air, and the chauffeur's worry was the dogs. No alarm system could match the dozens of dogs waiting in the cages and runs that surrounded his target.

Now that he was on his way, committed and prepared, the chauffeur felt calm. He also felt ashamed of the lie he had told his wife, that he had an employment interview with the night supervisor of a small electronics plant. He had never deceived her before, nor had he ever left her alone at night, but if she had known the truth she would have tried to talk him out of his mission to save their collie. His composure, reinforced by the accommodating fog closing in around him, was mainly the result of his second visit to the clinic that afternoon, a visit he now realized to have been crucial to his success. He had discovered the service path leading to the rear gate behind the clinic, used no doubt to deliver supplies. It was a way to reach the outside door of the ward without going through the grounds.

He had also managed to accomplish the purpose of his afternoon visit without his furtive approach to the exit door being noticed. While the outside door of the ward remained open he had slipped behind the clinic long enough to stretch a length of transparent plastic tape over the bolt socket in the door frame. When the door was pulled shut for the night the spring bolt would be prevented by the tape from seating. The door would appear to be tightly closed, but he would be able to open it from the outside with the blade of his penknife.

His fixing the exit door had been his worst moment so far. As he stood silhouetted by bright sunshine in the doorway, Laddie had recognized him. Fortunately, there were no other dogs in the ward, but the slightest sound from the collie would have brought someone from the clinic. There had been no sound, but the expression in the caged dog's eyes had brought the chauffeur around to the clinic entrance to pay a proper visit. Once again he had been reassured by the veterinary assistant that her patient was making good progress. Again, she could not allow him to speak to the doctor or to claim the dog himself. As he left he was shocked by the girl's duplicity. She must have been well aware of the collie's fate, yet only his digestion concerned her. Taking him illegally was the only way to save him now. It made the chauffeur all the more determined to succeed.

Beyond the downtown area, the freeway veered north, while the coastline curved west, and suddenly the fog vanished. The evening sky was lit only by the first stars and a half moon, however, and the wreath of trees around the Society's grounds would provide enough cover. He turned off the freeway, crossed above it and turned again onto the street leading to the Humane Society. It was a dead-end street, ending at the parking lot with an extension leading to the Animal Shelter beyond, and deserted after dark. As he made a U-turn and parked the station wagon in front of a private house so that it faced the only way out, he realized how obvious his car must be, but there was no place to hide it and no alternate escape route. Like many through streets before the construction of the freeway, this one had been amputated. But in a way, this would be to his advantage. The Society's grounds were a pocket set against the freeway bank. Not only were there no houses beyond the rear fence, the traffic sounds would cover his approach.

Wearing black-leather chauffeur's gloves and carrying a large pair of wire cutters, he made his way along the fence until he reached the locked service gate. He was now close enough to the exit door to see it pale white in the moonlight, but he still had to prepare the way out. He could easily climb the fence, but he would never be able to lift the collie over it, so he had to cut a hole they both could crawl through. His clippers, made of the best steel, were strong enough to sever the links in the fence, but it was also important not to shake the wire as he cut. So far the compound was silent and totally dark except for lighted windows on the second floor of the main house.

He worked quickly, grateful for the moistened ground under his feet, which absorbed the small cracklings of fallen twigs. When he had cut a semicircular piece from the bottom of the fence he pulled it carefully toward him, bending it out of the way so that he could crawl through. He placed the wire cutters across the hole to remind him to retrieve them on his way out, then slipped under the fence. It was then that the dogs began to bark.

The barking began near the front of the grounds, but it quickly spread through the runs and cages as one dog after another took up the challenge. And it seemed to ebb and flow in great waves as one group of dogs fell silent, then renewed their frantic uproar. The variety was bewildering. There were deep, hollow barks separated by seconds of silence; hammering, breathless barks; and barks ending in trailing moans. To the chauffeur's left came a sorrowful baying, while just beyond the clinic came such an aggressive volley that he was sure he had been seen.

He stood just inside the fence, frozen in deep shadow, afraid to move, yet certain he had already been discovered. The exit door lay a dozen yards in front of him across a patch of cleared ground faintly silvered by moonlight. The nearest dogs would certainly see him the moment he crossed to the door, but who else would? And why had the dogs farthest from him been the first to bark?

The custodian's plan for rescuing his dog involved tactics he had used many times before. Rather than attempt a silent approach through the grounds he intended to stir up as much noise as possible. That was where his partner came in. The old man knew that the Society employed a night watchman who lived in an apartment on the second floor of the main house. He also knew that the man was a retired police officer, like himself, with one of the softest security jobs, a comfortable place to live, and nothing but a collection of unwanted animals to protect. But, as he also knew, the softer the job, the duller it became. A man trained to face danger needed to be tested. He needed the company of men like himself and a better reason than a paycheck to stay awake and alone in a world asleep.

The Society's watchman had been delighted to receive his old police buddy's call the previous evening, to be remembered at a time in his life when he thought he had been forgotten. And he welcomed the suggested visit as a chance to talk about old times. As far as the watchman was concerned, it couldn't have come at a better time, the end of the television season and the beginning of the reruns. Thus the custodian's partner arrived to visit, walking through the front gate and up the steps to the veranda, where the watchman greeted him. To the chorus of barking dogs they entered the house and climbed the stairs to the watchman's apartment where they settled in facing armchairs to talk. The barking beyond the closed windows of the sitting room sounded as if every dog in the city had come to celebrate their reunion.

While his partner entered the grounds first, setting off the dogs with his footsteps and loud greetings, the custodian waited outside the parking-lot wall. But it was his own arrival in the grounds that caused the barking to continue. The watchman, however, was too absorbed in his visitor to pay any attention. Like someone living near a railroad track, he had stopped listening and so no longer heard.

The custodian walked calmly through the bedlam searching out the two places he thought the collie might be. One was the block of quarantine cages and open runs where dogs that were awaiting the results of rabies tests were kept. He had no idea how sick the collie was or where he would be isolated, so he stopped long enough to look through the fence at the dark shapes lunging against the wire to bark at him. None was a collie, so he continued across the paved area toward the clinic. His dog must really be sick if he was still being kept there.

The old man's passage through the open areas of the grounds was as determined, as heedless of the excitement his dark bulk aroused in the kennels, as if he were making his regular nightly rounds at the school. He made no effort to hurry; he had all the time he needed. His partner would keep the watchman occupied for as long as it would take to find the collie and lead him out to their car. Nor, as he approached the small white building at the rear of the compound, did its locked doors faze him. Locked doors were a specialty of his.

Ever since he had been employed at the school he had been called upon once a week or so to open a locked classroom. He had master keys to fit every door in the school, but often enough a teacher locked herself out or lost her key, and he could make her look foolish and himself something of a wizard by demonstrating his ability to pick any lock he chose, thanks in part to his police training. The ease with which he opened locked doors without a key also helped, he believed, to remind his employer of how vulnerable her precious school was and how important his presence to its safety.

He was not surprised to find the clinic door locked with an ordinary mortise lock like the classroom doors. After all, it was an old wooden building containing nothing but medical supplies for spaying cats, hardly a target for a drug addict. He stood before the door only a minute before the bolt clicked back and pushed his way into the dark anteroom. He had been inside the small building once before, but only to meet the veterinarian. He had glanced briefly into the back rooms, but now he remembered only dark enclosures with cages. He took out his flashlight and approached the door to his left.

He heard no sound as he worked the lock, causing him to wonder whether things had changed since his last visit. If the rooms were empty, where would they have put the collie? He pushed the door open and sprayed the beam of his light around the walls. A dozen pairs of emerald eyes met the light behind cage doors. The room was filled with cats transfixed by the light, silent as night creatures caught in some desperate act. He closed the door quickly. He hated cats.

He remembered that the small operating room was at the front of the building, so he turned to the door opposite the cat ward. The cat door had been an ordinary wood-paneled affair. The door he now faced was of metal siding and soundproof, but once again its bolt, seated in the metal door frame, offered little challenge to an expert. As he worked his pick into the keyhole, he thought he heard a faint ring of metal beyond the door, but he paid it no attention. The bolt slid back. He turned the knob and pulled the door toward him. At that moment a strong shaft of light struck his eyes. He stepped back, pointing his own flashlight into the room, but all he could see was the white light he faced.

Although he had been taken by surprise before, it had been years since he had called upon his reflexes. And always before the surprise had been possible, no matter how well he had anticipated his adversary. But there just couldn't be someone pointing a bidding beam in his face inside a locked kennel. The old man stood squarely in the beam, stunned and blinking. If his opponent had been aiming a gun at him, he would have presented a perfect target.

The chauffeur had just located the collie's cage and slid the latch to pull open the cage door when he heard the click at the end of the passageway. Quickly he turned his light on the door in time to see it opening. As his flashlight beam found the figure in the doorway, a strong burst of light caught him crouched at the cage door, revealed and terrified. The light he faced dazzled him so that he could barely make out the outline of a large man, not his face or what he might be holding in his other hand. Obviously the chauffeur had been caught. The barking dogs had given him away seconds before he could lead his dog out of the ward.

The faceless face-off lasted no more than a second or two. The custodian was the first to take the initiative. Challenge was his prerogative, no matter which side of the law he happened to be on. He hadn't brought his gun. That would have been dangerous if caught and unnecessary either way. But he had his phlegm-thickened voice of authority.

"Who are ya? What're 'ya doin' here?"

The chauffeur didn't answer. Instead, he slowly rose to his feet, his light still holding the figure in front of him. The burbling voice was familiar, but he was too frightened to be sure. He began to back slowly toward the exit door ajar behind him. As he retreated before the light in his eyes, he felt the collie brush past his leg. Encouraged to know the dog was with him, he made the final few feet to the doorway. Then, as he felt the yielding ground beyond the doorsill, he turned off his light and slammed the heavy door.

As he ran across the open ground toward the fence, he caught a glimpse of white ruff moving with him. He grabbed for the collar and missed, so he made his way to the fence hole, calling softly to Laddie to follow. As he reached the hole and crawled through, the exit door flew open and the light beam strafed the clearing, but he was through the hole before it dropped low enough to reveal the severed wire.

Hidden now behind the trunk of a large tree, the chauffeur could look for the dog. He was still frightened and in such a hurry to get away that he had forgotten his wire cutters, but to leave without the collie never occurred to him. And as he watched his pursuer spraying the light back and forth on the other side of the fence, he realized that the man was also searching for the dog.

And then he knew. The tortured voice, the barrel-shaped silhouette in the center of the moonlit clearing could only be the school custodian's. Relieved, the chauffeur stepped out from his cover, ready to summon the old man to join him in the search, but as he was about to call out again he saw the flash of white legs moving away from the fence hole into the cover of the trees. The custodian saw it too. He tramped heavily toward the fence, knelt, and wedged himself through the hole. Beyond the fence he got to his feet and lumbered on, gurgling a warning as he came. The chauffeur heard the threat. The old man was not his ally. They were adversaries, competing for the same prize.

The chase began in silence, both men reluctant to call the dog while they moved close to each other behind him. There was no doubt in either's mind of who the other was, or that it had become a contest between them. In the wooded area beyond the fence, the chauffeur had the advantage. Not only had he explored the perimeter in daylight, he was faster and he knew which way the collie must go. The freeway bank was fenced to keep dogs and cats from venturing onto the highway. There was only one way out of the pocket they were in, and the collie would find it. Obviously he had been frightened by the lights and running feet just as he was about to follow the chauffeur back to his car. If the chauffeur returned the way he had come, he would catch up with Laddie at the street.

The custodian ran in the opposite direction, skirting the corral until he reached the dividing fence between the Humane Society and the new animal shelter. There he realized he was trapped. He cursed his mistake. All this additional fencing had been put up since he had last seen the place. He decided to follow the fence, making a wide circle of the shelter grounds, a long detour that finally brought him back to the cul-de-sac where he and his partner had parked their car. As he stopped to get his bearings he heard the call.

"Laddie. Here, Laddie. Come here, old boy."

The old man ran as silently as he could to the opposite side of the street, then along the grass border in front of a dark house, trying to locate the chauffeur and the collie so that he could place himself between them to intercept the dog.

It was then that the three saw each other. They formed a triangle on the frontage road, each revealed by moonlight to the others and equally separated. The custodian stood at one side of the short stretch of road halfway between the Society's parking lot and the place where the access road turned sharply to the right. The chauffeur had moved up the opposite side of the street to a point near his station wagon. Ahead of them in the center of the street just before the curve was their dog.

"Laddie," the custodian shouted, a command.

"Laddie," the chauffeur cried, a plea.

Duffy stood in the center of the empty moonlit street in the classic collie pose, facing left flank supported by upright white forelegs, skirted hips rising above white-socked rear legs cocked at the tail curve. His head was turned toward the callers, his muzzle lifted, his ears cupped to the sounds. As he stood between the men, his nose quivered, sorting out their conflicting scents. Whatever he saw or heard, his nose was the final arbiter.

Then he turned his head away, lifting his muzzle still higher into the night sky where a soft breeze might carry other, stronger messages.

Again he heard the calls.

"Laddie," softer now.

"Here, Laddie," a coarse reminder.

It was up to him. Out of reach, beyond cajolery, he was being asked to choose between two humans and the two lives they personified as they waited for him to turn left or right. And the lives reflected in the urgent voices were as close behind him as the men. He was familiar with their sequences, their satisfying routines, their flavors of surprise and disappointment. Like every dog conditioned to dependence and obedience, his choice had been made dark eons ago. To turn back toward the human was inevitable. To turn away was not to be a dog at all. But which human?

Still he hesitated, tasting the breeze, savoring its variety, the distances it measured, seeming to deliberate, perhaps even to imagine no choice at all.

Then, as if there had never been a doubt, as if he had faced the callers not to be persuaded between them but to give his answer, he turned and trotted up the center of the road and out of sight around the dogleg bend.

Chapter Twenty-eight

Duffy was a country dog. That is to say, the major portion of his life had been lived where the space between humans is greater than it is in cities and in overdeveloped suburbs. But the country is also manmade, cleared and partitioned, and movement between one place and another is directed as effectively by dirt roads and fences as by city blocks. Duffy was used to following human paths, accepting their destinations as his, and avoiding proscribed shortcuts even when his senses directed him a different way.

As he reached the first intersection at the head of the dead-end street, he was faced with the human alternatives as to which path to choose. Behind him was the ward cage, a place to be avoided. To his right a broad four-lane avenue lay open toward the ocean, its borders clogged with small commercial buildings, lighted gas stations, and parked vehicles. Even at night it was a busy thoroughfare filled with movement and the sounds and smells he associated with confinement. To his left this same broad pavement rose to become an overpass above the freeway, dangerous to foot travelers because like many California roads, it was not built for pedestrians. Ahead there was no road open to him, only the dark fenced banks of the freeway south. Perhaps because the left turn led upwards, away from the lights toward the empty night sky he chose it, moving against the oncoming traffic along the narrow curb over rivers of moving headlights toward a distant wall of protective darkness.

As he set off along the narrow strip leading across the overpass he was very obvious, a dog alone where no dog belonged, his collie markings sharpened in the glare of each approaching set of lights. And although his pursuers were not far behind, he trotted on with head lowered against the tide of white eyes as if all that lay behind him was forgotten. He had chosen the least likely path a dog, by human reasoning, would take. He had not been disoriented by the crosscurrents of human travelers, nor had he sought cover. Those who noticed him on his way saw a collie as intent upon his destination as they were. The two men searching for him looked for a different sort of dog.

At the high point of the arching overpass he could see far ahead. The broad street continued through banks of lights and intersections, but it led toward darkness, a wall of night blacker than the sky. He went on, following the paved channel through the lights. Such well-traveled streets were new to Duffy. He had never learned the city dog's fear of vehicles, but at this late-evening hour traffic was light and he was fortunate. And the farther he moved inland, the fewer cars he met. He managed to cross at a major intersection against the traffic light, and once past it the road narrowed to wind through a quiet residential neighborhood where the low-roofed houses were already closed for the night.

He continued along the human path, sidewalks defined by plantings for a few blocks, then tarmac between low fences leading into blankness. A mile beyond the last street lights the road abruptly ended. There was no crossroad, no continuing footpath. Beyond the white barrier marking the end of the road was an avocado orchard rising to the crest of a pillowlike foothill with another rising just behind it. No longer outshone by ground lights, the half moon now revealed Duffy's horizon, a towering precipice stretching from one side of the sky to the other, its base set in cushions of low hills, its vertical so sparsely covered with scrub vegetation that its rock hide was washed by moonlight.

Duffy had come as far as his human path permitted. There was no way around, only a turning back. He stood at the road's end probing the breeze carrying hints of whatever lay beyond this stopping place. Although he had walked only two miles, he had been climbing the gradual rise from the coastal flatland to the first hills, enough effort to prompt him to open his jaws and to pause for rest. It is doubtful, however, that he considered turning back. A dog's compass holds him to his course as resolutely as a bird's.

With the soft tongue click he used to acknowledge a human question, an affirmative response, he walked around the barrier and into the enveloping shade of the avocado trees.

He continued north as if the mountain wall ahead were as chimeric as the bottomless night pools beneath the fruit trees. He followed tractor furrows to the top of one small knoll, then down the gentle slope only to begin a steeper climb to the next. Now and then loose clods in his path required an extra spring to carry him forward, each an effort he made reluctantly. His footpads slipped unevenly into broken ground, sinking deep to make each stop more difficult. The tilled orchards extended almost to the base of the range. Only when rock stanchions broke through the topsoil did the neat tree rows end. So too did the horizontal surface of the earth that had borne him this far.

At the foot of the cliff he chose a small depression between two outcroppings filled with the droppings of a slanting clump of greasewood. There he would rest. Like most four-footed animals, Duffy relaxed in stages. First he lowered his haunches to take the greater part of his weight, while his forelegs remained stiff to hold his neck and shoulders high. After a last glance at the skyline, he allowed his forepaws enough small steps to bring the rest of his body to the ground. Finally, if no sound threatened to disturb him, he flung himself on his side, relaxing every muscle before his eyelids closed.

He slept so deeply that his toes curled, then his feet twitched and his eyelids fluttered. He was exhausted. After four days without food, he had eaten his first few bites earlier that day, only to turn away from the bowl when his shrunken stomach knotted with the pains of its own emptiness. The parvo symptoms were all but gone, but to physical weakness had been added traumatic uncertainty. Duffy's digestion had always fallen victim to the crises in his relationships with humans. He had undertaken the most arduous journey of his life hollowed by illness and enervated by long days of imprisonment.

He slept only a few minutes. Perhaps he was awakened by some sound, but if so it was too slight to alarm him and it was not repeated. More likely it was his own clock telling him he was fit to continue, that the night had become his ally, the friend of all hunted creatures. He set off along the base of the coastal mountains keeping as near to the rising peaks as he could, even though walking would have been much easier if he had remained in the lower foothills where the ground had been worked. His way had become a detour, a westward search for a northward opening in the mountain wall. Had he reversed his course he would have found the pass he looked for two miles to the southeast, a winding road over the summit, but to have turned back toward the city lights in order to move at last away from them would have required knowledge he didn't have. And his experience told him that in nature's walls there were always openings.

He moved at a fast walk, head and tail extensions of shoulders and hips, an arrowlike shadow against the cliffs intent upon covering ground. His broad chest and long legs would compensate for the nourishment he needed, at least for a while. He was built for distance he had never had to cover. And the advancing ground fog moistened his throat as it crept inland. He heard nothing, saw nothing moving near him. This was border land beyond human use but still too close to human settlement for coyotes and deer, bobcats, and foxes to penetrate. Only the renegades, the castoffs from opposing societies crossed where Duffy walked, and these misfits were doomed.

A few miles along the way he entered the shadowed rim of a pocket canyon stretching from the coast to the foot of the range, marked by a winding road with houses and outbuildings scattered under stream-fed oaks and cottonwoods. The buildings were dark, the road empty at this midnight hour, but the rising hills that boxed the settlement on each side of the road contained its scents. As Duffy made his way to the canyon floor he savored the lingering remnants of wood-smoked dinners and collected water, of dogs and horses, all the familiar odors he could not resist.

He moved cautiously. Dog smell warned him away. His inclination to approach whomever he met as a friend no longer impelled him confidently forward. He wasn't looking for the welcome collies expect. He wanted only to steal a wild thing's share of the human leavings, then be on his way. He walked across an open yard toward the strong food smell. At the side of a garage he found the can, its lid tilted above the remains of a backyard barbecue. He dug his nose into smeared paper napkins and paper plates until he found the half carcass of a chicken. As he reached deeper, the plastic trash can toppled toward him, spilling its contents at his feet. An inside dog barked. An outside spotlight flooded the yard. Duffy filled his jaws and ran.

He climbed to a rock shelf above the lighted yard. There he stopped to tear and chew the mouthful he carried. As he watched, a large dog ran into the yard, nosed its way to the spilled trash and grabbed a bone. A man shouted from a doorway. The dog shied into the shadows. Duffy swallowed his stolen meal. For the first time in his life he had taken what was not offered.

The hot seasoning on the chicken flesh left him thirsty. He circled the lighted yard toward the water smell and found a small corral with a pair of horses standing in a corner. As he slid beneath the lowest rail, he heard a nervous *ahem,* but the horses' readiness to run no longer interested him. He made for the trough and drank until the bark of the dog and a moving flashlight forced him to move off. He returned to the high, barren ground replenished by his stop, but not tempted by the life it offered. His old way of coming to call wherever humans congregated had been replaced by his need to be free to continue his journey.

Beyond the canyon the topography changed. As fog swirls disappeared and moonlight once again revealed the rolling surfaces, Duffy climbed to a dry, forbidding plateau. The crests of the hills were so closely crowded together that they formed a single lumpy platform midway between the distant seacoast and the mountains. No earth folds carried runoff to this wasteland. No trees took root. The great blisters of seedless ground were fat with their own packed contents. As Duffy entered this undulating desert the mountains to his right seemed lower, little more than foothills themselves. He turned into them until he realized that the wall remained insurmountable, that only his path below it had risen.

The coastal fog chose easier passage over the range. So did the far-off traffic on the northbound freeway. Ahead, against the sky, a conference of peaks marked the turning of the coastline, but between Duffy and this turning point were miles of trackless waste. And neither his reserves of strength nor the slight refreshment could carry him far enough. Still, the comforting darkness persuaded, and the inimical succession of empty mounds repelled. No creature had ever stopped and started again where not even a boulder's shadow offered protection. Ahead, always retreating, was a shadowed crevass or a dark oasis that disappeared miragelike before his eyes.

Between his midnight stop in the canyon and the first paling of the sky to the southeast above the black floor of the Pacific he had traveled nearly ten miles in actual distance and several more over ground that was never level and never without necessary detours. He was no longer moving steadily but in sporadic fits of resolve between more frequent pauses when he sank to his haunches, his eyes searching far beyond his capacity to reach his next goal.

Then the coastal shelf changed again. Instead of racked foothills it swept shoreward in a broad ramp of wild grasses pinned with live oaks and traced with fence lines. And a narrow road rose from the sea, snaking inland, rising with the terrain until it disappeared into the mountainside. Duffy, limping now from a thousand bruising rock particles, crossed what appeared to be pastureland, although no animals grazed, and through sheltered glens, although he saw no houses. He walked at the edge of this fertile carpet just below the first steep banks of underbrush until he reached the road. It rose sharply ahead, but he could see no end. It seemed to lead into the mountain, at least farther than any natural gate he had come upon.

He turned up the road, the first prepared path he had walked since leaving the city limits. Almost immediately, it became steeper. He could see no crestline, only the rising seductive archway through the trees, tempting him toward the top, its precipitous incline beyond his strength to climb.

He had to rest. He sat in the center of the road, then let himself slowly down to take the weight off his bleeding pads. Finally he lowered his head to rest his chin between front paws. He would close his eyes just long enough to allow his haunches to gather the propelling force to climb the road.

He heard the far-off growl of accelerating motors. He lifted his head to look back down the swath of rising fields. Two pairs of close-set headlights dipped toward him, their wide-eyed glare fiercely penetrating under the brightening sky. Painfully he pulled himself to his feet. The white eyes were on him. The snarling shapes loomed just below him, moving fast. With a last desperate spring, he scrambled into a gully and up the bank where he sank into a tangle of low brush.

Trembling at the rush of angry sound, he watched the helmet heads, the goggle eyes, and the circling pincer arms flash by. He wanted to run, not up the mountain road but away, back toward the soft dawn. He tried to lift himself from the jagged bed of branches, but could not. He sank back to lie above the roadside, utterly exhausted.

Above him, along the only path to his destination, the sound of the prowling motorcycles rose and fell toward the summit. Duffy no longer listened.

Chapter Twenty-nine

When Duffy raised his head, the sun was high. One side of his aching body was warm, the other chilled by the dampness his coat had absorbed. He curled a front paw toward his mouth and began to lick the wounds in his pads, but the blood had congealed and his tongue was too dry to moisten the cuts. He reached out to chew the young grass spears near him, an instinctive recourse on an empty stomach. The blades were tender and dew coated, their juices welcome even as they collected at the back of his throat to tickle and gag. He coughed and shook his head.

This brought him wide awake, alert to his surroundings and his place on the bottom shelf of a mountainside overlooking the sunlit slope to the sea. He faced downhill. Before him lay open fields stirring with spring grasses, fence lines marking human boundaries, and the empty road falling to rock barricades along the shore. The scene was both strange and familiar, not country he knew or a road he had walked, but still a world like his world, filled with cats and water bowls and soft places to lie. And he could reach it so easily. It was all downhill.

Stiff-legged, he rose from his brush bed to stretch. He placed his forelegs together, then leaned back across gathered haunches, his tail rising, his jaws opening in a wide, squeaking yawn. The soreness in his leg muscles and the weight upon his hindquarters reminded him of the long night journey. He sat down again, turning toward the mountain behind him. The silent rise reminded him of the helmeted hunters. Fear of the mountain returned, fear unlike any he had known within his human circles. He had never turned away from anger, however much he feared it, because nothing in his experience suggested such an alternative. Disapproval and reprimand were inextricably woven into his vital human connections, the source of all gratification.

But fear of what might await him inside the alien wildness of the mountain was born of newer knowledge, of dark cages and of pain more unbearable even than the smack of a broom handle across his back. It was fear he couldn't face as he faced chastisement, because it was of unknown causes and unknown consequences.

Yet his compass turned him toward the mountain road. Until he had come upon it, his westward course along the base of the range had never faltered. The long way had been the right way. The mountain wall continued to the horizon, away from the cage and the pain, but now it was the wrong way. As he turned to face the mountain, he felt its pull. He had to face his fears also because something beyond his understanding told him that life would begin again on the other side of fear.

He returned to the road. Steep as it appeared, it was the only path to the summit. It required thrusts of strength his trembling haunches lacked, but at least it wound its way upwards allowing him to move horizontally, taking advantage of the four-legged animal's forward distribution of body weight. Filtered sunlight dotted the road here and there, but the high brush and overhanging branches deepened Duffy's sense of foreboding. He climbed slowly, head down as if he expected to be discovered at every turn, and as each blind turn revealed a steeper climb, he paused to suck the night-cooled air into his lungs.

Now that he was inside the mountain, it was no longer silent. Its impenetrable coat of high chapparal and stunted trees was alive with rustlings, small crashes, and startled scamperings. Duffy had never ventured into wilderness before. The scents were stronger, the sounds furtive. It seemed that every creature except him had reason to stay hidden. With better reason than they, his upward path in the center of the road made him all the more uneasy.

He had hardly started when he heard the sound of an overtaking engine behind him, following and moving fast. He plunged headlong into cover at the roadside just as a blunt vehicle rounded the bend below him. He had been seen by the two occupants of the Jeep. They stopped and one tall man got out to walk to the edge of the brush where he stared straight at Duffy without seeing him behind his screen.

"Must have been a fox," he called to his companion. "No dog could be around here."

With a surge of noise they resumed their climb while Duffy waited for the raw stutter to die away.

Back on the road, he followed the Jeep. Vivid memory warned him to turn back, and once on the road he did turn, one foreleg lifted, the prospect too real to face. But he continued on, driven upwards as if already he heard his name rising from beyond the crest.

The ascent to the ridge at this point in the chain of ridges was deceptively easy. As if the long wall had risen not from clashing continental plates but had been swept high from the ocean floor, it lifted gradually, providing the grade that allowed the only road to the summit. The absence of verticals gave the illusion of reduced elevation, but the crestline above Duffy was no lower and the length of his climb was extended by the winding path he had chosen. As he neared the top body curled and his spine arched, his forward steps no longer synchronized strides. His head and tail hung heavily, and drop by precious drop the fluid dripped from his tongue.

He felt the level shelf before he realized he had reached the summit. Suddenly his legs no longer reached for higher footing, and the sky tipped down. He stood on a sill of bunch grass and sank into its yielding softness. He could move no farther. From his shelf he looked down upon the coastline and his climb. Behind and to his right, the mountaintop flattened to form a broad tabletop set by human hands. He could see fences, paddocks, and the line of low roofs. He could also hear voices and catch the hot smell of oil. He had climbed out of a threatening world only to find himself within its ramparts.

He lay outside the enclave. In another, remembered life he would have been delighted to approach this high oasis where welcome must be found. How confident he would have been, and pleased with himself, a visiting collie come to receive his due. That was another dog, however. As he rested he looked longingly toward the inner circle of humans, feeling its pull, yet unwilling to step inside.

The sound of exploding motorcycle engines so close to his shelf startled him. He tried to pull himself to his feet in time to reach the fringe cover, but his heavy haunches refused to respond. As he lay helplessly before them, the cyclists sped past, back down the mountain road without seeing the dog.

His rest seemed to resettle Duffy to his course. After some time, he rose to his feet, slowly and without fear, turned away from the temptations inside the mountaintop fences and crossed the road. There the summit table narrowed to a ragged trail that followed the crestline. He made his way along this pathway walled on either side by a tangled forest of interlocking branches. He was moving southeast between peaks when to his left, the branches parted to frame the sky. He turned north again and walked to the brink of a plunging track down the opposite side of the range.

At the lip of what had once been a truck trail that scaled the almost perpendicular north slope, Duffy looked down. Immediately below him the parallel tracks, gutted by winter rains, fell away into a base of undergrowth, the accumulation of years without fire. There a country road began, leading to a wide riverbed where spilled water from the reservoir dam flowed in sparkling ribbons over apple-sized stones in the very shadow of the range.

He lifted his eyes. The road beyond the river was straight, a black lane across the valley floor. On either side he could see the patchwork patterns of spring fields, some disked and as dark as chocolate, some already deep in oat grass, a few dotted with grazing animals. And between chalkline fences and boxtop houses, live oaks, like boutonnieres, were set at random.

Chapter Thirty

Duffy came down the trail in a hurry, the sun already waning. The entire day had bloomed and faded as he traveled, watching his step, propelled by gravity and new certainty. The old tire tracks led straight down, but rain had so eroded the twin surfaces that at times he slid, at others stumbled into deep ruts. No matter. His tail was high, the foot of the mountain always closer and as he chose each small step he was already taking long anticipated strides toward his goal.

The vertical tracks became a smooth road rising and falling across tumbled foothills to the river bank. There was a crude bridge to service outlying ranches, swept away every few years by flood and replaced at minimum cost, but Duffy picked his way down the broken bank to drink thirstily in the first shallow channel, biting noisily at the flowing water and soaking his pads. He moved then to the next channel and drank again, unable to resist so many streams presented one after the other, when not one had crossed his path before.

He made his way across the stony bed to the opposite bank where he regained the road, now a blacktop rising from the river to a familiar junction. It was early evening and the traffic along the straight road was light, farm vehicles moving ponderously from field to field, pickups, each with a possessive dog riding in its bed. No one seemed to notice the collie moving purposefully along the unpaved edge of the road. Country dogs, like country people, move through postcard scenery on business. A dog on his way belonged as much as everyone else to this interspecific society, and Duffy was not an unusual sight.

But Duffy wanted to be noticed now. He had found his way home. He was pleased with himself and everyone he passed looked friendly because everything he passed looked familiar. There was the corner field where one night he had joined the midnight goose raid. The four marauders were gone, of course, and like the muscle tissue which had long since encapsulated the shotgun pellet he carried in his stifle, his memory of that night had been overlaid with other, starker memories. He passed the sheep pasture, but the woolly gray bundles under the live oak revolved their jaws complacently and never noticed him.

Night had fallen, dark and heavy, when he came to the entrance of the back road he had traveled, tied to the door handle of the white Chevrolet. The day's dust had long since settled on the empty road. Past the row of cedars, past the stand of huddled mailboxes, he came to the house where Princess lived. Certainly she would come cowering to greet him, but the abject Labrador was probably asleep in her doghouse.

He turned down the long dirt road. In the front pasture the cattle lay near the fence, their dark backs to Duffy. He walked by, but none stood to watch him pass. In the lower pasture, the two horses grazed, but neither raised a curious eye to the passing dog.

He reached the driveway, lighted by outside spotlights. He saw the yellow gleam of cat's eyes flash briefly before vanishing in the hedges surrounding the lawn.

His walk took on a jaunty strut as he moved through the breezeway, past the water bowl, and around the corner of the house, expecting at any minute to be hailed. Still no one appeared. Doors were closed, windows dark, and the house was silent.

He stood before the wide window of the master bedroom. Inside he could see three small bodies curled close to the sleeping lump of the man. His tail swept back and forth. His ears fell back in his collie smile. His dark eyes shone with joy.

He offered one small announcing bark.

The bed exploded.

"DUFFEEEEE!"

About the Author

Irving Townsend was born in Springfield, Massachusetts, November 27, 1920. He moved with his family to Southern California in 1962 as an executive producer for Columbia Records. He retired to his "ranch" in the Santa Ynez Valley in 1970 to write. Two of his books, *Separate Lifetimes*, and *The Less Expensive Spread* are available from J. N. Townsend Publishing. Irving Townsend died in 1981.